PAPER DOLLS

RACHEL MORAN

Cobra Books
USA

Cobra Books, COBRA BOOKS, and the cobra logo are trademarks of Cobra Books.

Front cover illustration by Jake Behrmann.

ISBN: 0615650058
ISBN-13: 978-0615650050

In Memory of Veronica Moran
August 25, 1949 - June 11, 2009

0.

Everything is gold. My plated accordion lungs. The neon fissures in my retinas. The fine-spun sinews of my arms. The glinting sun, the ionic smack of salt on my tongue.

I only hear the lap of waves, the bellows of my breathing. My circuitry surges, electricity in the water, but fear is the mark of fitness, so I expand my rib cage. My torso forms a sideways obelisk, a protrusion of air and musculature that sinks back into me. I turn my head to the side.

The watery egg timer of my ear blurps under the waves. A billion friendly parasites propel a school of dumb, organized fish down my stomach. I yank my arm up and over and tighten my obliques to raise the hips as I kick. This is just one crawl stroke.

I swim for miles, four or five at a time, in open water, every day that swimming is allowed. No one knows I can do this. It is a bad idea to tell people I can do this. They would try to rein me in, pester me ineffectually to stop—"It's dangerous!"—lose faith in my human credibility—"You can't go that far!"

People would not be able to fathom skimming foam for leagues. They would be maddened by the intrinsic limitations of imagination and harass me for words to describe an idea that urges the thought of a sensation, an obviously idiotic, impossible, paradoxical desire I could never satisfy. I can't tell anyone how anything feels.

I begin in the same spot every day. The tides of Germans and Swedes and various Midwesterners—noticeably original or derivative in their brief bikinis or oversized t-shirts—loll and roll at the water's edge, lost in pinnepedian dreams. They never notice me.

I move toward the shelf at a moderate pace. My heart rate increases. My jolly sting-ray shuffle, a choreological sweep of the foot, raises the sand to scare off the cartilaginous shark-cousins. This is the only period of schism in my unfortunate swimming ritual. I'm scared for the wrong reasons.

I'm scared, because I think I should be scared, because if I have to kick up sand in pre-emptive self-defense, it means something harmful could happen. I'm not scared because the nerves of my arches feel grains of sand ripple from a nearby, quivering denticle (don't bite me, little tooth!). I'm scared because I've heard caution from other people.

They have transferred their fear—*they*, the murky mass of people who love to wreck shit with their doomed sense of boundaries. I'm not that scared, anyway. I have not generated this feeling alone; therefore, I do not own it. I am not really scared at all. I reach the shelf where the sand drops at an underwater cliff, less than a hundred feet from shore. The majority of the world begins here. I begin here.

Today, I cut myself on the way out. I was shuffling, shimmying, shimmering, when the water glinted, sharp and dazzling, like a knife. The crescent of muscle from my waist to my groin contracted. I conjured clear green beach glass, an old Heineken bottle in the sand, but I felt infinitesimal scurrying in the water around me—finally a grain of sand had really rippled! I flung myself forward in the water, cursing the pleasant ease with which I had imagined the beer bottle, some frat-boy gangbang littering the beach, when, of course, the answer to everything is always the most obvious one—a sting ray—but I had been shuffling, God dammit.

The ray rose, a vertical self-expulsion from the sand, like the imagined take-off of UFOs. It coasted forward, its wings dithering beneath me, its swaying stinger grazing my ribcage, so that the light grooves of venom stored in its tail sizzled my skin, and, then, it was gone.

I swam to shore, the sand only a few inches under my belly. When I had no room left to stroke, I rolled onto my tailbone, my woefully blunt tailbone—no concealed weapons for me and my weak, upright notochord. I crabbed up to where the water couldn't reach me, trailing a carmadine streak that dissipated quickly. I touched my ribcage.

Already, it was swelling, the fine incision gaping like the curl of a fish's lip, rolling into a tiny scroll. I did not hurt. I felt the cut, but the sensation was my body signaling a wound. More signs of fitness.

My toe had a deep slice, directly into the tip, as though a double-edged blade had entered point first. I would lose a dime of skin soon, but not while the flesh was still white and flapping, not while my blood was seeping into the sand.

A concentric design of childish sand art spread near my ankle and the slurping of the water. I crossed my leg onto the opposite knee. I remembered that bleeding wounds require elevation over the heart, but that would require lying on my back and lifting my legs to the sky, blood streaming from the spillway of my Achilles tendon. I did not want the attention of tourists, tired of blinking at the sun.

At present, I was just the crook of a girl, a bent neck, the strings of a bikini around a fantastic tan, a coil of dirty blond hair that insists on blue eyes (but, sadly, they're gray). I was not more noticeable than the Germans with their rambunctious Frisbee playing and ridiculous barrel torsos, their topless children and quick sunburns.

Really, the only people I ever had to watch were the local rednecks, a generation out of Ohio and into Pinellas, with no discernible hair color, but so ready to talk, as if I knew them or saw any value in discussion of the heat or the price of beer at different holes up and down Gulf Boulevard.

The bleeding stymied slowly. My toe was beginning to throb with venom, a phenomenon that prevented the clotting, but forced the blood into an occasional viscous spurt. I nearly lost my patience and squeezed it, but, no, my reliable toe figured its way through the attack and stemmed the loss of serum, after almost twenty minutes of increasing apprehension about the likelihood of some strolling yokel.

I was so nervous by the time the blood clotted that my teeth were chattering. I looked at my ribcage. I looked at my toe. I was bloodless to all appearances. I inhaled dramatically. I pressed my palms into the sand. I tried to isolate the awareness of my injury from the anxiety over potential conversation about my injury. They were a bit entwined at the moment, but, then, OK, everything was OK, and I could see beyond the nystagmus of uncertainty. I stood and stamped my foot. The pain was reflexive, automatic, a warning that my foot was not capable of bearing that sort of pressure right then. I sat back down and scuttlebutted into the water.

The salt stings my toe. I have to remind myself that I am powerless against sharks out here, anyway, that I am tempting them by being out so far, by being so comparatively slow, by insisting on the vanity of jeweled tassels on my bikini bottoms, and, now, by being on the verge of bleeding, if not doing so without awareness already.

A shark may chomp me and kill me. Nothing much will change about the world if that happens. There is nothing but water and sun and salt and maybe blood—no, definitely blood, but maybe blood leaking out of my body. I swim past the final scythe's point of Tierra Verde.

This is far, farther than I have ever made it in one stretch. All I have to do now is haul one arm over the other, expand and expel the lungs slowly, turn my neck in syncopation with the rise of my hipbones for only a few more yards, maybe five hundred or so, a quarter of a mile—but there is nowhere to go if I tire.

This stretch is all or nothing, and, in defeat, I roll onto my back and paddle toward the shore, to the sand, and come out of the water, hips like diving knives, breasts like scallop shells. A fourth-generation Italian stares at me like he's staring at the sun. I smile like I could swallow him. His eyes widen. He nods. He looks out to the horizon.

He didn't see me that far out—maybe a hundred yards, but he doesn't think that far. I have a long walk back and I think about running, but I know if I could run back, I could swim the last quarter mile to where there is land again.

The sun is so bare. My shoulders are so bright. My tongue is salty and fat. My saliva is dry. Everything is possible, if not right now, then later. Everything is possible as long as I take my time. Nothing seems real, so I trust the chimerical beach kids from Munich and Detroit, fewer all the time, frolicking and not realizing that they hate each other and will hate themselves later, much later, and, then, after an hour of walking in a dazed glory, there is another man surrounded by many tan kidlings, screeching and giggling.

He shoos them away and takes a sip of a Mai Tai in a Burgundy glass (this classless fucking beach) and he's just a little drunk, just a little over the exact easement of the bar, technically loitering in a no-alcohol zone, with his strawberry hair and auburn beard and golden skin that clearly took years of local tomfoolery to bronze like that, across his wide forehead and narrow smile, full of chipper dentistry.

He doesn't see me yet, so I lean against the side of the bar near where he's wobbling and warbling into his chummy rum. Razors of horrible, violaceous bamboo trim the bar and prickle the skin on my arms. I look at the bamboo, hurt, surprised. The stalks are cut down the highway, like the wrists on a teenage girl who is finally tired of crossing the street (more ludicrous, wrong, purple decoration).

I bend one knee over the other again and look at the flat disc of skin, only remaining attached by the pressure of the bloating poison underneath.

I rip it clean off, tear it with a soft yanking that sets my teeth against each other to the point of squeaking, and then there is blood everywhere, all in the sand, all down the sole of my foot, and I hobble out, quite truly, and collapse into a yogic position that belies the raging poison in my sole, no, soul, no, I am fine, I am fine, and then I am actually pitching backwards and rolling forwards, at least one of the soles or soul so fully exposed that if no one sees me now, well, we all deserve what we get, and, then, he is over me, and his breath is nothing but tropical goodness.

I say to him, softly, as if I'm asking for him to give me the same, "Mai Tai?" and I pass out when, really, I just wanted to fuck him, but one of us is so stupid.

1.

I'm trying to think about what I'll look like at midnight and, then again, around four, and whether or not Alex will think I look prettier earlier or later.

My eye shadow looks good, and I smell nice, like cupcake frosting, but I should have deep conditioned my hair yesterday, because the ends look like shit. Maybe it won't matter.

I'm nervous. I hope we're actually dating now. This is our third date, but the fifth time we've hung out in a month. I think we're dating now.

I hate my eye shadow, after all. Brown does not work on brown eyes. I take it off, so it's OK that Alex is late, because now I'm not ready, but I have party jitters and I really want him to be here. He is a half-hour late. I should go outside. Be ready to go, but not impatient. But I am impatient—but a half-hour is more than kind of rude. The rest of my makeup looks good without the eye shadow, muted and shimmery. I take a beer and go outside.

It's sticky out. I consider going back inside, before my clothes start to stick to my skin, but then Alex comes loping up the sidewalk. Every bubble of anticipation spirals into a beautiful helix that pops like a glass of champagne.

"Hi!" I cry out and I'm jumping up and I know it's silly, liking guys is silly, but I'm just so happy he's finally here.

He hugs me. His arms are warm and strong. His t-shirt is so soft over his chest. He smells waxy. I look up at him.

"Hi," he says. He kisses me. His kiss is cool and wet. He tastes drunk, fun, like he's been having a good night.

"Do you want a beer?"

"Yeah."

We go inside. The doorway feels warm when I pass through it, like it's adorned with a garland of stars that flex and twinkle, bright and shiny, to show me how the beginning of our love looks.

My grandmother told me once that stars can die, but you can still totally see them in the sky. That's what guys are like—they give off all this heat and light, even if they're not really there. This is what Alex is like, too. He looks like he's here, but I don't know for sure.

He leans against the counter, and I bend over to get his beer. I hope he is looking at my ass. I turn around. I can feel my pupils changing shape, spiking at the bottom and indenting at the top, forming perfect hearts as I hand him the beer.

He's lighting something, a cone-shaped joint. The smell is vile, like the slaughter of goats. His face splits into a grin to accept the beer. He's still holding a lighter to the joint. The kitchen fills with an awful, burning fog. My pupils round out again, losing their happy inversions and elongations.

"What are you doing?" I ask.

"Smoking," he says. "My friend Ray got some dust. It's bangin'. Do you want some?"

I laugh. The melody of my laughter pushes through my throat like air through a trumpet. I want to sound happy, but my tongue is flattened as wide as possible in surprise. He could see my molars if he were looking at me. The back of my throat, where he can't see, constricts. The smell is the same as when the intestines drop from a kid. By the time I am finished laughing, he has sucked in a hit. His eyes are opaque. I can't tell if he cares when I say, "No, no, I'm good. I took half a Klonopin today. Thanks, though."

He cracks the beer on the counter. I lean against the refrigerator.

"You look good," I say. The corners of my lips press into my teeth.

I wish he would try to fuck me here in the kitchen, so I could look down, say no, what about my grandmother, and take him to my room. He smiles and pulls again on the joint. His eyes are blacked-out television screens, dumb and convex. I can't see his mind at all. He tips his beer.

"Are you excited about tonight?" I ask.

"Fuck yeah, I am!"

He slams the beer down on the counter, comes at me in one step, and pushes his mouth onto mine. Finally, but he tastes like the sour, creamy soup that boils up from offal. I do not want to think of home while he is here.

The dust has done something to his tongue and mouth. He's biting at me like he's a velociraptor, some insane, extinct, rapacious thing that can't eat enough. I can see something charred in my mind. The smell of his joint is entrancing me. I want him on me and off me at the same time.

He pulls away and grabs my shoulders and blows out a magnificent rumble of air. He shakes his whole body hard, shaking me with him. He lets out a whoop.

"This shit is good!" he says. "Tonight! Tonight is going to be good!"

I laugh again, but I'm nervous because of the way he tasted and I'm wet from how he pushed me and bit me. I can't escape the smell of acrid flesh. I can't erase the shadow of an animal in a painful lump from my mind. I can't tell if he feels excited by me or by tonight. I came here for a better life. My laughter barks into a cough.

"C'mon, you all right?"

"I'm fine. The air is all thick," I smile.

"That's party air! C'mon, do you know how much fun everyone is going to have tonight?"

He picks up a beer and flips it upside down over his face. He swallows it in a succession of gulps, his Adam's apple pushing at the throat, a fine spray of beer sticking to the strawberry down of his beard. I want to ask him if we're dating. I want him to tell me something good.

He shakes his head in wonder. "Do you know how hard my friends have worked for tonight?"

"No," I say.

"Oh God, yeah, like weeks of work. Everyone's involved. It's really cool."

"Oh, that's great."

"Yeah! But, listen, I should probably go now."

"You're going?" My insides contract again, hard and stunned and disappointed. The wetness in my panties congeals, thick and sticky.

"Yeah," he says and then he tilts his head, still smiling. "Oh, shit. Julie. I'm sorry. I thought we were just having a beer or something. But, listen, just come at, like, 11:30. Aaron and Jeffrey go on at midnight, so I can introduce you to some new people and stuff, too. I have to go help my friends right now."

He is looking around the kitchen. He isn't looking at me.

"No, totally," I say. "It's no big deal. You have to help your friends. I can't wait to meet them."

He nods up and down with the same smile, his chin rocking his ears back and forth. I can see his bottom teeth.

"Right," he says and grabs me around the waist and kisses me in the hollow spot between my cheek and ear. He pulls me out of the house with him. The walkway is covered in shattered glass from the broken bulbs of my imagined celestial trellis.

I have no idea why anyone likes anyone.

2.

We arrive at Art, and Aaron and Jeffrey are at the door. They hand out g-strings with silkscreens of their dog's asshole and puffy haunches. We kiss hello. Their cheeks and hands are sticky.

"Thanks," I say, taking a g-string from Jeffrey.

"Gimme that," Alex says. He cups his nuts with it and swivels his hips.

"Is that a banana hammock?"

"You know you love it," says Jeffrey.

Aaron licks his ear.

"Not as much you'll love what's next, though," he says. "We're performing a symbolic pantomime."

"That's genius, guys," says Alex. "Those things can get really literal sometimes."

"I know! We're going to elucidate what 'now' means," Aaron says. "You know that singular moment of joy when we call something art? We really only mean that specific instance of perception when it's art."

"Well, you can always remember the good things you saw," Alex says.

Aaron tilts his head. "If you do it right, it's impossible to remember artistic joy. Moments of beauty must continually occur! You'll see!"

Alex smiles in confusion. Someone shouts at us to move. The chemical musk of drugstore cologne threatens to trample us. I raise my hand to my face, as if I'm holding a cup.

"Literal pantomime," I say. I move inside. "I need a drink."

"Wait! Vanessa!" Alex calls, but I push past the people ahead of me. I have a headache.

Everyone is theatrical in neon rayon and sequins against a backdrop of geometric paintings splashed with more neon. A dull pang vibrates under my clavicle. The lurid, incessantly fluorescent sameness of everything is a spoon digging into the mushy muscles around my thyroid. I've seen exactly this, had exactly this night a million times—or maybe I just prefer dark colors.

My skin puckers. The fuzzy hair on the back of my neck springs up and falls down as if a roller coaster exists just under my skin. I am both trapped by the crowd and entirely alone. There is something wrong with me. These people here are my friends. I am having difficulty feeling . . . something, them.

I look back for Alex. He is gone already. I need a drink badly.

I start to move again, but the lights dim on the spectral, glowing colors of the paintings and people with their static, acrylic paint and skin. I can't tell how far away anything is.

The paintings fade, then flicker back, under a ceiling of black lights. I lose all sense of time. A childish insecurity flashes through my mind, but I can't remember what it is. The artwork beams in the darkness and illuminates the room. Still, everything feels untouchable, just out of reach. I am looking for the profundity, allegedly implied by the lack of dimension in the materials, the illusion of depth created by the lighting.

The people confuse me, too. They are all wearing Cosmetoptics and sporting back-piece tattoos. Flat is the new meaningfulness.

The center of the room crowds before I get too far. Chrissy touches my shoulder with her chin. Her fine, light hair fans and sticks to my shoulder, clinging again back to her body, like sparkling, wet gauze. Jason reaches out and squeezes my hand, the meat of his thumb pressing against mine. He is damp with coke sweat and smacks his hand back into his pocket. Erica's feet turn inward. She rocks into the arrow of her toes and bobbles back onto her heels. I am surrounded by friends.

Torchlight flares and startles the room. Our crowded friendship melts and combusts as we flatten against the wall.

Jeffrey is in the middle of the floor, in the center of a circle cleared by fear, in a *cheongsam* and a bun. His toes are encased in *tabi* socks, split by *geta* sandals. His little umbrella is aflame, coated with some magic resin to protect its webbed skin. He cowers under the spade-shaped pyre. His knees twist under the skirt of the *cheongsam* at a bracing angle, awaiting collapse or preparing to spring.

Aaron is over him, in a giant, electric-blue robe, on stilts. He wears a confusing whiteface, black brows painted over his eyes, a garish mouth exaggerated around his own. He swings the torch in pendulum strokes, grazing through the parasol fire.

The two fires hiss and flare at each other. Aaron blazes fierce trails just behind his wrist. The smell of paraffin twinkles and dusts over us in the crowd. I think of waxen, extinguishing stars falling to Earth. Still, Aaron and Jeffrey remain in place.

Suddenly, Chrissy pulls on the ends of her hair and shrieks. A small chunk is lit, a hair-brush fire of yellow straw that crackles and singes in her palm as she shrieks again. She stares at the center of her hand, aghast at her burnt-out future and lost rope of hair, but the room is transfixed by the crouching Jeffrey.

Chrissy trembles, locked in a tower of disbelief, but, even in the dark, I can see her anxiety. She looks lovely with her mouth rounded and open. Her eyes are wide. Her brow is spread.

No one else has turned toward her, despite the high-pitch flames and incendiary shrieking. Everyone is nervous, unsure of where to look after his or her instinctual retreat from the fire, its insistence on staying only barely contained. Everyone feels foolish with fear.

The threat has settled into the comforting crackle of a campfire, now popping jovially in an upside-down heart shape, atop the umbrella still. Jeffrey remains poised. Aaron holds the lessening torch under his chin, like a child with a flashlight telling a ghost story, his whitened face gleaming sickly.

Their chow, Snuggles, barks from her cage in the corner. She is crazed from being enclosed near fire, from the presence of so many smelly people she can't lick. People turn to the cage, fearful she will break free and bite, but Aaron and Jeffrey ignore her. They direct their fires at the walls as eerie minimal techno fades up.

The crowd turns, confused, straining to see what Aaron and Jeffrey want them to see, but it is too dark. The paintings are only vaguely luminescent without the black lights on them. The silhouettes of colors are weak. No one's work is distinguishable from anyone else's. It's all just flashes of hot pink and orange.

Snuggles rattles at her cage, ramming the door. A metallic echo haunts the room and blends with the sonorous plink of the techno. The snapping sounds from the fire atop Jeffrey's parasol finally die, but the clatter of the cage and the rumbling *soto voce* of Snuggles' growling rise. Jeffrey remains unperturbed, subservient. The music blends into another track. Everything seems rehearsed, gloriously and horribly rehearsed, until Aaron wobbles on his stilts and looks at the cage. He is distracted, but he spreads his arms and rebalances.

The torch swings out in his hand and swallows the oxygen overhead the first row of the crowd. People push for space away from the flame again, but it moves on quickly. Everyone is embarrassed, sheepish once the flame is onto the next person's space.

Aaron teeters, grabbing for something in his giant robe with his free hand, and Jeffrey sees his moment to escape. I feel the radiating nerves of my friends around me and I prepare for them to startle. Jeffrey's tensed shoulders indicate approaching drama.

He springs, his *geta* click-clacking resolutely, but Aaron hears the noise, crisp against the dog's harsh, hollow, resonant barking. He focuses his attention downward on his impending runaway. The crowd is still confused, but tries to look composed, deep in intellectual consideration. Light frowns curl. Eyeballs scan too slowly.

Aaron isolates Jeffrey with a swing of the torch, his balance regained. Jeffrey is trapped again by fear or pageantry. The torch rears up to Aaron's face once more.

The crowd has edged toward one wall with Jeffrey's approach. They are entirely unnerved by now, not by the awkwardness of Jeffrey's role or his charred parasol, which he still uses as a shield, but, still, by Aaron's torch coming near them. Chrissy is breathing unevenly behind me. Jason has only just noticed that she is upset.

"They planned this," he says to her soothingly. Snuggles continues to bark and howl, slamming into the sides of her cage.

Chrissy nods, wide-eyed still, and opens and closes her mouth again. Jason puts an arm around her.

I look again for Alex. He is only about fifteen feet from me, but he hasn't noticed me, either. He is next to Ray and Luke and a girl I've never seen. She has long, wavy hair and a dark, beachy burnish. Luke says something to her. She looks up at Alex for confirmation. He smiles at her. They are directly opposite the retreating crowd, behind the fire. They have nothing to fear. They aren't even paying attention. The rest of the room is in shadow.

Chrissy sees where I am looking and looks back at me, a look of sadness. I smile at her. Ray is telling the girl something that involves his hands, but she doesn't appear to be listening. The dog is distracting her. Chrissy smiles back at me.

"I'll be right back," she whispers. She darts from Jason's arm through the crowd to Ray, who lowers his hands upon seeing her and nods and puts his arm around her.

Alex grins at him, the white of his teeth glowing. He never notices the defeat of Ray's puppeteering. The girl says something to Luke, but her shimmering tan drifts toward Alex. His simplicity is contagious. Her body mimics his as she faces Ray again, who continues his tale, but he is less animated, propping up the sagging Chrissy and her destroyed head strings.

The crowd's attention ripples and scatters, comes back to the fire. People are becoming angry with the obviousness of their discomfort at the flames. The torch's path has jagged the circle into a milling and disoriented fringe of people who don't know where to look in the semi-dark. The low noise of voices rises. Snuggles quiets. In the center of the room, Jeffrey waits, like a rabbit, unsure of whether anyone is paying attention to him. Still, no one understands the analogy.

Aaron stamps a stilt and then suddenly jackknifes. The crowd crackles to attention. His robe floats like the arm of a dancing ballerina behind him as he falls. His garish red mouth opens in surprise, but the little gape is his face's only show of disaster. His heavy, oil-paint brows cannot animate. The outline of his mouth cannot intensify and only drops a bit with his jaw. His throat emits a tiny wail, barely heard from near the ceiling and through the ether of addled gasping below him.

Jeffrey clacks away, bounding into the crowd, but his *cheongsam*, a regrettable choice with those *geta*, restricts his thighs and allows only his knees to propel forward. His calves snap up toward his sateen-bound ass. His *tabi* socks and feet inside them fly off the wooden planks of the shoes, and he plants facedown in the parting crowd, knocking, as he goes, Aaron's left stilt from under him.

Aaron drops. The imperial robe fills with hot air from the torch, its fear-mongering magnificence swinging up and around as he wildly unscrews his own shoulder in flight. He looks like a frantic goose doing his best to avoid alighting the meticulous binding at the robe's edge. His stilts splay in both directions, leveling the crowd. People pile on top of each other and scramble to get up.

Jason tries to grab my hand, but his clammy palm only slips away. He runs around the back of the disintegrating circle of party patrons toward Ray and Luke and Chrissy and Alex. Alex pulls the girl with them out of the throng of people. They retreat into the darkness. Luke and Ray are gone. Chrissy shrieks again, and Ray pops back from the eclipse for her. I stand still as people scrabble, screaming around me. Jeffrey is nowhere in sight, and, then, Aaron is on the ground. He has made almost no noise.

The torch rockets down, gulping oxygen in its descent. Its flame bursts, a wonderful, careless comet. A path of mundane neon from the paintings dots the background, but against the flare of the performance, the paintings are children's refrigerator art.

The torch whispers like a missile and lands on Snuggles' cage. It explodes on impact and consumes the dog instantly. Her howls implode. The smell of salami and burnt hair fills the room. People scream more, the low shouts of men swallowing the hysterical punctuations of women.

The lights snap on, and Jeffrey appears next to the burning cage, his *cheongsam* ripped over one hairy thigh, his bun fallen on the side of his head, makeup dripping down his face. He sprays a cloud of nitrogen from a fire extinguisher on his dog. He looks terrifying and bedraggled and desperate. The dog chokes out a final, scraping bark amidst the pearlescent ash and foam. She falls silent. She is dead.

The room empties out the door into the street. People are pushing and yelling, replacing the extinguished imminent danger with their unobservant rush to leave. They curse at strangers to move, bottlenecking the door as they offer arms to pull acquaintances forward in the crush. Jeffrey sobs next to a moaning Aaron, who does not move in a broken heap under the robe, the stilts lying out behind him.

I don't see Alex. He has done his best to make sure as many people are as safe as possible, I know. I am the only one standing still.

The conventional neon art remains surprisingly intact.

3.

Today is Saturday, August 4, and the temperature is 96 degrees. The forecast is 101.

The morning light in the salon keeps my headache at a low simmer. My first real appointment isn't technically until noon, but walking here once the sun is that high is suicide. My hangover makes me feel like a raisin, black and ugly and dehydrated, with a sticky, pungent center.

I push thoughts of Snuggles away. The smell of her thick, wavy fur remains charred in my brain, but I tell myself that there is nothing to lament. She only died because she distracted Aaron and Jeffrey into stumbling with the torch, because she went berserk, but of course she did. A dog in a cage in a crowd of people spooked by fire will go berserk. Her death, if anything, is like all deaths in a way—a conclusion of her nature.

This rationale does nothing to remove the rasping echo of her final bark when Jeffrey extinguished her. The cadence of pain in her last yelp bubbled through the rush of foam like she was underwater, boiling. The memory of it warps the sun through the window, so that the salon is a boiling cauldron, too, but, then, Chrissy is at the door, smiling weakly, with two coffees in her hands, and I can forget it again.

I open the door and take a cup from her.

"Morning, sunshine," I say.

"Ugh."

"OK, sure, me too."

We sip at our coffee. Mine makes my headache tighten, and I put it down.

"Sit down," I tell her.

"Oh my God, Ray didn't even notice."

"Is that the worst thing that happened last night?"

"No."

"Did you tell him?"

"No."

"That's probably why he didn't notice. He didn't ask why

you're here so early?"

"He's at Art."

"Oh, wow. Did you guys go to bed?"

"No, Ray and Alex did a bunch of blow back at the marina with some other people after the fire and then they went back to Art to help Aaron and Jeffrey clean up. Well, Jeffrey, anyway. Aaron is in the hospital. You didn't see Alex?"

"No, he texted me, but I told him I was fine and wanted to go to bed."

Chrissy looks at me in the mirror. I am smiling.

"Are you OK?"

"I'm fine." I look like I am smiling still. "Are you OK?"

"Noooooo," she wails. "I'm missing a chunk of hair!"

I look at her bright yellow head.

"Yes, OK, you are. We'll fix it."

I pick up the singed chunk and quickly drop it and stick my fingers into the hair behind her ears and lift it up so that her cheeks relax. She unconsciously admires herself, how her face looks with the tension gone from the nasolabial folds.

I bundle the ruined hair into the golden cascade in my fist and reach for the scissors in front of her. She notices, but she is still looking at herself, so I slice through the spill of hair and, again, quickly, so as to minimize what she will think is trauma, let go of it and bundle the back of her hair, too, and chop it to the same approximate length. She sees the blunt ends, the falling sheets of hair in the mirror, and shrieks again in the lesser acoustics of last night.

"What the fuck?!"

"It's fine," I say, soothingly. "I'm not done."

"That's a *lot* of hair!"

"You lost that hair yesterday. This is not the traumatic part."

She gapes at me.

"Really," I say.

She starts laughing, shaking her head. I laugh with her.

"Aaron and Jeffrey lost their dog!" she says. She is giddy. "They killed their dog!"

"I know," I say.

"I don't even know what happened," she says. "They're both at the hospital now. The gallery is a mess, too. The walls are black where Snuggles' cage is."

"Is it still Snuggles' cage if she's dead?"

Chrissy looks at me again. "I don't know."

"Anyway . . ." I comb her hair out flat, parted in the middle.

"We should do something," she says.

"Like what?"

"Like, a party or something."

"We could."

She looks at her hair, lank and wet against her face. Her lips quiver. She is about to pout at herself in the mirror. Everyone is always so sexy.

"Is your coffee working?" I say. "Mine is making my headache worse. Let's switch."

"To what?"

"Something better," I say. "Hang on."

I leave her in the chair. My brain is shrinking away from my skull as last night's copious alcohol leaves my body.

Chrissy seems to have forgotten the last memorial we attended—the awkwardness and drunkenness and then egregious drug use to compensate for the awkwardness. When it was over, everyone filed out of my living room as if they had been in a church, even though most people had left four and a half hours earlier, before Ray threw down two eight balls and Luke started DJing.

I check my phone. Alex has not texted again. It has been six hours. He has either crashed completely or is so destroyed, he has lost all sense of time, and is at some random party person's apartment downtown or in Ray's garage at the marina, huffing blow off a mirror, feeling super-connected to everyone who was part of the fire.

I return with two glasses of cheap, pink wine that one of the other stylists bought. I will have to replace it, which means I will have to buy this cheap, pink wine. This seems ludicrous to me for some reason, but I am probably tired, too, now.

"Here you go. Your hair is starting to look really good," I say.

"How can you tell? It's plastered to my face."

"The edges are clean. You'll like it. Drink up," I say. I take a large gulp and reach for another pair of shears.

"Oooh, this is good!" she says. "So, we should have, like, a party, not just for Snuggles, but for Art, too. The money can restore the gallery and pay the artists who lost work!"

"I didn't know the art burnt."

"Well, it isn't going to sell now."

"How much did Ray have up?"

"Oh . . . I don't know."

I smile at her, anyway. The cheap, pink wine is already working. My headache feels so much better. The scissors sing in Chrissy's hair.

"What if we did it on Egmont Key? It just reopened," she says.

"When was it closed?"

"Last year."

"How do you close an island?"

"They were going to use it as a sand berm if the burns didn't work."

"Right. Well, good thing the burns work, then."

We are lucky in our bubble of a beach town. We are a spit of shore drift that clings to the wang of Florida, but there are advantages to being a peninsula upon a peninsula.

The loop current, even at its closest variable in winter, is always heading away from us. We are rarely ruined by hurricanes. The water that rests here is always warm. When an offshore drilling unit explodes in the Gulf and the well is still profitable, the surrounding beaches are soaked in oil, but we remain in paradise. The black clouds that rise over northerly Sand Key are not ours. The burning pools drifting south to Egmont are far away.

"Can we take people swimming?"

"Who swims?" she says.

"I don't know . . . People."

"There have been swimming advisories for three weeks now. No one wants to swim."

"What are we going to do out there?"

"I don't know! Drink? Tan? Talk about Art? What do we do?"

I swallow more wine.

"Listen, we have to do this," she says. "Ray is hiding our boat, OK? We run a marina and we have to hide our own boat. The guy who runs the public slips let us put it behind that artificial shoal, so it can't be repossessed."

She stares at me in the mirror. She is drunk.

"We're, like, completely out of money. People are selling their boats to old people and snowbirds who take them to, like, Orlando and Michigan."

She pauses and takes a deep breath, "We're fucked."

I take another drink.

"Do you want to come out tomorrow with me and Alex?" I ask. "I wasn't really planning on going to the Key, but I guess we could."

"We have to get people back out there, back on the water," she says.

"What does this have to do with Aaron and Jeffrey?"

She continues to stare at me. I can't remember when we became friends.

"Vanessa, we have to. Aaron and Jeffrey need our support now, and people need to remember what we're losing. We're all losing . . . everything."

I rub her scalp vigorously and let the hair settle around her cheekbones.

"Look, though, your hair looks really awesome."

She looks at herself in the mirror. Her feelings show on her face. She blanks out immediately. It is approaching mid-day. Last night is obliterated in the glare of sunshine and fantastic hair.

"It's all curly! How did you do that?"

"I just paid attention to your head," I say.

She grins, and I drink the rest of my cheap, pink wine. She flips her hair around and smiles at herself.

The afternoon passes slowly. The plate glass window at the

front of the salon feels like it could melt when I touch it. I am a little drunk and then I am a little drunker, and I always like the smooth, lifeless feel of the glass under my fingertips after they have wiggled through the soft, warm hair of one girl after another.

They are all the same, all the same, and I finish another bottle of wine with a client whose name I only know because I wrote it in my book years ago and just continue to rewrite it for every third Saturday of the month. Someday she will cancel and then I won't write it anymore. I can't make myself care about her.

She is drunk, too, by the end of our appointment. She says she doesn't have her wallet, but I can see it inside her purse. She is waiting for me to say it's OK and she can pay me next time, but I don't say it, because it's obvious that's what is going to happen, anyway. It doesn't matter if it's OK.

She leaves embarrassed, and her drunkenness confounds her embarrassment. I wonder if I will see her again and realize the guarantee of seeing her again was to excuse her lie and her theft of services. I was cutting her hair on credit before she even sat down and, now, because I wouldn't excuse this, I will never get paid for this work.

By three o'clock, I am punchy. I am still the only stylist in the salon, a more and more frequent occurrence as months pass and people run out of money. Clients that used to come biweekly now come monthly. Clients that came monthly now come every three months. Stylists in other chairs are now waitresses or bartenders 'just until the economy gets better.' The economy is not getting better.

A girl comes into the salon and asks the price of a cut. I tell her, and she nods and thanks me, looking sad.

"Sit down," I tell her. "There's no one here. I can do it for free."

"No, no, I couldn't do that," she says.

"Yes, you could. My next appointment is at 3:30 and it's a friend. It's not a big deal."

"Oh, no," she says. "I just realized I have something else to do is all. I can come back later."

She is nervous now. She leaves quickly. I go to the front of the salon and lock the door after her. I press my forehead against the glass and look at my phone.

Alex has texted me, "I fucking <3 you."

I text him back, "<3 <3 <3," and sit down on the floor and try to think of nothing until Dani and Erica arrive.

They are just as drunk as I am, knocking on the door, pulling on the handle and rattling it in the frame. I am not sure if I fell asleep. When I open the door, they tumble into the salon, giggling.

"There is nooooooobody here," Erica says.

"Hello, hello, helloooooooo," Dani echoes into the room.

"Hi, guys," I say.

"Hope you don't mind I tagged along! I brought stuff, though!" Erica says. She waggles another bottle of wine. She puts it down on the counter and claws through her purse and dumps a bag of coke on a hand mirror.

"So, I guess we will not be looking at the back of your head with that," I say to Dani.

"We can! C'mon, girl, just huff it up!" She scootches next to Erica and watches in anticipation as she crushes and cuts the coke.

Erica elbows her. They giggle more. The sun streams in through the window at a blinding angle. We line up and snort. The coke is like star sparkles, hot and explosive, across the pink wine-fog sky.

"Wow, thanks," I say. "Dani, sit down."

I brush her hair out. I can smell smoke in it.

"So, we'll just trim it," I say.

"I want bangs," she says.

Erica comes up and takes another line. Dani flails in the chair.

"Bring me one, too!"

Erica passes me the mirror, and I hold it for her while she sniffs. She takes it from me, and I take a second line, too.

"OK," Dani says. "I know it's not, like, super cool to talk about it, like, right off the bat, because we just got here, and I wasn't there, anyway, but what the fuck happened last night?"

"Oh, yeah, I noticed you weren't there," I say.

"Jason and I got in a big, stupid fight. I could not even stand to look at him or be near him or even think about him. Oh my God, he was being such a fucking douche." She pauses. "Why? Did he look unhappy?"

"I don't know. I got there with Alex right before they started. Things fell apart pretty quickly."

"Oh my God, Vanessa. Erica thinks they did it on purpose."

I look at Erica, who has destroyed the cork on the wine. She jams it into the bottle, stabbing at it with a pair of scissors. She shrugs and nods and continues stabbing.

"You think Aaron and Jeffrey purposefully set fire to the gallery and killed their dog? Even though they could have killed everyone inside, including themselves?"

"Of course it was on purpose. They're artists, Vanessa, in the truest sense of the word. Haven't you seen how dedicated they are to performance and exhibition? The way they involve the entire community in a new understanding of art? They make it accessible to us, because they're generous with their talent."

Dani raises her eyebrows. I tap at them, and she lowers them as I snip across her forehead. Her jaw trembles. Her nostrils flare. Her pupils dilate as she tries to diffuse her awareness of the scissors so close to her face.

"Take a drink," I tell her. She does, and her body relaxes.

"They could have planned it. No one got hurt," she says.

"Their dog died," I say.

"An animal is not the same as a person," Erica says. "Everyone knows Aaron and Jeffrey share an intense love that none of us match with our own partners. Dani, you and Jason fight constantly. Vanessa, you and Alex never appear in public together. Luke and I don't understand each other's artistic values. He totally just uses music for popularity."

She stabs the cork viciously one last time, and it crumbles into the bottle.

"But Aaron and Jeffrey transcend ego and daily strife in their partnership," she continues, "so to sacrifice a portion of what they love in order to show the community the strength of that love is the highest use of art there is."

"That *is* really beautiful," says Dani. "Snuggles is like Jesus. They sacrificed her to teach us about love."

Erica nods importantly and pours us more wine. I think of Alex standing with Luke and Ray yesterday, the way that girl with the bronze hair looked at him. She doesn't know anything about me. Erica is right. I don't know what to do with Alex in public. It is impossible to take him seriously when he is so uniformly chummy. If everyone's awesome, no one is.

I brush out Dani's hair and leave her with the strands in her face while I take another line.

"Chrissy wants to have a party, like a memorial service."

"That would cheapen their sacrifice," says Erica. "To resort to ritual when they were so brave and novel is offensive."

"She wants to go out to Egmont Key and have a fundraiser to restore the gallery." I don't really want to tell them this. I just want Erica to shut up.

"Shit, really? That's awesome," says Dani. "How are we going to get there?"

"Boats," I say.

"I thought no one could go out there. "

"Chrissy says it's open."

"But we all just party here now," she says.

"We used to know more people with boats, too," I say.

"Where did everyone go?" Erica says.

She sniffs loudly and swallows her drip. I can't recall whom I meant, these people with boats who left.

"The Midwest," Dani says. "Long Island. New Jersey. Places people are from."

Erica nods.

"People are from everywhere," she intones.

I scissor into Dani's hair with a precision that defies sobriety. The coke has made my focus meticulous. Her hair, so fine for such a dark color and otherwise strong features, is an asymmetrical sculpture. I slice upwards to flatten the strands at a hard angle from her ear. Her petulant mouth and square jaw appear nearly cartoonish. She is watching me snip like a psycho. Both our eyes are huge, like telescope lenses at night.

"What are you doing?" she asks.

"I'm making you look like a *hentai* figure," I say.

"What's that?"

"It's a style of really beautiful Japanese girl in one of the country's recently globally recognized creative movements."

"Oh, sweet, girl!"

"If you're going to offer Aaron and Jeffrey a memorial event, you should ask them how to incorporate their aesthetic," Erica says. "They may not want a competing value to distract from their restoration."

"What's the competing value, Erica?"

The coke is clumping into shards of glass in my nasal passages. It melts again in my throat. It bubbles through my blood. A thick hum rises in my ears.

"Aaron and Jeffrey structured a subtle and provocative call to action. If Chrissy organizes things, it'll be a crass lament for marine consumerism. I mean, c'mon, Vanessa, everyone knows Ray's business is failing."

Dani looks back and forth between us, uncertain. We are silent for a moment and then Erica continues, "I'm sure Chrissy doesn't realize that subconsciously she hopes to draw energy from Aaron and Jeffrey's strength in order to somehow save the marina."

"Erica," I say. "You know Aaron and Jeffrey will never let you suck their dicks, right?"

Dani's eyes get even bigger. She breaks into giggles. Erica is looking down and then up at Dani, and then, somehow, we're all laughing.

"So, yayyy, party!" Dani says.

Erica nods and shakes her head and smiles. I continue to snip Dani's hair into sharp lines and fantastic angles. The style continually flattens around her face, teasing the appearance of her cheekbones into impossible heights. She looks nearly unreal by the time I am done.

"It looks fucking awesome!" she tells me. She whispers to herself in the mirror, "*Hentai.*"

After I hug them good-bye, I stare out the plate glass at the waning sun, sizzling in its mid-afternoon glory. I have drunk three bottles of wine, done at least a twenty of coke, and made no money today.

Chrissy has texted, "Thank you so much for fixing my hair! <3"

Alex has texted, "I can't wait to see you tomorrow!"

I text them both back at once, "Right on. ☺"

4.

She's bucking underneath me and then, somehow, she's on top of me, so I throw her down hard, and she lands on her side, on her shoulder, underneath me again. I am not letting her get up this time. I jack her knee up as hard as I can, and her stomach tucks in as her hips widen to fight me off.

She smiles. She thinks she's got me with the other heel about to slam into my lower back, but I grab that leg, too, and bundle her thighs together with my left arm. I pin her at the pit of her knees with my right arm, so that her legs cross. Her left knee touches her shoulder.

She tries to toss her head, but she can't even do that. I slap her right cheek. There is a loud crack, a handprint already turning purple at the cheekbone.

"What were you smiling about?" I say.

She shrugs and grins again, so I slap her again. She huffs like a little princess, and I slam my cock into her. My balls bounce against her asshole. I want her clit to hurt. She cries out. I smack her again. She doesn't do anything this time but tighten around my cock.

"Now, that's a good little slut. Shut the fuck up," I tell her. My voice stops after every word, "and let me cum."

She does, finally, and the whole world disappears as I splash into her shiny, wet cunt. I don't even see her, even though I'm looking right at her. Everything is just a golden haze of her hair and her face and her tits and the back of her legs and her pussy slurping up my cock, pumping around it and milking it, until her breathing becomes louder and jagged at the end of each exhale when she cums. I stop and feel her pussy spasm and jerk around my cock, and I look at her, very seriously.

She rolls her hips toward me and rises up on her ass cheeks, crying, as she finishes cumming. When she relaxes back down onto the bed, I slap her again, hard, with an incredible crack that makes my stomach lurch with power and lust.

"I told you to shut up."

She lowers her chin, her eyelids, and I pound back into her, so that she ripples around me once more, quiet and soft this time. She reminds me of a lamb somehow, and this idea makes me cum, which is fucking weird, but I pull out and spray all over her face, while she keeps cumming underneath me with her fingers inside her pussy.

When we're done, I flip her over from the hips and smack her ass, lightly, and kiss her neck, but she doesn't taste like anything. I pass out for several minutes and when I wake up, she's got her head resting on my arm, facing me, smiling, with her eyes closed. She's breathing evenly. I pull my arm free, slowly, and get out of bed.

My head is swimming. I am not used to this strange house— I've only been here . . . I don't know . . . three times? I'm not even sure where the bathroom is in the dark, but I find the kitchen by its wide sliding doors that lead to the lanai and I open the fridge and crack a beer. The refrigerator is chilly, but it re-orients me. The house has the same layout as Vanessa's.

I take the beer to the bathroom. It almost drops when I put it on the toilet tank. I grab it and catch a flash of my face as I'm leaping for the beer in the mirror. I look silly and tired. I feel a little crazy and empty inside.

The air hangs in front of the bathroom window. It's thick and damp. We aren't that far from the beach, but it's still insanely humid. I piss a bright, yellow stream—it's practically orange—and flush hard.

I tiptoe back to the bedroom. I feel like I might laugh. I grab my pants with one hand and keep drinking my beer with the other. I take a big swig in front of the bed. She doesn't move, so I put my pants on and I tiptoe out. I almost laugh again, but I still feel totally weird and I don't want to wake her.

I sit down outside. It is so hot out, even at night. The yard is dead. I think her grandmother planted the wrong grass. It's weird that her grandmother is here, too. It's still early enough that I could go out for another few rounds. I need to leave, but I'm spent. I check my phone.

Luke texted an hour ago, "Yo, party, son?"

I text back, "Where are you?"

He hits me back immediately, "Sippin' on Star!"

I have no idea what that means, and it depresses me. I'm never there when my friends figure out the next big thing.

I down the rest of the beer. I don't need to go out right now, anyway. I have to be up early to go boating with Vanessa tomorrow. My skin is tingling from fucking. I look up at the sky and down at the grass and back at the house and wish I had another beer, anyway.

I didn't want to come here. Julie is already desperate. I wasn't really part of the show last night. I never am. She just thought I was. They put my name on the fliers, because I help them set up, like always. Somehow, she invited herself. I had to come over. Desperate can become hysterical fast. She could have fucked everything up. She still thinks it was my show, too.

I used to think I was talented because my art shows almost always sell out. I had a painting of houses around a lake at night. The houses were lit up with candles and lanterns and lampposts along a road. They were all symmetrical with no real architectural style. They had Venetian windows and multiple dormers and pilasters, but they were all exactly the same.

The lake was in shadow. I used black and dark greens and blues and grays to paint the world of the lake from the perspective of above. I painted the still, iridescent bodies of sleeping bass and the glowing aura of the water around them. I showed the net of algae that rested, dark red, at the edges of the lake. The best part, I thought, was the alligator, illuminated in the saw grass.

I called the painting *The McMansions at Deer Lake (Avon Park)*. I thought it was brilliant. The alligator was a warning against the artless bulldozing of central Florida. The lake showed true beauty. The parenthetical in the title admonished the laziness of a state that gave four lakes the same name.

I thought of this painting as my masterpiece, the one that made my talent instantly recognizable. I gave it an insane, sentimental price, so it never sold, but I didn't care. I thought it was an important enough piece to travel.

After the first few shows at Art, I realized my friends didn't see it that way. They always asked me to hang out with them—plan stuff, set up, and promote—but they never asked me to show anything.

At first, I thought it was because they knew I was busy with my own shows, but then Erica curated a show about the misrepresentation of art in order to sell something else. The show was called "Bait and Switch." The call for submissions listed sources of inspiration as "paltry, red-herring federal grants, Chihuly's indentured servants, and landscapes in the lobbies of condo towers."

She couldn't find anyone who fulfilled the vision besides her, Jeffrey, and Ray, so I volunteered *McMansions.*

"I know it's about more than bait-and-switch tactics, but a McMansion is the ultimate bait and switch, anyway. You think you're getting a beautiful home, but there's no real aesthetic value in cookie-cutter houses. You've been duped," I said.

"Thanks, Alex," she said. "I'm looking for really complex diametrics right now, like how Jeffrey uses geometry as multiple cultural references or how I've shown the weakness of subjectivity in the uncultured masses with found objects."

I looked at the wall behind her. Jeffrey had drawn a large, colorful piece with a Spirograph. Erica had glued trash to plywood.

"That's what the lake represents," I said. "It's ironic because there's something truly beautiful right in front of the houses, but no one cares. They only light up the houses, because developers told them they're beautiful."

"The perspective makes it hard to understand that, Alex. You've made the lake so wonky and dark, but the houses are perfect."

"But perfect in this context is subjective, too, Erica!"

She shook her head slowly. "I'm sorry. I do hear what you're explaining. This piece is very representational, though. The uncultured masses my work addresses may just think it's the same condo art we're lambasting with this show."

"Condo art?"

She smiled. She looked gooey, as if her face were made of warm plastic. "Because it's houses on a lake. It's scenic."

The gallery had just opened, but they had already developed a style together. I didn't get it, but then I did. They were actual artists, testing ideas and perceptions. I was a lucky sell-out.

I keep trying to get galleries to take these mobile sculptures from me. Ray had a bunch of scrap metal at the marina once, so we torched it into big squares and then welded chain to the squares to make a giant mobile.

He took it down a few days later, because he had to sell the scrap, but it was still the coolest piece I ever made. I want to do a series of them, but make them look like women, dangling in the breeze, the way girls look at clubs or bars or wherever.

Luke texts again—"Bro!"—and I whip around to look at the house. It's totally still, and I shut off my phone. I have to get out of here.

I was sure this would end last night. I was just going to tell her I didn't think it would work out, but she disappeared after the fire, too, so I just ended up blowing rails in the marina with Ray and Luke and some gallery groupies, guys and girls we didn't know who knew us.

I am hoping if I just never call her again, that will be that. She's just some chick from one of those carny towns in Volusia. We banged at the beach. Big deal.

I stand up and go back inside, quietly, almost disgusted with myself, but I still feel a sick thrill, a sense of accomplishment at having nailed her again, anyway. Julie's house is completely still, as if it's much later than it really is. My shoes are by the door, where I left them, but I hop on my tiptoes back into the kitchen and grab another beer, just for the hell of it, and let myself out.

I put on my shoes in the middle of the street and crack the beer before I start walking home. The sky is purple. The air is humid. I turn my phone back on, but no one cares what I'm doing right now.

I'm pretty excited about going boating tomorrow, anyway.

5.

I wake up, and Alex is gone. I look out the window thinking of his scratchy, strawberry beard and turquoise eyes. The moon shines gently on tufts of tall, dry grass along the fence. I look at my phone. It's not even one o'clock. I thought maybe he would stay.

My legs and hips are tired and a little wobbly. My joints feel loose and liquid from how he spread my thighs. I think of how my hips popped. My neck feels bruised, and it hurts to swallow. My lips are dry.

I sit up and untangle the sticky sheet. The air is still and damp in the bedroom. It smells like salt and sweat. I put my feet on the ground. The floor is cooler than the rest of the room. I walk to the mirror. My skin looks golden and bright. My face is full and glows, like I'm about to start sweating, but I don't think I have any marks from where he slapped me.

My torso looks tight over the ridges of my hips. The flesh covers the bones fully. I pull back the wings of my hips, look in the mirror, turn around and look at my ass. A handprint welts the skin.

I dress quickly, shorts, a tank top, lip gloss, earrings, a giant ring. I take the ring off. I put it back on again. I go out into the hallway to the other side of the house. My grandmother's door is closed. I can't feel if she is awake or not.

Everything overwhelming about my mind is starting to fade now that I'm here. I am relieved. I only need to pay attention to the present. I almost knock on my grandmother's door, but I feel weird telling her I'm going out, so I don't.

I see myself in the mirror as I leave. I think I look pretty good tonight, and I think, even though Alex left, it's because I think I can be happy here.

Downtown is humid and nearly empty. The red light over The Bait Bucket is garish, but it beams steadily. It looks welcoming in the wet air.

Kim is at the bar, talking to a skinny dude in an oversized t-shirt and baggy shorts. He has sharp cheekbones and colorless hair, almost brownish-grayish, like a pale rodent. His tattoos are jailhouse watercolors, the lines too fine and blurred.

I had a boyfriend who looked like this. He was from Deltona. His name was Rob. It hurts to look at the doppel-Rob. I thought Alex would be here. He said he hangs out here.

"Hi," I say to Kim. She is my only friend right now. She is always smiling.

"Hi, girl!" she chirps.

The skinny guy looks at me, up and down.

"So, y'all wanna drink?"

"I thought you were going," Kim says. Her ear floats up to the ceiling, pulling her smile sideways.

"I got time for one more," he says. His eyes stay on my tits.

"Do you want one?" I ask Kim.

"Yeah! You just got here!"

I look around the bar. Alex is not here. None of the people I met at the show last night are here. The crowd is middle-aged, weathered. There is no music.

"Maybe we should go somewhere else," I say.

"Stay," says the guy. "I'll get these. I'm Jeff."

"Julie," I say, but I feel like I'm not in the room somehow. I put my hand on the bar to steady myself.

"Are you OK?" Kim asks.

"I don't know," I say. I am pushing away thoughts of Rob, scanning for signs of Alex or his friends. I am sure he said his friends are always here.

"You look a little . . ." she turns to Jeff, still smiling. "Hey, we're going to pass for a minute."

He ducks his head sheepishly, still staring at my tits.

"Anything I can do?" he asks.

Kim sees his eyes. "No, we're fine. We're going to leave."

He looks up at her abruptly. Her face is sallow, set in its grin.

"Sure, then, see ya around," he says. He pecks her on the cheek. She stiffens, but her smile stays where it is. He lopes off, one hand on the back of his head as he walks.

"Do you want to go?" Kim asks.

"No," I say. I can't leave yet. "I feel OK. I think I just didn't like that guy. Is that weird?"

I laugh. The sound is harsh and stunted.

"Oh . . . yeah . . ." she says.

She looks above the bottles. A giant fish hangs over the bar. The mouth looks surprised. Its eyes are dried discs. They're burnished to a dull golden-green from hanging by the smoky ceiling for so long. Its eyes are the same color as Kim's eyes.

"Let's get that other drink," she says.

"OK."

"Where were you before?"

"Home." I lean in. My smile pulls my cheeks to match hers. "This guy came over for a few hours."

"Really?"

"Yeah, he's pretty cool."

"Wow. You've only been here a few weeks."

"Yeah, he's cool, though. He's an artist, so he doesn't really hold back."

"Is this the same guy that took you to that party last night?"

"Oh, yeah, but the place caught on fire! I kind of lost track of him and—"

"Wait! Julie!"

"Yeah?"

"Are you banging Alex?"

"You know him?"

"Yeah! I hooked up with him at the Alden in the spring!"

I look for the bartender. I don't know how much to say now. The fire seems far away. I had almost forgotten it entirely. I want to tell her everything that happened last night. I want to tell someone everything. The same lightheaded feeling returns, as if I'm not fully here. I haven't taken anything today. I wasn't expecting this. I thought Alex would stay.

The bartender leans on the far end of the bar. The streetlight throws a dull pallor on his greasy curls. He shakes his head at his customer, laughing as he walks away slowly.

"What is he doing?" I say to Kim.

"Seriously," she says.

I am staring at his fat, red face. He stops halfway down the bar and begins mixing two drinks.

"Oh my God," Kim says. She squeezes my arm. Bubbles burst up my triceps and crystallize in my brain. She is staring at me, her face startled, like the fish overhead. "Doesn't Alex have a girlfriend?"

"I've been with him two nights in a row now," I say. I am shaking my head. "I met a bunch of his friends." I am still shaking my head. I can't stop.

The bartender looks at us, but he keeps stirring. I should have taken a Klonopin. He makes his way over to us and puts the drinks down in front of us.

"Ooh!" Kim says. "You read our minds!"

The bartender smiles. "They're from him, down there." He points at the man who made him laugh before. The guy waves at us. Kim giggles.

"We definitely need more alcohol," she says.

The guy stands up and walks toward us. He looks old, but like he works out.

"Hi, ladies. You looked like you were having a serious conversation, so I thought I'd come down here and lighten things up for you."

Kim giggles again. She sounds pretty, like a harp.

"We were just talking," I say. I can't tell if I'm still shaking my head or not.

I try to look at this man. I think his eyes are dark blue. I keep seeing Alex's eyes, fuzzy and opaque in my kitchen, then globe-like and frosted in my bedroom.

The same popping sensation from when Kim squeezed my arm bursts into my head, but now its popping noise comes from the frosted globes of Alex's eyes in my memory. The globes rise from his face like bubbles into some new part of my brain and explode, soaking the inside of my mind in a wet, silver-gray lens.

I feel like I am looking through something cold and alive, a tempered glass womb, but something that still comes from Alex. I look around frantically. He isn't here. None of his friends are here. I don't know why I'm here anymore.

"I'm Paul," the guy says. "I saw you last night."

I try to look at him again. I don't remember him. He smiles. His teeth look acid-washed against his tan.

"You were standing outside that ridiculous art gallery with a thuggish looking guy with black hair."

"Oh my God! That fire," says Kim. "You were there, too?"

"Tragic. Guess that's what happens when you think you're invincible."

"I didn't see you," I say, as Kim says, "It *is* tragic!"

Paul looks at me and winks. "You know, if you like me, I won't tell if you have a boyfriend." He turns back to Kim, "Tragic is the only word. Arrogance like that is always its own reward. Artists, right?"

He smiles again. His teeth chatter with his grin. He runs a hand through his hair. Kim looks giddy.

"So, what do you ladies do?" Paul asks.

"I'm a make-up artist," Kim says.

"That must be why you're so pretty," he says.

She giggles again.

"What about you?" he asks me.

I look at his craggy face and thinning hair. I am trapped behind the wall of convex glass in my head. I cannot think of anything to say.

"She takes care of her grandmother," Kim says quickly.

Paul looks at me again, carefully. His pity shows. He swallows from his drink, looking at me, over its rim. He is mocking me.

Suddenly, I feel as if the frosted glass womb inside my mind is made of sharp light. The light is going to explode, too, and I am going to cry tears of thick, silver uterine lining. But I don't know what it means this time. This cannot be happening again. It is happening again.

"Guys, I have to go," I say.

"Oh, are we boring you?" asks Paul.

"No. I'm . . . I'm tired," I say. My voice breaks, but Kim doesn't think anything is wrong. She is still smiling. I blink hard.

"OK," Paul says. He isn't looking at me anymore.

I lean over to kiss Kim, but she isn't looking at me, either. She's gaping at the hollow anchor charm in the middle of Paul's chest, and I kiss her good-bye anyway, clumsily. She blinks at me with dead, green eyes.

Outside, in the hot night, away from the smoke of the bar, I don't want to go home to the dusty smell of my grandmother's house. I walk the mile or so down to the beach.

There is a flock of teenagers squawking in the sand. I lie down and look up at the sky. Its navy blue is instantly comforting. My body sinks into the sand. The rush of the ocean vibrates under my skin. Tiny grains of sand shift around me with each lap of the water. The children tumble on top of the sand, too. If neither of us moves from our rough, granular positions, these kids will be wrestling and fondling each other on top of the same sand that touches me now.

I remember the last time I saw Rob. He had gone hunting for hogs with his brother near Deleon and he came down the road carrying a turkey feather, long and fine and gray.

The sun cut through the moss in the trees, so that a diamond pattern of light skipped over his colorless hair. He slashed the feather through the air, and its oily vane made the wind whistle from afar. I felt awful when I heard it. He was too far down the road for me to have really heard it.

When he approached, he handed me the feather.

"No hogs," he said. "Just an old turkey. We're having it for dinner tonight if you want to come by."

I took the feather from him. He kissed me on the cheek as our hands touched. The fluff near the quill covered my vision, so that everything was downy and hazy and white. I saw the brown face of a girl who loved him and wished he would come visit her more. She was tall for her age, taller than her brothers and sisters, who were older and had different fathers. None of them were born yet. She had Rob's flat, narrow eyes.

We had been together five years, then, since I was fourteen, and even though it made him feel good to share me at a party sometimes, I still thought we would get married.

"Where were you, really?" I asked him.

"Huh? Oh, we camped up the west end by Harry's Creek Swamp."

I looked down at the feather in my hand, up at the moss in the trees.

"Have a swig," he said. He offered a bottle of bourbon.

"I don't want it."

"Have a swig," he said again.

"I don't want it," I said and I couldn't control my voice. I sounded angry.

"You should have a drink. Why's your mama drink?"

I thought of my mother, sitting on the plaid orange and blue couch in our trailer, watching TV, letting nothing come near her. He was trying to be gentle, but he hurt me by saying it. I couldn't speak.

"See, ain't nobody fittin' to think like that," he said. He offered the bottle out again. I turned back to our trailer and walked toward the low, spatulate palms in front of it. The sun still danced a diamond pattern.

After that, he went to Miami, and I didn't see him again, just like that, and every guy I dated after that always showed me something similar. A secret kid, another girl who relied on his promises. Violence. Always violence. Everyone always holds violence.

Then, one day, years after Rob was gone, my mother turned off the TV and told me to go stay with my grandmother.

"Why?" I said.

"Why?" she repeated. "Aren't you tired of all this? Just go."

So I did. It's better here. Sometimes, I still see the things people have inside them—things they don't know yet, but they already own the thoughts that later manifest, so I can think them, too, but I don't feel as troubled by it here.

It's as if they think less here. They just live.

The teenagers roll nearer to me until they're just a few feet away. One of the girls is upset. She sounds like she has been drinking and she's beginning to sober up. She's just realized she might get in trouble. She can tell she smells like boys and liquor—intoxication.

I try to remember if I ever felt that way, scared of my parents, but I don't think I did. My father worked slaughtering goats for a while, but, then, later, they always just sat on the couch and drank or sometimes bickered about nothing. They didn't bother me too much.

My grandmother was around while I was young, but then she moved here, and my father, her son-in-law, wouldn't go. He said we didn't need her, but my mother just drank even more with her mother gone.

The only thing about them that scared me was that they didn't care about anything. But that's different. They never did anything to me.

The girl is leaving now, walking up the beach alone. I close my eyes and open them again. I prop up on an elbow to watch her walk away. Her shoulders are far ahead of her hips. She's trying to walk fast, but she's drunk and can't move as quickly as she wants. A boy follows her. The rest of the group pauses for a moment. One of the girls quickly says something, and the others laugh. It doesn't seem like the boy is going to do anything bad to the girl. He wants to be near her longer, and it sounds nice to hear the rest of them laugh.

It sounds nice to have friends here.

6.

I wake to a text from Alex that says, "Be there in 20 minutes."

I blink, and the room comes into focus. The sound of paper flutters over the window, a soft *whippety-whippety* sound. Breeze this early is unusual, but I'm glad for it. I'm alone without it.

I sleep better when I am alone, but it's so much easier to act normal when I wake up and Alex is next to me. When I wake up alone, I realize I am always alone, no matter who is there some other morning. When I wake up alone, I feel like I will never be able to figure how other people connect without turning into a row of flat cutouts.

Alex looks at me in the morning, looks right at me. Even though later in the day, I will know he was just blinking awake and I was there, I also know that he connects with people. If there is any chance of believing that other people's minds exist, that there is another real person in the world, that is when I believe it.

I listen to what other people say, but their words turn into hills of white noise. I peer into their pupils for glimpses of rooms or even hallways, but they become unnerved and pull the blinds, looking at the ground or to the right of me.

It seems entirely possible that the rest of the world is aliens or robots, or that I am and just don't know it, or that some creatures that look like me are one thing, and others are another, and I haven't found the creatures that actually are the same species I am.

Most of the time, I think people look like odd machines. Programmed, but still programmable.

I text Alex back, "Meet me at the marina in 30 instead."

He texts back, "<3"

I call Chrissy. She doesn't pick up.

I text her, "Are you at the marina? Meet us in 30?"

She texts right back, "Can't, but will be there all afternoon. See you when you return?"

I feel like I should be disturbed that she always texts right after she doesn't pick up, but I am just relieved she isn't coming after all.

The sun is blazing and bright enough to give me a headache before I am at the boat. Alex is not here yet. He will be late anyway. The water is still, almost stagnant in the heat. I take the cover off the boat and spray everything down. The hose hisses aggressively, pounding the boat so it rocks in the hoist.

The boat is a 1968 Super Florida, an Italian tribute to the carefree optimism of Americans who worshipped the sun and the new reliance on foreign manufacture. Mine is the last model free of fiberglass, and it gleams in maple and mahogany. It was a graduation gift from my parents, who could afford it, but only just.

At first, I thought they must have wanted it for themselves, years ago, before I was born. They had me late in life, and the boat would have looked good in the canal behind their Old Southeast home with its Spanish tile roof on its pink brick street.

But, no, the mild countenance they wore when they gave it to me betrayed no excitement. It was an appropriate gift—austere, expensive, meaningful, and lasting, like a college education.

They wanted me to go to graduate school, but they didn't have any course of study in mind for me. I didn't see the point in anyone paying for it when all I wanted to do was snip out paper dolls and cut elaborate outfits for them.

I made paper-girl battalions and cut them rows of matching machine guns or machetes. I cut square dancers with flying braids and constructed a line of suitors for them, each with his arm behind his back. Chains of paper people scallop the molding in my house still, dressing windows and doorways, like garland for a holiday that never comes.

Back then, the only time I felt fully absorbed by anything was while fucking or cutting things. Only then did I find a parentheses of time when I did not think the things I am always thinking. Everyone dies. How can beings that don't control the course of their existence be real?

By the time my parents gifted me the boat, I had already

enrolled in beauty school without telling them. Scissors made sense. I could cut things and change their form. I could slice the world into more attractive forms again and again. I could give a definitive beginning and end to forms and if things changed, grew, split or fried, it didn't matter. It just meant that I always had a way to feed time, that parasite that clings even after shelter and food and water are gone.

I was going to tell them on a Thursday night, August 19, that I wouldn't be moving to some dense metropolis to study some arcane, useless topic. Beauty school began in another week.

They wouldn't be upset. They would nod and smile and ask me how I had decided that. Whatever answer I gave would be swallowed along with the most expensive Zinfandel on the menu. They were kind people, and even though I thought of them as one insipid person when I was young, they never noticed people's decisions as good or bad.

They didn't make it to dinner, because a Silver Meteor traveling from Miami to New York hit their car on the tracks in Palatka. They had been vacationing in Jekyll Island, Georgia. Witnesses say my father tried to beat the crossing gate, and, while I don't think anyone at the scene was lying, I know this was unusual behavior for them.

Sometimes, I try to imagine what could have been happening, why they tried to beat the train. I never heard them fight, but they lost all placidity when they were late—but, also, they were cautious to the point that if something seemed even mildly risky, they simply didn't do it. They never debated heatedly the worth of any particular course of action or bore each other resentment for their shared life of predictability and calm.

Whatever happened when my father decided to race that silly wooden stick was a genuine impulse. He did something that showed he was more than a cutout, and they died, together, since they were the same pallid person, anyway. No one can beat the engine of death.

I drop the boat into the water and turn it on. I haven't been out in it with other people all summer. I am less and less social the louder my friends become, the hotter it gets. It is so hot out already, and while I feel the same irritation my parents would have felt that Alex is late, I am actually grateful that I can get ready to go by myself.

When he bops up the dock in a pineapple-print bathing suit and a smile, I am able to smile back. He swings his legs into the boat and hugs me and kisses me. He feels vibrant and foreign.

"Chrissy was going to come with us, but it turns out she can't make it," I say.

He looks back at the dock house, "They're not there."

"She will be this afternoon. Ray has to hide his boat now, but she said she'll be here."

He looks down and nods his head.

"What?" I ask.

"I just think it's too bad," he says.

"Oh. That's why I told her to come out with us."

He grins at me. "That was nice of you!"

I gaze back at him. His eyes gleam with the same brightness that shines from his pupils when he wakes. He seems so foolish sometimes.

A manatee's scarred back surfaces next to us, a tan bandage of tough skin around white gorges. Another bobs up to the surface. I kill the engine.

"Wow! Hey, guys!" Alex shouts at them. They bobble under and puff back up, trying to submerge.

"You're threatening them," I say.

He looks overboard again, but they're gone. He looks back at me, confused, and I have to look away.

"They don't understand what you're doing," I say.

He laughs and calls over the edge of the boat, "Sorry, guys!" He turns back to me, "They must be worried I want a ride!"

He looks right at me, that childlike smile blotting out the sun. We meander north and cut through St. John's Pass. We round the inlet of Treasure Island in silence. Alex is looking at the backs of houses. I am looking at the entrance to the Gulf of Mexico, a turquoise bathtub that flashes white from the sun's reflection on the glassy surface.

I open the boat up all at once, and we head south. Alex

comes up to the helm with me and rubs sunscreen on my shoulders. I take off my top for him. He rubs more lotion on my tits and rolls my nipples in between his index finger and thumb while he kisses my neck. He takes his cock out of the top of his bathing suit and pulls down my bikini bottom just a little bit, so that he can tap his cock in the crack of my ass. I roll my ass cheeks into him, so that I can rub it for him. We continue like this for another minute, until he pulls away.

"Damn," he says. "You're gonna have to stop the boat if you're gonna keep doing that."

"I wasn't doing anything," I say, but I am massaging my own cervix with pelvic contractions even as I say it. I can't look at him.

He pushes his cock back into his bathing suit and rubs it through the fabric. He sits down in the passenger seat. "It's beautiful out here."

We are charging through the water, so that my hair becomes a snarl of salt at the back of my head. There are no other boats near us. The shoreline is free of the speckles of people that crowded the beach last year. The water is clear around us. The wake smells like salt and fish.

We hurtle past the motels and bars on Gulf Boulevard, where forlorn and relocated divorcees gulp shot specials in the afternoon. We bounce past places that are all exactly the same—Postcard Inn, Sandbar, The Alden, Tradewinds, Sirata. The only facade that looks different from the others is the decaying and closed Bongos, and I wonder if the others will topple soon, too.

No one comes here anymore. Oil never stops chugging into the water. We just burn it and disperse it, and no one wants to come here to see the tourist-less beaches and remember what idiots we all are.

We go so fast past these reminders of where we used to live that the boat catches air. Alex tenses next to me, but I don't care and I only decrease our speed at the Don CeSar, a regal ridge of soft, pink towers at the edge of Tierra Verde.

"That was crazy," Alex says.

"I know," I say. The boat hops in the water and then levels out to match the gentle waves. The soft perfume of benzene

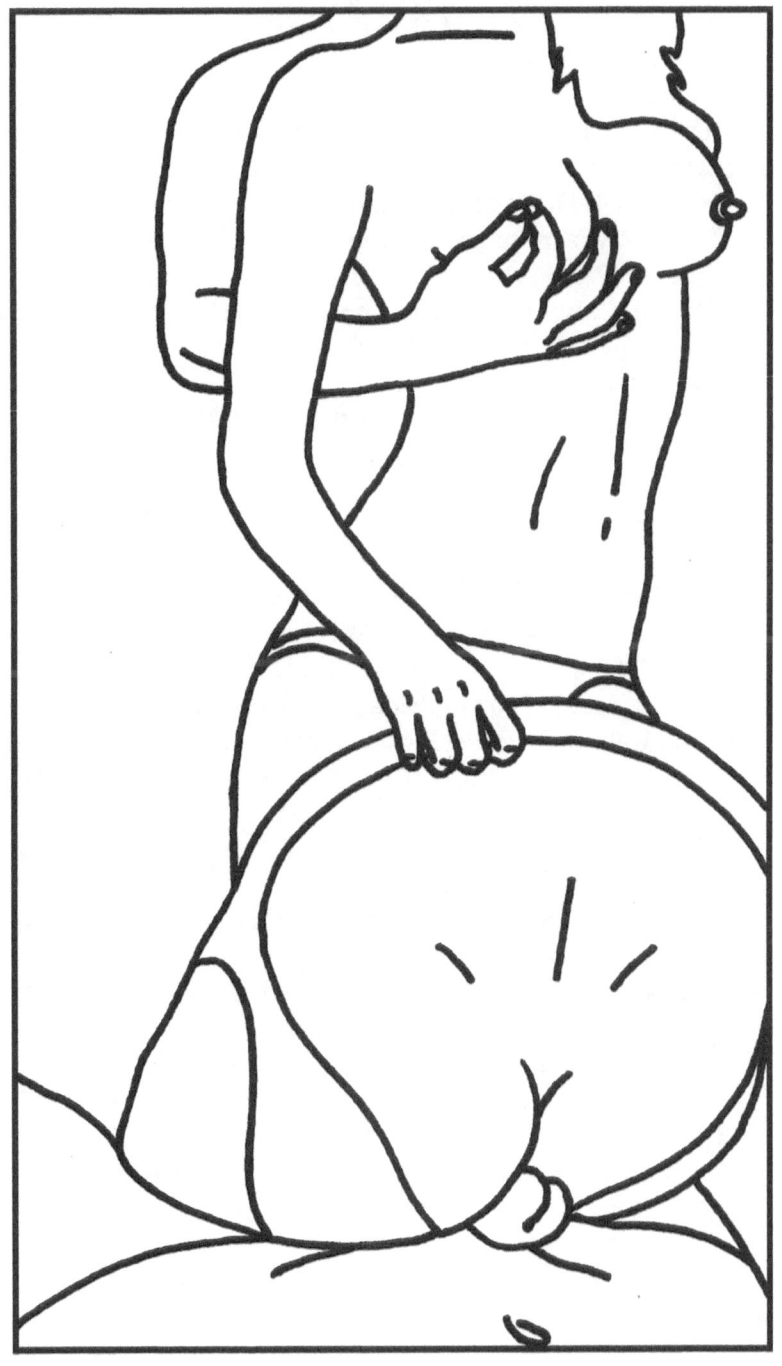

comes from the west, but it's only barely noticeable, a far-off burn. I continue south.

"Where did you go last night?" I ask.

"Oh, I just had to get ready for today, get organized for next week, that kind of thing, so that we could relax today."

I nod. He is looking toward the shore at the Don.

"This is my favorite place in the whole world," I tell him.

"The Gulf?"

"Yes, but, also, this specific spot here, in front of the Don, in the water."

"How come?"

"The current runs parallel to the shore through this whole area. When the weather is this hot, the current is as reliable as it can get."

He stands and smiles at me, his hands behind his back on the gunwale. "Girls like reliable."

"It's not so much that," I say. I motion to him to stand at the wheel. I start pulling the anchor out.

"Here," he comes to help me. I trade places with him again and let him toss it over the side. Once he secures it, I take his hand and walk back to the deck with him and sit on the platform. I drop into the water.

"What are you doing?"

"Come in."

"Hell no."

"Why not?" I'm treading water, still topless.

"Your boobs are floating."

"OK, so come in. Do you want to check the anchor again?"

"No, it's fine." He goes and checks it again, anyway.

I swim around the side of the boat. I have to crawl.

"Where are you going?"

I can't answer him. I just continue swimming until I'm in front of the bow, a safe distance from the hull, but close enough that he can hear me shout.

"This is what I wanted to show you! Come out!"

We are still within the same current we followed south. It pushes its way toward the next county, but stays parallel to the mainland. A cross-current intersects it as part of its path around Egmont Key. Finally, a tiny stream from the shallow, shark-infested water of the adjoining bay trickles out to the north of the Key and converges with the two larger currents.

These currents create a natural whirlpool, a halo of saltwater. It forms an outer ring of pressure that creates a gentle brim only on the surface. Underwater, the ring no longer exists. The water flows with the rest of the Gulf.

Alex does not like that I am out here, though. "You're crazy. I'm not going out there!"

I stroke back to him, slowly. I am swimming against the current now and I should crawl to make it back with any efficiency, but I am looking at him as I swim.

He is not scared for himself. He is worried that something might happen to me. I can see the plaintive look on his face. I wonder if he can see the isolation in me too clearly this way, out in the middle of such vastness. I swim back, keeping my face on his.

His discomfort is like a mask that peels away as I get closer. I almost believe I see something unique in him for a second, and it almost feels like a current of hope, but I can't think of why I would hope for anything.

I hoist myself onto the swim platform. He bundles me up in a towel and hugs me and kisses me.

"You are fucking crazy," he says again. "There are sharks out there."

"I suppose."

"No, they're bad now, worse than before. They swim closer to land now, because of the oil. The fish they eat are all dead out there," he motions with his hand toward Tierra Verde.

"It's not nice to call rich people fish," I say. "They have feelings, too, just different ones from you."

He laughs nervously. He is embarrassed. "You know what I mean. There. Out there." He points west. "The fish are dead out there, and the sharks are coming here to eat the ones that are still alive."

"OK, it's only noon. Sharks feed at dusk."

"God, could you stop being so stubborn and just stay in the boat?"

"OK. Sorry. OK . . . Chrissy wants to throw a party on Egmont Key," I say.

He relaxes at the mention of a party. I wanted to show him something amazing, something real, but, instead, I freaked him out, and, even though it brings us back to talking about the same thing as always—oh my God, let's throw a party—talking about Chrissy is easier than talking about myself and seeing his eyes finally become as smooth and far away as the horizon.

"What for?" he asks.

"She wants to do it for Aaron and Jeffrey, as a fundraiser."

"That's a great idea!"

"Really?"

"Yeah, it's seriously a good idea! Yes!"

"Do you think it would actually . . . raise funds? And that Aaron and Jeffrey would like the idea, too?"

"I bet they'd love it. They might be a little shy at first, but I bet they'd feel really connected and loved."

I look out at the perfect sky. I cannot imagine Aaron and Jeffrey feeling love. They seem so waxen, despite their boisterousness and productivity.

"OK," I say.

"We should definitely do it! I'll help! I'm going to go see them tonight. Aaron's getting out of the hospital tonight."

"What happened?"

"He broke his arm. They cut open his muscles to reconstruct some shattered bone, but once they found out he doesn't have insurance, he was on his way."

"Oh, that sounds bad."

"It is, but it isn't, you know? We'll all take care of him, and he'll be OK. This is a really good idea, though. Why don't we put on a show, too?"

"What kind of show? There's no electricity out there."

"I've wanted to make these metal sculptures of women forever, but, like, really abstract, where I just connect shapes with chains to show the movement of women. They would look really shiny and cold, but because of how I build them, they'd be kind of warm, too . . . because of the movement," he trails off.

"You mean like what Ray did with that scrap metal?"

"We did that together."

"Oh, OK. I didn't know you could do stuff like that," I say. "Cool."

"I think I could do it," he says quietly.

I pull on the anchor, but I am tired from shouting and then swimming back. Alex sees this and pulls it up for me and puts it away while I sit down.

"Wait! I know!" he says. "We should do it together. The idea needs a life force! What if I didn't make the sculptures women? What if I made sculptural armor around real women?"

We stare at one another for a moment. The sun is directly overhead. The boat rolls back and forth in place. The current is pulling it south still, but it will bob to the west if I don't turn on the engine soon. I continue to float.

The heat is magnificent. The top of my head sizzles, but all I feel is that I am beginning to break through some pile of dung, like a miraculous scarab beetle called to the sun. It is because someone else's emotions are all around me. I wonder if this is what love feels like, this ability to feel one other person, even when everyone else feels like mindless, industrious cockroaches crawling over a wasted expanse.

"What if we had models, like a runway show, and you did their hair? It's perfect, because Aaron and Jeffrey can still be involved . . . and Chrissy can do stuff to bring people to the marina for her and Ray."

"What about Snuggles?"

"Who?"

"The dog," I say. "No one remembers the dog."

"Oh . . . I don't know." He looks back toward the shore. The white tips of the Don's turrets are invisible in the sun from this distance. The stucco is a blur of pink fluff.

"We're getting pretty far out," he says.

I turn the engine back on.

"Well, anyway," I say, "who would go? I mean, there's

nobody out here, anymore. People don't really like coming out here."

"We're here now," he says.

"Right," I say.

He looks at me with raised eyebrows.

I look straight ahead and don't say anything for a second.

"Do you want to check it out? See how far we can get before we find oil?"

"Haven't we gone too far once we can?" he says.

"No, we'll smell it, I think."

"If you know what you're doing."

"I think so," I say, even though I don't.

I open the boat up again. The shore is one clean line, and we move even faster than before. The salt abrades my skin. The boat skips higher than it ever has at the mouth that pours the bay into the Gulf.

We reach the eastern side of the Key in minutes. The island is inaccessible, except by private boat. It looks pristine, its old lighthouse rising into the sky. The water around it is clear, beautiful. I peer over the gunwale. The sun streams over my shoulders and into the water. I can see down at least twenty feet.

The cawing of birds in the sky is loud and rhythmic. Long-winged shore birds make wide triangles in the air. They wear different patches—over the eyes, at the skull, across the napes—but they stay together, watching the black plovers with their dramatic, dark stomachs, flying higher in the air.

The only threatening flock is the large herring gulls. They repeat the same circle, each pecking aggressively at the bird in front, and swooping toward the water without diving into it.

There have never been birds like this before. This is what happens when we stop coming here. Birds nest all along the shore.

Alex is silent. "I haven't been here in years. Probably not since, like, March two years ago or something," he says finally. He is looking at the lighthouse, the crumbling remains of an old fort. "It's still incredible. Can we get out?"

The boat is off. The only sounds are the water and the birds and Alex's voice.

He is smiling goofily, and I am thinking about smiling back, when a gull swoops towards the windshield of the boat, screaming, its throat bulging in front of Alex's face. He ducks.

"What the fuck?" he says.

I look up. A pelican has chased the gull downward. It swoops in front of us, too, its mean eye unblinking on the side of its thin, contracted beak. It splashes through the water's surface and shovels up a mouthful of saltwater that it discards in a gray dribble that blows back into the boat. Its dingy wings are immense and intimidating up close. The tips of its feathers are dark gray, almost blue. A putrid scent rushes behind its black, webbed feet.

"Jesus!" Alex says.

Its bill looks dry, shriveled. I realize too, suddenly, that it hasn't caught any fish, that, overhead, the gulls are more aggressive and numerous than usual, that below us, the water is empty. There are no fish at any visible depth. The striped mullets that used to jump along the shoreline are gone. The short, sloped fins of kingfish are nowhere.

The birds have come to where there were fish a few weeks ago. They have eaten this spot free of fish for now. There will be more later—at dusk, or the birds wouldn't be here at all—but there is not enough for all the birds that are here now.

The pelicans do not want the gulls here. The beach birds are watching the plovers.

I look at Alex and dab some sweat off his forehead.

"Bird bath," I say. He smiles, easily soothed.

"Do you mind if we go back after all?" I ask him. "I forgot to pack us a lunch and I'm starving."

"Yeah, sure, no problem," he says.

I circle around the southern tip of the Key and back north. He pushes his cock against me again as I drive the boat. I let him drive for a while and stand behind him and jerk him off until he can't focus. He finishes himself off as we whiz past Pass-A-Grille. Cum splatters the boat's mahogany bridge deck, but he doesn't notice and he falls asleep until we get back to the marina.

I am cleaning the deck off when he says, "So, are we doing this for Aaron and Jeffrey?"

He sounds casual, but I can tell from the stunted flap and affricate of their names that he wants to do it very badly.

"Maybe tomorrow we can go see them at the gallery."

"Oh, I can't tomorrow. I'm leaving for Athens, remember?"

"You are?"

"I told you."

He says this as if I have accused him of something. I turn off the hose. Everything is silent before I speak.

"No, you didn't."

"Yes, I did." The pitch of his voice rises.

"When?"

He looks past me. "I don't remember."

"Me, either." I shake my head pleasantly.

"Well, either way, have a good trip," I say. I am smiling now.

"We can still hang out tonight," he says.

"When are you getting back? I thought you were going to see Aaron after he gets out of the hospital."

He pauses for a moment. "I'll be back Thursday, but I can come to see you after I see Aaron tonight."

"Don't worry about it. I'm going to see Chrissy tonight. Did you notice they're not here?"

"Yeah, I noticed," he says.

I finish snapping the cover over the boat. The marina is half empty, and the fuel pump has been removed from its big metal case by the dark dock house.

It is only 3pm on Sunday, August 5. The mornings have been clear for weeks. The rain is always done by five. Midnight is always purple and green and cool. There are no approaching or forecast hurricanes. There should be people here, but we are the only ones.

"C'mon," I say. "Let's get out of here."

I feel as if the day has duped me, like the world keeps tricking me in some way I don't understand.

7.

I'm bored by the time I hit Ocala, which isn't such a great thing, because I have no radio, and it's another five hours at least before I get to Athens.

Ocala is better than Hillsborough, which is just a clusterfuck of McMansions, but traffic is in a holding pattern, and no one will let me change lanes. Every time I put my blinker on, someone gets in my blind spot, as if it were personal. This is supposed to be horse-farm country, but I don't actually see any horses—just miles and miles of boring grass.

I think about stopping in Gainesville for a beer or something, but there are cops everywhere in Gainesville, and I can't get a DUI. I don't have the money to bail myself out and I don't want to come back up here for court, but, more than anything, I can't go to jail today, because if I don't go to my own shows, I don't sell any paintings.

I noticed this at the very beginning of my career. My first show was a total success. I sold almost every piece on the wall—granted, the economy was a lot better, or we thought it was, anyway—but, then, at my second show, nothing sold. Partially, it was because I was still pretty new to painting for an audience, but, also, I didn't bother to attend.

I sort of acted like a douchebag at my first show, accidentally. When the last piece to sell got its red sticker next to it, I pumped my fist and said, "Yessss!" A couple of people turned around. Only the gallerist knew for sure what an asshole I was being, but I felt like a fucking idiot. It was just so obvious I hadn't expected the work to sell, so I avoided my second show and fulfilled my own expectations—almost nothing sold.

I found a place far away enough from my second show's gallery to take the same work, but I attended this one after all, because I wanted to fuck the gallery owner, a slim, black-eyed reed with alabaster skin. Almost everything sold again. I didn't get to dip into the owner, who was all deceptive, wet eyes and dry business, but I got it, then. Show up and talk and people buy stuff. The art might not stand up that well on its own, but if I can talk to people and try really hard, they will buy it.

Sometimes, I can see they feel sorry for me.

The highway is humming along at 70 miles per hour, a reasonable speed, but it's annoying, anyway. People are driving too slowly in the left lane. A Toyota is doing 65, and when I flash my high beams, it hits its brakes like an asshole, instead of just moving over.

I think about just slamming through it next time it hits the brakes like that. That would probably keep it out of the left lane for good, but, instead, I pass on the right, and now I've broken two traffic laws, all because some self-righteous jerk is going ten miles an hour below the speed limit in the left lane.

I miss Vanessa. In reality, I'm riding the brake toward Gainesville—college students, muscle cars, more McMansions— but, in my mind, I'm with her. She is in the van with me, right now, just here with me while I grind my way toward Georgia.

Luke is funnier than she is. Ray would have drugs and he sings when he's high, which would make the time go faster, but what I am imagining as I drive is that we're here together, sitting bored in traffic, both of us knowing that we have hours to just sit here and do nothing but be irritated at how slow other people drive. I'm staring at traffic. She's staring out the window. We're together, anyway.

I shake these thoughts and shut off the air conditioning and roll down the window. The window is manual, and I crank it hard. It glides smoothly into the door of the van, even though my arm is powering around hard and fast, but then I have to put up with the white noise of rushing air in my left ear.

I crank the window back up. I wonder if I could get myself all the way from Ocala to Gainesville just cranking that shit up and down. I try it a few times. It agitates me, pumping my arm that way. I should have hammered Vanessa into her mattress before I left last night.

I consider if I can manage jerking off in the van while I drive. It's high up enough that the only people who would see me would be truckers, but if I got over to the right lane, they wouldn't care about looking over, and I don't really care if one of them sees me.

I yank the wheel to the right and cut across lanes without my blinker this time. The car two lanes over hits its brakes, but no one honks or tries to block me like they do when I signal like a normal person. It occurs to me that all my attempts at honor or accomplishment are met with passive-aggressiveness or pity.

I unbutton my pants and stroke my cock with my right hand while I drive with my left. This gives me some illusion that the vehicles on the left can't see me pulling my cock out and squeezing it up and down in my fist, but soon I'm not even thinking of them.

I'm thinking of that day at the Alden when I used my belt as suspension cuffs and Julie said, "Restraint is a virtue," and I said, "I thought patience was," and she laughed. She was absolutely fearless in there. I had only known her for an hour at the most and I had her hogtied to a ceiling fixture in a motel room. She wasn't scared at all. I almost thought I wouldn't be able to satisfy her. I felt like I was looking at a centerfold the way she hung there like a fucking doll, stretched out and willing.

I'm jerking my cock so hard now that I shut my eyes for just a second. I open them, and the white noise of the highway screams past my cheeks. There is an old BMW in front of me. I should let go of my cock. I could let go and start again and still cum, but it's only 11AM, and it's already so fucking hot out, and the heat spreading through the windshield and through my brain is making it impossible to do anything but think of how wet she was when I grabbed her pussy with my whole hand and squeezed it.

I take my other hand off the wheel and brace the van to stay straight with my knees. I push down at the base of my cock and pull past the last searing flash of light in my head and cum in jagged breaths, bending over the steering wheel. I'm grasping the wheel in both hands now, panting as my abdomen clenches and cum spurts over my pants, and then I'm practically in the trunk of the BMW and I slam on the brakes, so that the person behind me slams on his brakes.

Both our tires squeal, and the car behind me, a Subaru, veers sharply into oncoming traffic to avoid hitting me. An old Ford pickup slams into the driver's side of the Subaru with a deadening thud. The driver tries to throw the Ford into neutral on the fly, and I can hear the gears grind as the truck skids the Subaru across the highway.

Behind the Ford, another car, a red sedan, jerks over a lane the same way the Subaru did to avoid the Ford, and the car in the next lane over, an SUV, pummels the red sedan.

The heavy thud and distressed shriek of crumpling metal send a tingle of adrenaline through my spine, and I slam on the gas, trying to focus my eyes through the post-cum haze in my brain. The BMW is gone, and I hear glass dance across the highway and brakes yelp helplessly as the red sedan spins out in my rearview mirror and crashes into the center guardrail at a frightening speed, crushing into its own hood.

The last thing I see as I charge down the next deceleration lane is a man getting out of the SUV. He bends his body to peer at the red sedan before its hood catches fire and then he runs toward the right shoulder of the highway, through traffic that is slowing and screeching like a child banging on a piano, all disjointed high notes and anxious tuning pins.

I race down the exit and I have no idea where I am, but it doesn't matter. I keep driving, shaking worse and worse as I follow a two-lane road. I see a sign that directs me to Micanopy and I take it, because Micanopy is a place with a name. The sign is blurred. My vision is still not good. My hands are covered in cum. I feel like I might pass out. I take a deep breath and force myself to drive a lawful speed and look at where I am, but my heart is thumping in my chest with the same dull, dead sound as the bulldozed Subaru.

Massive oak trees knot their roots together on the side of the road. The occasional laurel tree sprouts between them, hardy trees in their own right, but sickly and snappable compared to the unbothered oaks. The oak branches hang low overhead. They dangle Spanish moss like an old woman with a limp handkerchief out the window.

I roll the window back up, but before I can turn on the air

conditioner, one of the trees drops a net of moss onto the roof of the van with a gentle *thunk*, and I become paranoid that, even if I make it out of here, the moss has trapped me and will snitch.

I keep driving until I see a sign for Route 441 to Gainesville and take it, relieved, only to find, after a few miles, that there is nothing on this road, no gas stations, no businesses, no signs for anything else, not even any cars.

There are wire fences and then wooden fences, holding back dry, gray-green brush. The land is as flat as a sheet of paper, and I can see nothing ahead of me, except a huddle of palm trees to my left, far up ahead. The sky is ferociously blue. The sun has burnt out all the clouds.

There is a bike lane, which freaks me out even more, because there are no people, but a bike lane means maybe there used to be people, and where the fuck have they gone, then? The grass is fried to the color of straw.

The inside of the van is sweltering. The brush straining against the fences is now a dangerous dark red. Spontaneous brush fires are common this time of year. I may keel over at the wheel. I take a deep breath. Sweat rolls down my moustache into my mouth. I turn on the air conditioner and instantly feel better.

I am being a total fucking pussy. I tell myself to stop it, but I'm still sweating, and my sweat is cold.

I cannot see anything for miles ahead. To my sides, there is nothing but red brush that turns brown when I come upon it, but then I see a cellular tower and know that as long as I drive the speed limit and get the fucking moss off the roof of the van, I will be fine. I decide I'm going to have that beer in Gainesville after all, but then think better of it again. The best idea is to get the fuck into Georgia and be cool.

I grab my phone from the passenger seat of the van.

"Hellooooo, great painter!" says Aaron.

"Hey, buddy, what's up?"

"I am divine — except for my shattered limb, but Percocet is a friendly butterfly with wings like whispers and kisses. So long as I don't startle anything, it's fine," he says.

"That's good, man, that sounds good. Well, I've got some interesting news for you, an offer, I guess."

"Offeerrrrrrraway," he says.

"We were thinking we'd throw you a fundraiser. Get a bunch of people together to buy tickets and take them out to Egmont Key in a couple of boats. It was Chrissy's idea first, but then I came up with this other idea to get a bunch of people involved, like, to do a fashion show. Remember that mobile we hung at the marina?"

"Ah, yes, it was moving. People pitied the female plight after seeing it and then it sold for scrap."

"People pitied what?"

"Women. Pitiful creatures."

"Oh . . . so, listen, Aaron, I'm going to do some sculpture stuff like that, but, like, dress girls in the sculpture, and then Vanessa can do their hair with some really crazy cuts and styles and stuff."

Sweat is still streaming down my face, even in the air conditioning. Aaron says nothing, so I continue.

"There's no electricity out there, so everything would have to be really organic. We could grill and serve drinks and stuff and let people go swimming or whatever and then take everyone back at the end of the day."

Still, he says nothing, and I feel that clammy fear that he is going to say something awful to me.

"What do you think?" I ask.

He babbles forth, as if jolted, "A fashion show! With clothes no one could ever wear! On an island! Well, hand me down and cast me away, we're having a part-aaayyyy!" He pushes the phone from his face with a sputter, "Jeffrrrrreeeeeeyyyyy!"

"Yes, dear?"

"Ray is on the phone. He is throwing us a heavy metal show!"

"What?"

"Heavy metal! Sculptures and girls!"

"Aaron?" I say.

"Yesssshhhh?"

"It's Alex."

"Alex?"

"Yeah, man, it's not Ray. It's Alex."

"Alex! Where did you ever come up with this charming idea? This is your idea?"

"It was Chrissy's first."

"Aahhh, Chriiiiisssssy with her lovely flaxen hair. Triple xxx's in that flaxxxen when you really look at her, am I right? But all of this is phenomenal! We will be there. We will help! You need girls. Girls flock to Jeffrey! It's dissshgusting!"

"All right, man, so let's do it! But, Aaron, maybe I should talk to Jeffrey right now. We'll figure out the details and you go pop another Perc and get some shut-eye."

"Jeffrrreeeyyy!" he squawks into the phone.

"Yes, dear," says Jeffrey, next to him still.

"Ray wants to talk to you!"

"Hi, Alex," says Jeffrey.

"Hi, Jeffrey." I tell him again what I told Aaron.

"Oh, I don't know, Alex. It's a sweet thought, but Aaron and I aren't used to that sort of attention."

"You're not?"

"We've never really been to an event in town that we didn't create. It seems crass to start now, just because our own place is a little burnt."

I wipe sweat from my beard. A puddle comes back in my hand. The fence posts are flying by, and I force myself to slow down again.

"Well, Jeff, you guys have had a tough time. You can take a little help from friends. There's a whole community of people who will miss Art pretty badly if it doesn't come back, and you guys have to keep afloat somehow if you can't have shows or run classes."

"I can teach classes in another studio space," says Jeffrey. "I can't take the charity, Al."

"Are you sure?"

"I don't think it's the right thing to do," he says.

There is a sudden rustling on the line. Wind cuts through the brush as the van rushes past, mimicking the noise on the other side of the line. The noise is nearly overwhelming. The land is still totally flat, and I have no clue where I am. I have to be in Alachua by now. I pray I am in Alachua by now.

Aaron comes back on the line.

"We are having the party," he says imperially.

"Hey, how's your arm feel, anyway?"

"Awful. We need a party, so that it doesn't hurt anyone," he says.

"Do you guys want to talk about it and maybe get back to me? I'm driving to Athens right now and I'm in the middle of Butt Fuck Nowhere. You can just call me back."

"Ahh, Butt Fuck Nowhere! We have reservashunzzzere tonight!" he slurs. "Hold, please. Let me check on our table!"

He covers the phone somehow, even though his arm is broken, and I can hear him and Jeffrey murmuring in urgent tones. I think about hanging up and letting them call me back, but I don't want to be driving through this hot, baked plain alone. I am seeing heat mirages, waves of nothing ahead of me, while Aaron and Jeffrey yammer at each other in whispers.

Finally, Aaron comes back, "We are on! Art gracefully accepts your invitation to a fundraiser on its behalf and hopes you will accept with equal grace our servitude in selecting the next girls-cum-art-installations for the event."

I laugh, but I feel a little desperate. "OK, sure, sounds good to me, man. Everyone just wants to help. Are you sure Jeffrey is OK with this, though?"

"Jeffrey, say you're OK." He puts the phone to Jeffrey's mouth, and Jeffrey says, "I'm OK."

"OK, guys, well, I'll talk to you when I get back, then. Aaron, take care of the arm and go easy on Jeff."

"OK, tootaloo, Ray, you're a complete doll! We love you!" and he hangs up.

I put the phone down. I am drenched in sweat and completely disoriented. The ends of my hair are wet. I can see in the rearview mirror that my cheeks are red. There is no end to the narrowing line of county road in front of me. It just tapers into nothing with a thick swath of brown flattening out to the sides.

Gainesville seems like a dream, like somewhere I will never reach, and then I remember I have to get out of Alachua, out of Florida, and all the way through Macon and Atlanta, before I hit Athens. The rest of the trip seems impossible, and then I remember the cars that crashed on 75. Now is as good a time as any to brush the moss off the roof of the van.

I pull over to the shoulder and climb out. Standing feels good. The temperature is insane here, and the heat makes me dizzy. Sweat rolls from my hair down my spine and over my eyebrows, down my back into my ass crack, down my calves from my knees. I feel beads of it pop on my rib cage and cascade toward my belly button, but I still feel better than I did in the van.

I walk around the back of the van to the passenger side. I'm nervous about alligators. I open the passenger door and step up on the side of the van to check the roof. The moss is gone. Of course it's gone.

I don't know why I'm being such a pussy on this trip. I need to get back in the van and get my ass out of here, back to somewhere that makes sense and is part of the plan, but, then, I'm shaking and, suddenly, I feel cool, but I know that's not a good sign, and then everything is a wonderful checkerboard.

I think of Aaron's trilling, skipping slurring, and everything goes black for a moment and when it all comes back, I feel just fine. I've stayed standing somehow, even though my torso is slumped over on the sizzling roof of the van.

I crouch down and get my phone off the seat and stand back up again. Just the slight elevation means I can see further down the flat road. There are road signs at the very end of my vision. Road signs mean a new road is coming up. I call Vanessa.

"Hello," she answers.

"Hi, how are you?"

"I'm fine. Are you in Georgia yet?"

"No, I'm almost at Gainesville."

"Oh, OK, Gainesville is fun. Are you making good time?"

"All things considered, I'd say so."

"Neat. Anything good happen?"

"Aaron agrees that a fundraiser is a really good idea. I just got off the phone with him."

"Oh, OK." She sounds uninterested. I tell myself to get over it. She's probably at work, distracted, and I'm lonely and hot. I need to get back in the van and turn on the air conditioning. She hasn't said anything else.

"So, we'll talk about it when I get home, then, OK?"

"Sure, that sounds great. I hope you have a nice trip."

I take a deep breath. "I really miss you. I wish you were here."

She pauses. "That's sweet."

She sounds so tentative that my heart floods with love. If she had just been here, none of this mess ever would have happened. I would just be on the highway, sitting in traffic, bored and thrilled, with her.

"I have to go. There are signs coming up that I need to read."

"OK, bye, Alex," she says and hangs up.

I squint at the signs but I can't tell what color they are—yellow or brown. I pray that they're yellow, because that will mean that there is either construction or a merge, and both those things mean Gainesville is close and I can get back on the damn highway.

I hop down from the truck and land on the asphalt, but, as I land, I feel a funny, bouncing sensation in my crotch. I look down, and my cock is out and bright red in the sun. It has been out the whole time.

At the sign for Jennings, the last town in Florida on 75, I hit the phone again. This time, the greeting is a warm coo.

"I only have a second, but I'm coming back to town Wednesday," I say. "I'm coming to your house first and I am going to pound the daylights out of you."

She laughs.

"Tell me yes."

"Yes," she says.

"Good," I say. I hang up and leave the state of Florida. I feel immensely better once I do.

8.

Blue, everything is a pale, sickly, wavering blue. Cold emanates from the blue, and, then, the blue or the cold, something shivery that crawls across my cheek, is on the rubbery, clammy wrap over my skull. My face. My skin contracts, then presses down into the cold. The skin cells like the cold. My skin is too hot, and my forehead lurches forward into more watery blue.

Something smells medicinal, and then my throat takes whatever that medicinal smell is and tries to squeeze the life out of it, me. Everything is fully alive and going to die. My third and fourth vertebrae jerk up to the sky, and my ribs hurt, and my face is so close to this clear lake and its nutty smell, and then my body tumbles over onto the floor.

I stand. I don't stand. My palms are on the floor. Something is punching the insides of my lungs. My back teeth are swimming. There is no horizon, just a wall. Vertical white lines crowd together and blur. One palm slaps somewhere new. My wrists are crossed. The crown of my head touches the wall. My brain burns and tries to escape through a hole where my skull is cold at the top.

My throat chokes, and then my face is in the lake, and my lungs are coughing, and my shoulder blades almost touch, and then my elbows do, and my forearm finds my stomach and presses. The heel of my hand smacks my face, and my lungs are coughing more and more hoarsely. My trachea won't let enough air in or out. My mouth fills with water, the taste that was the medicinal smell.

A phone rings somewhere close, on top or to the side of my leg. My hip jiggles. My tongue spews the water out, and my esophagus expels in segments a half-digested, paper mache earthworm that thrashes against the roof of my mouth.

Loopy, gaseous bubbles rise and pop in the air. The gooey, squirming axons in my brain are whispering, burrowing worms. The phone continues to ring, ring, ring, irritating *annelus*. My hand picks it up. My voice speaks. I stand up, and the pond is filled with scum, my insides.

I swallow an Oxycontin with a cold glass of Riesling. I want peaches. I am in a kitchen. I think it must be mine, because I know where everything is, but I can't find any peaches. I am going to have to find the peaches.

I try to remember a trip to a store, find the traces of a recent path to the produce section—it could have happened—but any of my body's recent industriousness is in the cryonics aisle with the ice cream and other baby treats, waiting for me to grow the fuck up and gestate a new version of myself, perhaps with better packaging. There are no peaches in this fucking kitchen.

I go outside, and there's a bicycle, so I get on it. A breeze pushes east, so I go east. The bike wobbles on the road. There is no shade, and then a gentle, bright orange shutter covers my eyes, and then I am gasping, and my legs are propelling the bike forward at steady pace that scares me. I slam on the brakes and get off the bike. I touch my legs. The sun is stark and merciless, and my eyes tear up and shut.

I am breathing slowly, shallowly, and I would like to go to sleep on a patch of grass somewhere, but all of it is scratchy and burnt and belongs to someone else. I get back on the bike and follow bleary signs with arrows. The sun is making my head hurt.

There is a crowd of beetles ahead, shiny, pushy beetles with feelers that pop up in the sun. They squeal and scratch. A squat, tough one trails away from the group, herding it deferentially so that a loud cockchafer, a coleopterist Cleopatra with wide, see-through wings and a gold band at the crown, can lead the swarm with his whirring and harping.

The bike propels forward. My legs cannot stop. My eyes are enveloped in the warm comfort of orange, and then I am floating through the air in a slow descent. The bike is gone, and the beetles are crawling all over me, full of howls and laments.

I wake up again. The sky is taupe and black in one patch. I try to sit up. Someone pushes me down, but nicely, and keeps a hand on my sternum. It is a man, but a mild one—I can feel the fog of testosterone. I am breathing evenly and more deeply than before. He puts a cool, wet cloth over my head, someone's t-shirt run under a freezing tap. I gasp. He clucks his tongue soothingly and sits by me for a moment. He is breathing loudly. He is nervous, has been nervous for a long time.

I hear him walk outside and I sit up and take the t-shirt off my head. My eyeballs are desiccated. Their collagen matrix is disintegrating. I close them instinctually, and the sensation of ocular corrosion disappears as I snap back to blackness, but I have no idea where I am and I open my eyes again. Seeing hurts. Fuzz begins leeching over my eyeballs, stinging the vitreous humors.

The black patch of sky trails into a corner and curls away as a ragged line of black plaster squiggles around a gaping hole with tall, narrow beams inside it. I am in a room and I think I may vomit again.

The walls have been demolished, so that all I can see are support beams and leftover lath with uneven plaster keys dripping, dried, in parts of the room where the studs remain. An industrial fan sibilates in a corner. I can hear the thrum of people outside. I am afraid to move, and my breathing comes quick and short again, and my stomach cramps with nausea as I see that one high wall has thick vines of glinting wire over it.

Someone has left before completely covering the wall's opening. Heavy-gauge steel wire overlaps in a basket weave—over two, under two, under two, over two—welded into place at cruciform joints, with high, wide holes in between each cross-section. The proto-plaid is closed with a tight herringbone weave—under one, over two, under one, over two, over one, under one, over two, under one; I am going to die. An acetylene torch lies on the ground next to a coil of the heavy-gauge wire.

I need to find a way out, but there is a mob out front. I cannot find a way out without passing the mob.

I hear people coming back. I put the freezing t-shirt over my face again and lie back down. I cannot see. I cannot hear. I cannot feel anything, but near-freezing water trying to rush through my veins, which are hot and stuffy. The ice water inside my boiling, clogged blood-tentacles is making my head hum.

I hold as still as I can. I do not want them to know I am awake or that I saw the wire or the torch. There are many people in the room now, and two of them are guarding me, but then I feel, through the sheer veil of the t-shirt, the creepy reaching of antennae. There are no people in the room.

The crowd of beetles from that other time and place has made it inside this place, through the opening gates of the walls and the tiny cracks in the lath. I shudder, and the stout minion beetle from before says, "Shhhh."

A high-pitch voice on the other side of me, full of anticipation, says, "What are we going to do now?"

"We aren't going to do anything until she wakes up."

The high-pitch beetle quivers. The crisp taste of fruit is in my mouth.

"When is everyone leaving?"

"I don't know."

I am growing more and more nauseous and, as the nausea swells, it drowns out any sense of self-preservation.

"We aren't making any headway like this. There's work we can be doing right now, but, instead, we're just sitting here."

"We're sitting here because of Vanessa."

"That doesn't make sense. She isn't going anywhere."

"Fine. Do what you want. It doesn't matter, anyway."

"What doesn't matter?"

"Nothing matters."

"What about everyone out there? They matter. They believe what happens here matters."

"What happens here?"

They fall silent. I feel like I am fading away into nothingness. My brain is so hot and staticky behind my frozen forehead. I am disappearing.

I jolt awake at the sound of my phone and see that I am alone and run through the open front wall and sprint down the street. There is no one out. I turn a corner. A car passes in the opposite direction. I turn a corner again. A man in a tuxedo jacket appears on the opposite side of the street and lights a cigarette. I cannot run past him. I have to turn another corner, but I know this isn't right. My knees are gelatinous. The phone rings again.

"Hello?" My voice is low, raspy. Something is stuck in my throat. I have not been breathing well today. I try to appear calm. I begin walking.

"I only have a second, but I'm coming back to town Wednesday," someone says. "I'm coming to your house first and I am going to pound the daylights out of you."

I look around to see if someone is watching me, from a window or a parked car, somewhere. I suddenly know where I am and why and I begin to laugh.

"Tell me yes," says my phone.

"Yes," I say and I hang up.

I walk toward the health food store to order a smoothie. Erica is outside, sipping a strawberry drink. She looks startled.

"What are you doing here?" she says.

"I wanted a peach smoothie," I say.

She blinks at me and sucks from her straw. Black seeds ascend into her mouth.

"OK, I'll go in with you," she says.

9.

The temperature is monstrously hot, unreal. From the window, I can see the Pier, the outdoor mall at the end of the Pier, built to look like a circus tent, searing the horizon with its ugly red and yellow triangles. Everything else is faint, bright white, blurred by the sun. Palm trees have silhouettes, but no color. They look like they are hovering, wavering in the air, but there is no breeze.

I cannot bear to turn on the lights today. The air conditioning is already wheezing. I have sweat on my upper lip.

Today is Monday, August 13, the first day in months that I have a full day booked. The heat makes people wish they were different, not so rubbery at high temperatures, lighter under the weight of humidity.

Kim comes in for a trim. She is one of my first clients ever and has never gone anywhere else from what I can tell, but she has dwindled from a monthly cut to a quarterly trim. Her hair is grown out from its aggressive wedge. She looks like a rabbit, a soft, goofy pet with a funny sheath over one eye. Her other eye darts.

"What are we doing today?"

"Oh, just a trim. A trim is fine."

"Just a trim?"

"I don't need more than a trim."

"Once you're in the chair, you might as well get what you really want," I say.

She nods, smiling nervously.

"OK. Maybe you could fix this part here? It's starting to look weird."

I lop at her until she looks less leporid and, when I am done, she is vaguely attractive, but I cannot see anything human in her. Her nose is too squashed and triangular. Plush bunny ears of hair fall over her narrow crown.

She blinks rapidly in the mirror when I am done.

"There's a sign at Art that says you're doing the styling for models for a fundraiser," she says.

"There is?"

Crepuscular rays stream in the front window of the salon and blind me momentarily. I blink back at her, and she reappears slowly, twitching her nose at an errant snip of hair.

She takes a deep breath. Her shoulders hunch up and her smile stretches. "Can I help? I do Aaron and Jeffrey's makeup when they have shows. I just had an unexpected break-up, too, you know? It would be . . . it would be good for me . . . if I could."

"A break-up?" I say. I keep one hand in her hair. Her shoulders lurch forward.

"Yeah . . . you know, that guy Jeff."

"I didn't know . . . you were seeing him, really." Her skull radiates nervousness and determination under my fingertips.

"I wasn't, really," she says, "but I'm not going to anymore, either."

"OK," I say. "I'm sure it'll be fine."

After Kim is Michelle, whom I don't know and who wants something "angular, to show off the jaw line." The only definition on Michelle's face is her jaw line, a large, protruding rhomboid, so I suggest something to soften the chin and bring out the brow line, but she insists.

"I haven't paid for a haircut in over two years," she says.

"What's the occasion?" I ask. "Do you have a special event?"

"No, you're doing that fundraiser for the crazy art gallery downtown, right?"

"I'm part of it," I say, "but why do you want a haircut today?"

"I feel real badly about what happened to that dog," she says. "You're givin' the money so they can get a new dog, right?"

"No, I'm styling models. For a . . ." I trail off. "A show of sorts. It's a bit conceptual, really."

"What? You think I won't understand conceptual art?"

She glares at me in the mirror.

"Well . . ." I begin, but I don't really have anything to say. I look around the salon. Everything is quiet for a moment. "I suppose all art is conceptual, right? So, anyone can understand art, because concepts are subjective."

"Oh, I get it," she says. She looks directly at me in the mirror. "Never mind. I heard you guys were real cliquish. I thought what I heard was OK, though. Somebody's hairdresser girlfriend cares about animals or something." She gets out of the chair.

"You've got me all wrong," I say.

"I can tell," she says.

She picks her purse off the shelf and leaves. She still has her cape on, but I don't try to stop her, because it is 99 degrees outside. The heat makes people crazy.

"Girl!" Dani says when she calls. "I am in your show!"

"Oh, great," I say, but she cannot hear me over her own squealing.

"Because you gave me that rad haircut a few days ago, remember? I'm, like, your first work of art after the tragedy!"

"I might have to re-clip a lot of it before . . . that day, though. Hair . . . grows, you know?"

"I know! This is so exciting, though! I can't believe you're really doing it!" she lowers her voice. "Erica is pisssssssed."

"Why?"

"She thinks it interferes with the literal and figurative spirit of Art or something."

"The literal spirit? Like Snuggles is going to haunt the party?"

"I don't know. I can't believe I'm going to be a model, though! Is someone taping everything? We can make a video montage and put it online! Someone has to! I'm going to be an actual model!"

"Dani?"

"Yes?!"

"A model . . . what?"

"Huh?"

"A model what? A model home, a model airplane, a Ford Model T? A model what?"

She laughs. "A model . . . person!" She laughs some more. "I'm going to be a model person!"

"I have to go," I tell her.

Sophie is pretty, plump, exuberant. I've never seen her before, either, but she laughs when I wash her hair. She tells me she can't wait to lose fifteen pounds.

"But, you wouldn't know, anyway. You've got a terrific body!"

"Oh, thanks," I say. I angle her hair just below the chin, so that she can begin to see what she might look like if she slims down.

"What kind of diet are you on?" she asks.

"Mostly salad, coke, and wine," I say bluntly. I have to re-snip the strand I just chopped. She is making me nervous.

She laughs as though I am joking. "That is so funny! I'm eating a lot of salmon in cans. I eat it with, like, broccoli and stuff like that, even though I don't really like it. I'm just really excited to be thin. I lose weight really quickly. I've lost three pounds in the last week."

I rub her head to give the top some movement before layering the front. She looks thinner. She is losing weight right now. Her hair is growing, too. I realize how bizarre it is that she is getting hotter—thinner with longer hair—just sitting here. I think about telling her this, how I would tell her this, but I already know there is no point.

"I mean, the ultimate goal is to be really thin, like model thin. Have you ever done any modeling? You've got a really awesome body."

"No, I've always been a hairdresser."

"Huh . . . do you think I could be a model? I mean, I'll have lost a lot of weight in a few weeks," she says.

"I don't know what it takes, I guess."

"I bet I could," she says, and I tune out everything else until she leaves, when she says, "Oh my God, are you online?" as if she just thought of it.

"Not much," I say.

"I will totally find you online! That way if there are any, like, events in town, we can hang out again!"

"That could happen," I say.

Anything could happen. Someone could break an arm and kill a dog being a total douchebag at a party. A train to New York could obliterate a car in the middle of nowhere. I shake my head.

"Anything is possible," I say.

"OK!" she chirps. "So, I'll find you!"

I pick up my phone and immediately delete every public account I have.

Ali, whom I have known forever, because she used to be my babysitter, comes into the salon next and immediately pulls her tank top away from her big, globe-shaped tits and blows on them.

She pulled this same move when I was fifteen and too old for a babysitter. She would lift my shirt and blow on my nipples and then show me hers and we would pinch each other and laugh and this is how she convinced me that it wasn't really babysitting, like I needed it, but babysitting, like my parents paid her to come over and hang out when they went out.

"Your tits look awesome," I say. I sound tired.

"Yeah? Do you want to touch them?" she lifts her tank top. The pale pink scars toward the bottoms are still raised. They are cool in the heat, almost cold when I run my fingers over the nipples.

My first conversation as an adult with Ali was at a pool party ten years later in September. She was topless, and her tits were smaller than they are now, but bigger than they were when she was eighteen. She had told Matt, the best friend of a guy I was seeing, that I had done all the coke and that's why she didn't have any to give back to him.

"You told Matt I did all your coke," I said to her.

"What? No, I didn't. I'm sorry, you must be mistaken."

"Do you even recognize me? You used to babysit me. Matt wants to know why I did all the coke he gave you. He said you told him I did it all, so if you meant someone else, we should tell him that right now."

She looked at me vacuously, her pale blue eyes cornered in the sun. "I don't know," she said.

"You don't know what?" I said.

"I don't know what I said to Matt."

"Please tell him I did not do your coke."

She looked at me pleadingly.

"Matt," I called.

He came over with a skinny, black-haired girl, also topless, with no tits at all, under his arm. "You got some more blow for me?"

"That's not who I meant," Ali said quickly.

Matt looked at me and then back at her. "Well, who did you mean, then? You said it was her. You pointed at her."

I looked at Ali and walked away and, from across the pool, took my top off, too, and came back with my purse. I sat down next to Ali and pulled out a bag of coke and a mirror for them.

"Here, no problem," I said. I poured the coke out and started chopping and offered it to the black-haired girl with Matt.

"Yeee-ah!" he shouted, pumping his fist. "Now, that's what I'm talking about!" He pinched the black-haired girl's nipple, and she swatted his hand away and did the coke.

Later, Ali said, "I don't know who I thought you were before."

"Maybe you thought I was you," I said, but I let her do the rest of the coke with us, and when everyone was ripped, we all started making out with different people than who we came with.

The black-haired girl and Matt ate me out together on a chaise lounge. The sky was bright blue. The sun sweltered overhead as I came. Matt's best friend stopped calling me after that.

"I heard you're scouting for models," Ali says.

I smile placidly in the mirror and continue chopping her hair savagely in front.

"Alex is doing body painting, right? I know so many beautiful women."

"All women are beautiful simply as themselves," I say. I hack the back of her crown, where she can't see.

"Well, of course they are," she says. "That's why body painting is so hot! I modeled for Swim Tiki's posters this year, you know."

"Oh, did you?"

"I wore body paint, too. It looked like a bathing suit, and I brought two really hot guys a tray of drinks. They wore a new resort line. You know how guys are wearing shorter inseams and a floral print? We shot it at the Alden."

"That's almost incredible."

"It was! So I know a lot about modeling."

"That's an important skill," I say.

"I know. I'm so lucky," she says. "So, should I come down to see about the body paint thing?"

I smile at her in the mirror. She looks like a hungry Chihuahua, begging to be petted, but just as ready to steal a bone and hide. She has always looked this way, even as a teenager.

"Do you want to go in the back with me? I have an hour before my last appointment," I tell her.

She freezes for a moment, only a fraction of a second, really, and then she agrees. In the back, I sit down in an extra hairdressing chair and adjust the height. I pull back her shitty, porn-star hair, my shorts on the ground, my thong around my ankle, and watch her lap at my clit and think how well-suited the cut is for her and how she actually does look good, humming into my vulva, acting like a dumb whore, not quite beautiful, but not bad, either.

As I cum, I realize with the force of a blinding punch that Alex should have been back five days ago, but I haven't heard from him.

I cannot remember a single thing I have done all week.

Ali is reapplying her lipstick in the mirror when another girl walks in.

She is the bronze-haired girl from the night of the fire, the one that laughed with Luke and Ray and looked up at Alex, the one who disappeared with him when he shepherded everyone to safety.

"Hello," I say. "Please come in."

She smiles at me as I lead her to the chair. My hand hovers at

76

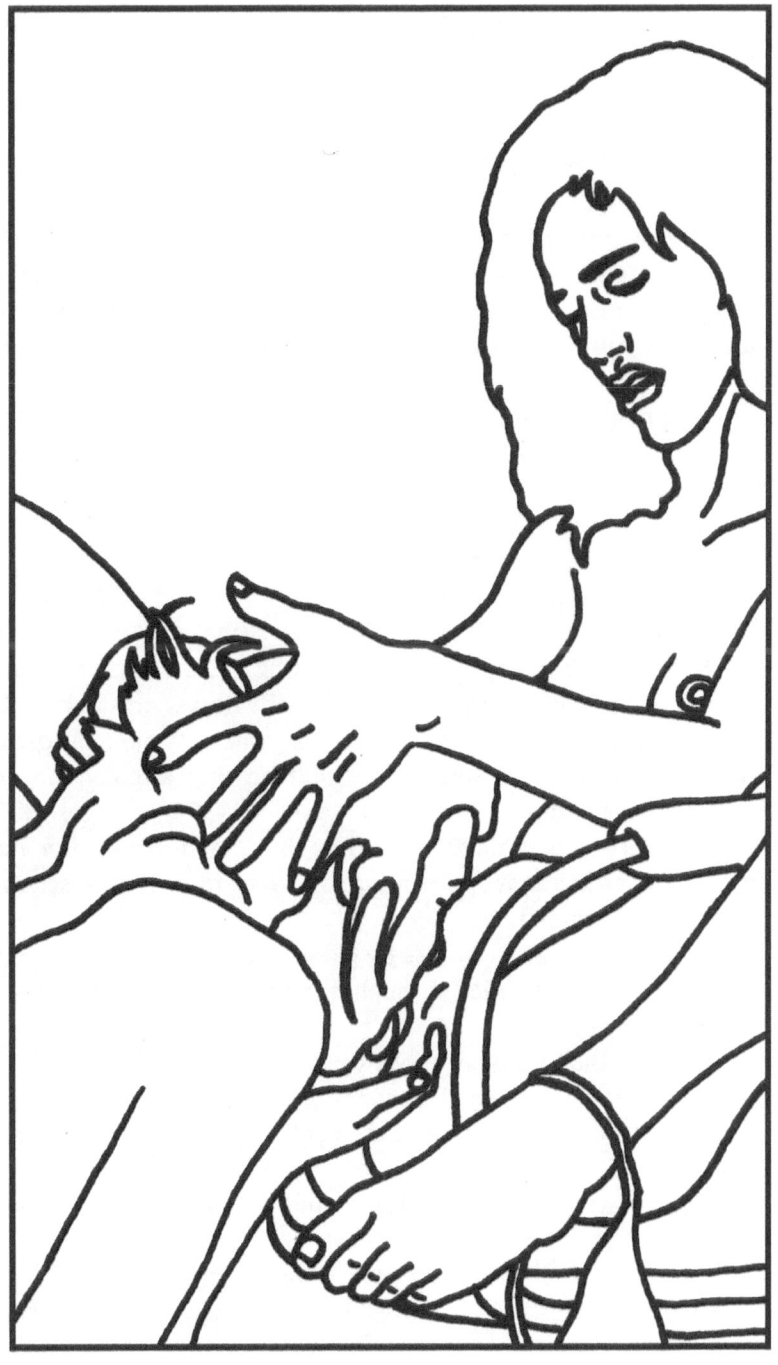

her lower back. I am still warm from Ali. My cheeks are still flushed. Ali looks at the girl.

"Hello," she says, appraisingly.

"Hi," says the girl back. She has the same shininess she had near Alex, as if she spends all her time putting on moisturizer and doing her best to look happy.

"I'll call you," says Ali, but I'm barely paying attention as she leaves. Instead, I'm looking at this girl with her perfect waves of hair that are dry and split at the ends. She has a heart-shaped face and almond eyes and long legs. She is pretty, and I am curious.

I begin picking up pieces of her hair. "You have a perfect wave pattern," I tell her. "Let's just take the dead ends off to bring it back to life."

"All right," she says.

"How did you hear about me?" I ask her.

"I know your friend Erica," she says.

"Oh, how?" I ask. We both sound so normal.

"She's friends with someone I'm dating." She looks at me and smiles boldly, white teeth glimmering in the darkened salon. I still have not been able to turn the lights on. "I've only been in town a few weeks, so it's not that serious, but he seems really cool, so who knows? Maybe it'll work."

"Who are you dating?" I ask her, but I pause with her hair lifted in the air, so that she looks up and sees me with the scissors poised over her head.

"Oh, well, I mean . . . we're just kind of hanging out."

I say nothing, but slice through her hair, so that little spikes of bronze fall to the floor.

I smile. "Did you hear about the show we're putting on? It's a fundraiser for Art, the gallery that burnt down."

"Oh, yeah. I was there that night. That's the night I met Erica."

"Well, we're doing a fundraiser and we need models," I say. "You should be a model."

"Oh, all right! I'll think about it. Thanks!" she says.

My phone rings. "Excuse me," I say and answer it.

It's my last appointment of the day, "I'm sorry, I'm going to cancel. I just heard about the show you're doing and I'm going to volunteer. You can just do my hair that day."

"I won't have time that day. I'll have to do the models' hair that day," I tell her.

"Right, I know," she says. "I'm going to volunteer to be a model."

"Oh, of course. OK, well, then, I'll see you then," I say and hang up and look at the girl in the mirror, who is looking back at me, just as curiously.

10.

I've been back for almost a week and I haven't called her, even though I said I would come see her.

Instead, I am by myself in my studio, painting her streaked blond hair and trying to show her cheekbones. Her cheekbones are nearly invisible when she looks ahead, but if she turns her face even just slightly, they are knives, straight and sharp and unexpected.

I'm pretending I had to sequester myself to sort out my feelings, that I had to be alone to paint, but the truth is I just freaked.

I was a fucking mess on the road back. The show was stupid, a bunch of small-town drunks with no money in obnoxious clothes. I sold almost nothing and only just paid for my trip.

The thought of arriving on her doorstep and telling her this did nothing for my cock and, then, the thought that she wouldn't even ask made me feel like a complete fool.

When I came to our exit on the highway, I paused at the divide for South 54th and the Bayway. A red sedan behind me slammed on the brakes and leaned on the horn. Its grill in my mirror seemed like an obvious sign, another impending fuck-up, and I took the Bayway home instead of going to see her.

In the morning, I felt guilty, so I started painting. I thought if I brought her a painting, she wouldn't mind that I had waited to see her. She would be distracted from asking about my failure in Athens. I would be distracted from the possibility that she wouldn't even care. I would have something else to show her.

But it took too long. I kept messing everything up. It didn't look like her. It didn't look like how I feel about her.

I had to paint over part of it, and that sent me to bed for nearly sixteen hours, forcing myself to breathe deeply while I lost track of day and night, and then three days had passed. I felt like I had to have it perfect before I could see her, but she hasn't called me, either, and now I wonder if she'll ever see it.

The first conversation we had, the first real conversation we had, when I knew we were more than just friends who were fucking, was at eight in the morning, walking back from a party, coming down off three or four hits of Ecstasy that we knew would flare up again when we got to my house.

"Did you see Ray and Chrissy making out on the dance floor? That was cute," I said. "Tongues all down the throats."

"Gross," she said wryly.

"Yeah, they're like Super Couple or something."

"Oh . . . I guess I've never thought of them like that." She looked up at a palm tree and smiled at the convex undersides of its fronds.

"They're probably afraid of each other," I said.

She looked at me sharply, interested. I hadn't known I was going to say it, either.

"I mean, they've never really been with anyone but each other and they have this extremely perfect life. Houses, boats, bikes, parties, art shows—they're young, rich, talented, and in love. It's a lot at stake."

I paused. She had known Chrissy her whole life, but she wasn't offended.

"It gives the other person a lot of power," she said, "but it's a checked power, because you exert the same power over them."

"Yes! So they have this very solid relationship, but only because it has to be very solid. If it starts to crack, they don't just lose the relationship, they lose everything."

"All eggs in one basket," she says, "but, also, there's nothing to say they couldn't figure out an amicable split."

"They probably don't want to split up, but, sometimes, they might want to be different people. It's just that they can't, because it isn't different people who made that life.

"They never take risks they haven't taken before. The marina grows only by buying or building more docks. Ray's art career expands only by trying new mediums instead of new ideas. Chrissy will never have her own job, because her job is orchestrating their life."

"But that's not a power balance. It's a paradox. Neither one has anything, but if they split up, they can still lose everything . . ." her voice trailed off and she said quietly, "It's like they aren't even people if they're alone."

"Well, they have all these other inhibitions, but making out like teenagers isn't one of them, because to each other they are teenagers."

She looked at me curiously, a vague smile on her face. I could feel myself blushing.

"Are your parents married still?" I asked her.

"No, they're dead."

"Oh . . . I knew that. I'm sorry."

"Thanks. Yours?"

"Very in love with everything to lose, but, actually, just very in love."

"So, it's possible."

"Yeah, it's definitely possible . . . are you hungry?"

"Do you have orange juice?"

"Fresh-squeezed."

"That sounds just fine," she said and she smiled dreamily at me.

I'm struggling with her hair. It's wavier than it should be. Her hair is like crinkle-cut French fries, dirty blond and sort of zig-zaggy, but I keep painting s-curls, snarled up in the back.

That's not what I'm trying to capture. That's what her hair looks like after we fuck, after I've had her on her back, rocking her body back and forth while she rests her head on her pillows or my bare mattress. That is what Julie's hair looks like all the time.

I've got the water just right though, finally, black and shiny and beautiful. I want to dive into water just like this. This water would feel thick around the knees if I tried to walk into it. It would have a heady, sweet perfume that would disorient me if strong waves came, but it would also leave my skin pearlescent and springy if I could make my way back to land again. This water is both treacherous and welcoming.

I step back to look at my progress and feel the sinking death of failure again when I see it from the other side of my studio.

I am a total loser, painting the vast, black ocean of love. No wonder anyone will buy these things. I have a ridiculous moment where I am caught between a gasp and a hiccup and I begin coughing, because I realize all I paint are childishly obvious metaphors and meaningless panoramas.

Luke comes into the studio without knocking while I drink a beer.

"Whoa, playa! What is that?"

"Oh . . . a painting, it's a painting."

"Word. For your next show?"

"No, I was just . . . working on it, you know?"

"Dude! You're back! I'm glad you're back, broham!" He clasps me with one arm and pounds my back, and it makes me glad I'm back, too.

"How was Georgia?"

"Oh, it was cool, you know? Cool. It's not as muggy up there. The people are a little more Southern. I had a long drive, but I stayed in an OK hotel. Free breakfast. I probably drank too much at the opening, and it was a weekday, too, which can be a little weird, sometimes."

Luke looks at me carefully. He is trying to figure out what drugs I have by the way I am rambling.

"So, um, I should have some dust around here if you want. Ray got me some dust last week that I didn't finish. Do you want some? I've got, like, half a cone around here . . . somewhere."

The corners of his mouth turn down, but it's a smile. He stops trying to figure me out and shakes his head.

"No, man, that stuff is crazy. Smells bad, makes you psycho," he says.

"Oh, did you get some, too?"

"No, Jason is just always doing a 'roid and dust combo. He gets all aggro and shit. Erica hates the smell on me, too."

"OK," I say. "OK."

I look around the studio, almost frantically.

"Do you want a beer?"

"Yeah, word—oh, shit! That's not—? Wait, is that—?"

He's looking at the painting again.

"You sly dog, you!"

"What?" I say.

He laughs loudly, triumphantly.

"What?" I ask again.

"Oh nooooooo, broham! What are you doing? Where have you fucking been all week? Let's get outta here!"

"OK, man," I say.

I try to act bewildered, and he lets me.

My last girlfriend, Mindy, was pretty. I liked that she wasn't gorgeous, but just pretty, with long, straight hair and a funny hook on her nose. She was too skinny, but she had straight, bright teeth and smooth, bright skin.

She made me feel like a genuine person, because I was really hot for her, even though she wasn't completely beautiful. Vanessa is beautiful. Julie is beautiful. They are innately fuckable. Most of the girls I fuck are not beautiful, but I don't really care. I just like that they want to fuck me. I'm not intensely attracted to them the way I was attracted to Mindy.

Mindy was into me, too. She was hot for me all the time. She changed my life because she loved my cock. She said it was the most perfect cock she'd ever seen, and the more she talked about it, the more I paid attention to it.

I started looking at it in the mirror and watching it grow as I jerked off. I would do my best to keep my eyes open when I came, so that I could watch myself shoot. I started comparing myself to different porn stars and I realized that she was right. I have a really fucking nice cock.

Its color surprised me most. It's pink, but a really masculine pink, a dull blood color. Every time I cringe at the strawberry in my beard or the pale copper that keeps my hair from being blond, I remember that girls smile when they see my cock.

In the end, though, Mindy and I broke up, because she was so sure I had this Super Cock, she figured I must be using it all the time, until, finally, I did.

She lived with me in Indiana, mostly because her dad was impossible to please, but we were happy, anyway. I thought that I might marry her, because she talked about it sometimes, and my art was starting to take off.

One day, I said to her, "Let's go somewhere that makes sense for who we really are."

We decided quickly. We were leaving Indiana and moving to Florida. She would finish school. I would paint. It would be a good life.

But, then, when we got here, I made friends, and she didn't.

She mistrusted everyone. She thought they were trying to do something to me or do something to her or take advantage of totally normal situations where no one was trying to take advantage of anything. She developed this paranoia that I was going to fall in love with one of these artist chicks that hung out on the beach.

I was still semi-fantasizing about marrying her, but Mindy didn't care. She was positive I was on the make. I went from this guy who loved her and moved her out of a boring, poor Indiana town, so that we could create art and adventures, to some scoundrel dog that would stick anything that moved.

I told my new friends a lot about her, about her smile, her theatricality, her super-close relationship with her mom. I loved her and I knew they'd all get along if she'd just give them a chance.

None of that ever happened, though, because Tara moved to town and was friends with Ray from childhood, and Tara was Mindy, almost exactly, only she liked all these new people I liked, and she was new, too, so, one night, I banged her on the sand.

I kept it up for weeks, until I had my arm around her in a bar, and Ray said something about how it was good to see us together. He was smiling broadly. He meant it, and it felt good to hear. Tara and I smiled at each other and back at Ray.

He nodded and hopped back and forth a little bit. He was drunk and he said it was a good fit, that it was cool that Tara had left Connecticut because of a break-up with Steve right when I had broken up with Mindy.

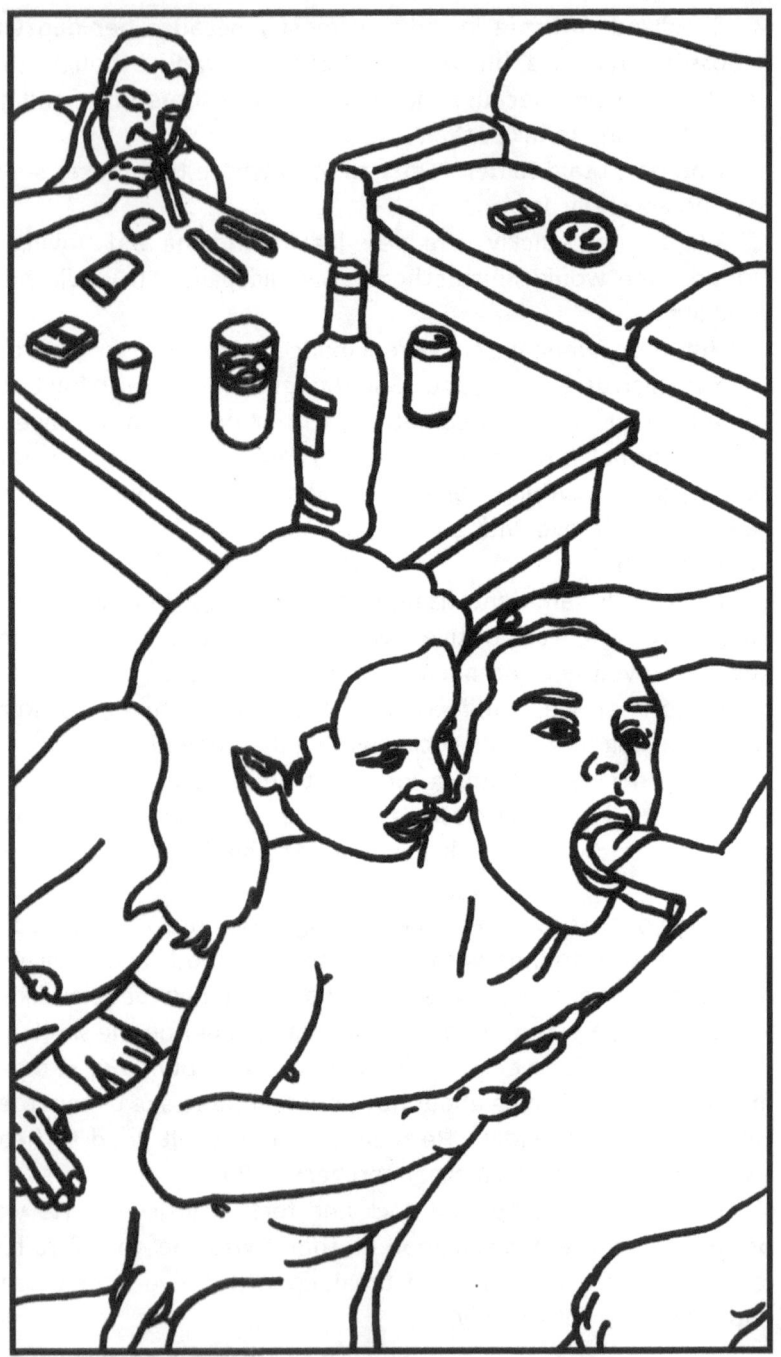

I was drunk, too, and I replied, wishing I would shut up while the words were still in my mouth, but totally unable to stop, "I didn't break up with Mindy."

They both looked at me, shocked. Tara ducked out from under my arm, smiling stiffly and looking at Ray for help. He just looked at me and muttered something to Tara about being sorry.

Tara had never heard of Mindy before, but she tracked her down quickly and told her of my attentions. One night, after hanging out with Ray and Chrissy and Chrissy's cousin, Tina, who Ray was secretly banging, even though she was dating his brother, Carl, I came home to find the locks changed and a backpack of paintbrushes and shorts on the steps.

I looked at the bag in front of our little bungalow and up at the window once. Her theatricality never did have much art to it. I wasn't sorry.

I called Jason, the only guy I knew who lived alone, and stayed on his couch for a few days, until he told me I could convert it to a bedroom if I would pay half the rent.

I had people hang out in my bedroom at all hours of the day and night and I didn't actually produce any paintings for months, because Jason is a crazy fucking cokehead, but I got my dick sucked a lot by guys and girls. It stopped mattering who was on the business end after enough 7AMs, and no one ever said anything to me, but they would say stuff about me.

They would say I have a nice cock and that I used it right. Rumors started about my painting. People started saying I came here, because I was on the verge of being famous and needed to refocus, because I was a crazy partier, too.

Later, they started saying I am famous, and I started getting even more play, three girls on my dick at once, back massages from guys while I pounded their girlfriends, a succession of coke whores who loosened up after a few lines.

I lived somewhere that made sense for who I was.

Things changed after Art took off. Aaron and Jeffrey started doing these shows and they never put my work in it.

We all go around pretending I'm too successful, too busy with other shows, to show at Art, but we all know the truth is I'm not good enough. I'm lying to myself and everyone else.

But they keep letting me get away with it, too.

Ray orders the first round at The Bait Bucket and he's short four dollars. I hand him the cash without saying anything, but he balks.

"Oh, no way, man, that's OK, I'll put it on my card."

"Fuck it, man, it's four dollars, I got it," I tell him.

His eyes open wider, and he looks straight ahead, and I feel like a dick.

We cheer each other, anyway, and take huge, loud gulps. Luke smacks the back of his hand across his mouth. Jason stands in front of me where the bartender can't see him, because I'm almost a foot taller than him. He pulls out a bag of coke and bends down and bumps out of the bag with his key.

"Dude! You're fuckin' nuts!" yells Luke.

He is loud enough for people to look at us. It's part of the fun, getting people to look at us.

"Gimme that shit," he says.

He snatches the bag from Jason and does the same thing, crouching down in front of me exaggeratedly, waving at Jason to cover him. It all just looks like a big joke.

We're laughing, and the three of us, me, Jason, and Ray, put our arms around each other in a huddle. Luke tucks down in the center of our circle and bumps himself out, too. When he comes up, he whoops and bobs his neck like a crane.

"You next, playa!" he says and he hands me the bag.

There's no way I can crouch down in the middle of them without someone seeing what we're doing. I nod at Ray and the bathroom, and the guys groan. I shrug, and we laugh, and Ray and I go into the men's room.

I stick my key in the bag and take a substantial bump.

"You cool, man?"

I hand him the bag.

"Yeah, man, how was Athens?"

"Oh, Athens. Shit, man, it was great. It was totally fucking great."

"Damn, man, wish I could say something even close to that. Who knows when I'll sell something again? All my shit got wrecked in the fire."

He snaps his fingers, the bag still dangling from his ring finger and the pad of his thumb.

"Eh, you're better than me, anyway," I say. "It doesn't matter if your stuff didn't sell this last time. You'll make more."

"I'm fuckin' broke, though," he says. "Fuck it. Up in smoke, up the nose."

He takes a giant bump, too. I taste the drip in the back of my throat. The coke is cut with baby laxative.

"The party will bring people back to the marina," I tell him.

"What's that gonna do?" he says.

I look at him. I can't think of anything, except that my intestines are churning from the baby laxative.

"I don't know," I say.

"It ain't gonna do nothin'," he says. "Let me get another hit."

I nod, and he digs into the bag again. He takes the bump quickly and dips his key again to give me one. I take it quickly, too. I can feel the shit inside me about to burst.

"Ready?" he says.

"Give me a second," I say. "Fucking baby laxative."

He grins at me. "And I thought you're the only guy I know who isn't full of shit," he says.

"I'm trying to fix that," I say and I head into the stall.

"Fuckin' a," he says and he leaves the men's room, laughing.

I am always convinced of the beauty and originality in my work when I start. I always think each new piece is my masterpiece, the one that will settle any question about my creative value.

It makes sense in a way. I wouldn't be inspired if I didn't really think my ideas had enough artistic weight to be something special. There's something backwards in this logic, but I can't figure out what in the hot, narrow stall of the bathroom at The Bait Bucket.

My lower intestine opens up like a snake. Three days of food, mostly microwave popcorn and gas-station hot dogs, tumble out of me like rocks. I stare at the metal door. I am too aware of myself. I am too wired from the coke to be this aware of myself.

But, no, that's wrong, too. The coke wires me and makes me hyperaware. It's just that I am too high to handle being this aware of myself—or anything, really.

I should know better by now. I should know that shitty coke makes me shit and that feeling inspired is not the same as having a good idea. But if I am inspired, then the idea must be good or I wouldn't be inspired. Just the simple fact that I feel inspiration means the idea must be good. Because it is good enough to inspire me.

But, then, I think, as the last brick of shit plops into the toilet that maybe I just don't know what a good fucking idea is. This seems to explain so much more than just my career.

Luke buys another round. We cheer again and slam them back. Everything begins to take on a loose and convex look.

"Yo, how was Georgia?" asks Jason.

"Oh, yeah, it was really good," I say. "Really good."

"Nice. How come you didn't call anybody all week?"

"He got bitches to run," says Luke.

"What bitches?" says Jason.

"He got that black-haired chick," says Luke.

"Dawn?" asks Ray.

"No, that was a long time ago. Why? You want it?" I push him.

"I got a steak at home, thanks," he laughs, "even if I am gonna have to grind her into a taco just to make her last."

We laugh.

"He got that crazy chick, Maria, chasin' him around," Luke says.

He looks at me carefully, the same way he did in the studio, waiting for me to give something away.

"Fuck that girl," I say.

"Heard you already did," Luke says. Him and Jason nod at each other.

I motion for another round. We are going through them ridiculously fast, even for us.

The heavy weight of drunkenness slumps over my shoulders with a sudden fuzzy feeling down my spine. The coke is wearing off, but the alcohol is keeping me going. I look around the bar. It's as dirty and disgusting as always, but it feels good.

"Guys, this is the first time we're together since the fire," I say. "Has anybody seen Aaron and Jeffrey while I was gone?"

"Oh, man," says Jason.

"What?" I say.

"Do you have to go there?" he says.

"What? Where? They're our friends."

Ray and Jason look at each other. Luke is looking at some girl behind us. They say nothing.

"What, guys? Did something else happen?"

"No, man, nothing happened, but, like, nobody's trying to bother them, either. They don't need to be reminded of that shit," says Ray.

"Reminded? How are they . . . forgetting? Their gallery burnt down. Their dog died. Aaron's arm is broken."

"C'mon, man, don't be like that," says Jason.

I stare at them, bewildered for real this time. Maybe the coke is making me emotional. But we're throwing them a fundraiser. I don't say this last part.

"Sorry," I say. "Coke got me all emo."

"Plus, you're a total bitch now, because you know you have a girlfriend," says Luke.

They laugh and whoop at me, together, hands slapping my back.

"I don't have a girlfriend," I say, but it sounds weak, and I don't want it to be true, anyway.

"Right, playa, I know," says Luke. "You got two, right?"

"Fuck off," I say.

They really know nothing about it, nothing at all, but I feel like total shit, anyway.

"Gimme that bag back," I say to Ray.

They holler after me on my way to the bathroom, and I do

enough of the coke that it's time for Jason to buy the round when I get back.

I am home again. I can't get in bed, even though I'm destroyed from the beer and crashing hard off the coke, because when I lay down, the whole room tilts. I am back at my easel.

Her ribcage and her back are exactly right this time, more muscular than she probably realizes, because she's got a slim build. The muscles striate gently in a chevron slant toward the waist, which is also tightly defined.

She is leaning forward ever so slightly, and in her hand is a glinting tang, but her fist covers the hilt. She looks as if she is waiting for something to come out of the water. She looks as if she is fully prepared to kill. She might show mercy, anyway.

In my mind, she is waiting for an inkfish of some sort, something hard to see in the black ocean, something that cracks open softer creatures. She is waiting for something that has a complex nervous system, but I don't know how to show this.

In my drunken torpor, the fact that I imagine this is enough, and I realize that my satisfaction with my imagination is my first real admission that Vanessa will never see this painting.

I've fucked up her hips, anyway. Those aren't her hips. Hers are narrow and offer two indentations on the sides for my palms to cup the hipbones. She has two gentler dimples on each side of the vertebrae above her ass for me to rest my fingertips, too.

The hips I've painted are wider and don't offer these places to hold. They are Julie's hips, just hips to fall into and off again. They aren't as interesting. They just look more available and are the most recent addition to my catalogue.

I feel the old, familiar sense of failure. While the painting is decent in scale and energy, it is not what I wanted it to be, which is a tribute and a question, a stupid way to say that I think I understand what she is when she's with me and when she's by herself and would she like to be with me more often than she is by herself, by any chance?

But I fucked it all up with another girl.

11.

The odor of tar hangs like a shawl, heavy over our shoulders in the heat. The scent of window cleaner prickles through the knit of the tar smell. We are a hundred feet from the water. There is no wind. This is the beach's new perfume.

Europeans used to flock here, lured by glossy fliers that advertised the club's proximity to the water. They would arrive in groups, strangely cheerful, wearing ugly, flashy t-shirts from the Pier. They would load up on cheap booze and invite us to their motels for bizarre, heatless sex that made them sweat and grunt.

They were pigs. We didn't care that they thought the same about us, but when they stopped coming in droves, we missed them—drink prices rose. Staten Islanders replaced them.

We understood, though. No one wants to cross a perfectly clean ocean just to sit in front of a dirty basin full of chemicals.

They were right. We are pigs.

We sit on low futons around a glass table and pull the metallic privacy canopy shut. Dance pop grates through speakers. Dani whines over a Cosmotini.

"So, then, he was like, 'Why do you even care?' and I told him, like, 'I care, because we live together, so if you won't get a job, it affects me,' and he was like, 'I've been looking for work!' and I was like, seriously, where, because all he used to do was snort coke with Ray down at the marina, which was great when Ray actually—"

She stops here and exhales loudly through her nose, "when Ray actually had work for him, but, you know—" here, she turns to Chrissy, "he doesn't have enough work for Jason, which is fine, you know? He has to take care of you guys first, obviously, before he gives his friends jobs, but, like, that doesn't mean Jason can just wait for Ray to fix his business and just not work until then, like, ever, and still just, like, hang out at the marina all day, anyway. Ray isn't paying him! They just sit there and fuck around online and do blow and shit."

Erica puts her hand on Dani's shoulder. She swipes at her nose with the free hand, sniffing and nodding empathetically.

"Ray is actually working," Chrissy sighs. "He just works . . . less."

"Well, if he's working less, he can't pay Jason. I know they've worked together for years, but he can't just do blow all day and come home all hot and sweaty and coked out. Ray doesn't owe him a job just because he used to give him one, and Jason doesn't owe him free work just because shit is hard. I mean, basically, he is still working there. He just isn't getting paid."

She rolls her eyes and continues, "It's bullshit, but he got, like, all stupid and defensive when I told him to get a job somewhere else. He was like, 'It's not just as easy as that,' and 'I wanna do something I li-ike,' but, like, fuck what you like. We need fucking money. It's not always about what people like. I like a man who works! I don't have that! He can't keep working for Ray for free!"

"Dani, he's not working for free," Chrissy says.

"Well, he's down there all the time and he comes home filthy with no money at the end of the week."

"Ray doesn't tell him to do anything. If he's there, he wants to be," Chrissy says. "And you're right, Ray doesn't owe him a job if the business doesn't support it."

Her voice is tight. We look at her, and her eyes are giant. Her hand is trembling on her knee.

"Oh, girl," Dani relents, "I don't mean like that. I just mean that Jason can't hang out with him every day like they used to do. He needs to find work that earns money and let Ray focus on getting what he can out of the place, before everything goes to total fucking shit around here, and we all have to move somewhere horrible and cold and sensible and unsexy, like Chicago or something gross like that. Somewhere with fat people."

"I'm not moving anywhere with fat people," I say laconically.

"Why not?" she says. "Fat people love having their hair done. They can't spend money on clothes, but they'll drop a hundred bucks on a blow-out for, like, some cow-tipping contest or something."

"What?" I say.

"What?" she says. "Did you know Alex is from there? Oh, well, yeah, I guess you did, but, I mean, can you imagine?"

I cannot imagine anything but here. I cannot imagine air that doesn't smell like naphthalene or sulfide. I can't imagine what trees look like without leaves or fronds. I cannot see the sickly white of people who never see the sun. I cannot understand a place where everyone has the same accent and has lived there forever. I am the only one who has lived here forever. Everyone else is from somewhere else.

I picture Alex, standing in the middle of a field with miles of sky behind and ahead of him. His head is filled with whatever simple, Midwestern things fill his head. Optimism. Faith. I think about calling him, but I am drunk, and then I remember why I can't call him.

I hear him tell me that he wishes I were there, the last thing he said to me. A swell of anger rises in my throat. That was nine days ago. I cannot bring myself to ask my friends if they have seen him. I swallow the rest of my drink, a Sidecar, the bartender's recommendation. It is pretentious and gross, like everything here.

"They have cow-tipping contests in Chicago?" Chrissy asks, and we all laugh, and everything is fine again.

We leave the booth, coked to the gills, smiling and sweeping the cheap metallic curtains to the side. The rednecks smile goofily. The Staten Islanders touch their hair and smolder. We cannot even look at them. We are too jittery for drinks after the blow.

I order another Sidecar, even though it is cloying and nearly undrinkable, but I force it down, washing away thoughts of Alex and the drip from the coke. Chrissy is out on the deck, smoking. Dani and Erica are still ordering next to me.

A tall, tan man in a white shirt approaches me and immediately leans in too close.

"You look beautiful tonight," he says.

He has no other night to which to compare me, and I only

look OK. I have been tired for days. I am extremely hopped up on coke right now. My eyes dart. My jaw sticks out.

He smells nice, though. He looks smooth and soft with just a little oil in his hair. His teeth are capped over old breadline dentistry. I breathe in deeply and can taste his gauche testosterone. I haven't seen a European in a long time.

"Thanks," I say. I try to look down, but I can't maintain it for long, because of the coke.

"Are you here often?" he says. He has a nice clip that makes "often" two distinct syllables. I can't place it. It doesn't seem very original to ask.

"Yeah, I come here with my friends," I gesture to Dani and Erica, who have moved back to our futons with the curtains open. Dani is bent down, picking something off the floor. "Our other friend is here, too, smoking on the deck. You?"

"All the time for as long as time permits," he says. This means nothing to me, really, but he is leaning back now, so that I can see the drop from his shoulder to waist. He looks nice, standing there. The line of his torso seems smoother and cleaner than the usual club Volk, like he works outside instead of pumping up at his hotel gym before coming out.

"We all live locally," I say, "so we'll be here for awhile, unless we decide to go to another spot."

"Ah, don't go without saying good-bye. Or!—" he lifts his hand, summoning the bartender. His fingers leave gaudy Eurotrails in the air. I follow his fingers, smiling. I am drunk enough that I can think of Alex now. I like this Euro enough that I can think of Alex.

"Stay here!" he says. "I need to get a few friends who don't know where they are, but I will return immediately when I get them."

The bartender arrives. Euro looks at me meaningfully.

"Will you stay?" he asks.

"Sure, we'll stay," I say.

"Please give her and her three friends what they want on my tab," he says.

The bartender nods. I circle my finger in the air the same way

Euro did, laughing as I do, so that the bartender knows we want another round. He nods again. I walk over to the futons to sit next to Dani and Erica and Chrissy.

"What the fuck," Dani says.

"What? He's getting us drinks and coming back with friends."

"That looked very . . . cozy," says Chrissy.

"I don't think I've seen you . . . talk so much before," says Erica.

"He's intimate," I say. "He's European. Obviously."

"He's not European!" says Dani.

"He's not?"

"No! That's Andrej, you idiot!"

"Oh . . . um, so?" I cross and uncross my legs.

"He's, like, Alex's best friend," Erica says. She looks sorry for me.

"What? What do you mean?" I say. I am stuck on the words "best friend." I can't seem to remember what they mean or what this might have to do with Alex.

"Erica, c'mon, they're not best friends," Chrissy says. "He spends half the year here and half the year in Croatia on some mountain where he's from. He comes here in the winter and grows bamboo. Some special stuff that never rots and comes in colors. You can buy, like, perma-purple bamboo that never dies."

"It's not winter," I say stupidly.

"Whatever," Chrissy says.

"Well, he's European, anyway," I say.

They laugh, and Chrissy puts her arm around me.

"Just be cool," she says.

"Why? What's not cool? I'm cool," I say. "I don't owe Alex anything."

They look at each other again, the same tension as earlier. Dani nods at me to close the curtains, and I do.

"You shouldn't be such a bitch," Erica says indignantly, but her look of pity quickly returns. "Luke said Alex painted you."

"Huh?" I cannot even make sentences anymore. "I can talk to whoever I want."

"You're not listening. He created a new piece of artwork.

Why do you think we haven't seen him?

"He's been working on it, but Luke saw it. It's you with a broken pair of scissors standing in front of the Gulf, only the Gulf is all black, and you're standing facing the Gulf, so no one can see your face.

"Luke said you look all tense and wild, like you're going to kill whatever comes out of the Gulf that's making it black."

"Oh my God!" Dani gasped. "Because the Gulf is going to be black soon! And you're going to save it when you have that party!"

"I'm not saving anything. It's a fundraiser for Aaron and Jeffrey," I say.

"But you know people aren't going out there anymore, and now they're going to, because people will go anywhere for a party!" Dani says. "You're going to save the Gulf and Alex painted it!"

We are passing another bag of coke around. Everything feels surreal. I feel like I am in another dimension, like my friends can only see a hologram of me.

"Erica, did you see this painting?" I ask.

"No, Luke saw it, but he told me about it as soon as he got home. Ugh, they were all so drunk that night, but Luke said that he met Alex at his place and Alex was working on it."

She lowers her voice, "Unfortunately, and I mean, we know this about Alex, but it doesn't exactly . . . you know how he's always striving to improve his execution?

"I mean, Vanessa, don't stress it, you know? He's definitely making something for you, but you need to know, too—Luke said he kind of made your thighs a little too thick—not fat, just thick— and your hair is curly.

"But don't worry. He said it's hot, too, and, like, obviously, he sees you as this completely beautiful thing, Vanessa, don't you get that?"

I picture the girl who came into the salon two weeks ago, the same one who smiled up at Alex the night of the fire, with her wide hips and scallop curls.

"It's not me," I say flatly.

"Yes, it is! Who else could it be?" Erica says. "Don't you understand how amazing that is? He created a tribute to your image, because he sees you as a column of strength and artistry in the face of the world's turmoil."

Her eyes gleam from the coke.

"He thinks the fire was an accident," she says, "and he thinks that you're going to help save things.

"The use of the Gulf is both literal and symbolic, because it's blackening with the filth of mankind, but at the core of his art, he believes that his vision of you and the work you'll do together for Aaron and Jeffrey on Egmont Key will overcome the uncontrolled turmoil in the world.

"I mean, he's wrong, but he loves you!"

Dani gasps. "That's amazing!" she says.

I think of that girl in my chair again, how pretty she was, how she told me she was dating Alex while I stood there with the scissors over her head. And, still, the only thing I feel about her is an intense curiosity. Alex likes her. He wants her. He painted her. She smiled so brightly when she talked about him. They fit together. They are both smilers.

There is no point in telling Erica and Dani and Chrissy that they probably haven't seen Alex all week because he has been with this girl. The thought of them together is almost comforting. She smiles when she talks about him. He paints her. They connect. This is who Alex is. He seeks connections with people. He wants people to like him. He makes it possible to be human.

I have the odd thought that I want to watch them fuck. I want to see what this connection looks like, but then I realize that my instinct for voyeurism is only proof that I will never connect with someone like that. The only reason I want to watch is because I will never feel that way myself.

It's what makes everything OK. It's OK that Alex never called me, because I never missed him. There were enough other people around. People always leave, but there are always other people around somewhere.

Anyone can live without anyone else. Whoever is not present is someone without whom you live and, therefore, someone who does not matter.

I look at Chrissy and Erica and Dani in front of me.

"Alex doesn't matter," I say. I have to pause, because the coke drip gets stuck in my throat.

"I haven't seen him since he came back," I say at the same time that Chrissy says, "Aaron and Jeffrey didn't set the gallery on fire on purpose."

We look at each other.

"That's not right," Chrissy says, but I don't know which topic she means.

"No!" Erica says and, again, I can't figure out the context.

"It's true," I say, confirming my own statement.

Chrissy looks at me, surprised, mournful. Dani gawks.

"But what about the show?" Erica asks. "You aren't doing the show anymore?"

"No, we are," I say, although I realize I don't know if this is true or not. My words are crumbling, hollow, like a hole in a tree trunk.

"There's some sort of confusion right now," Erica says. "Alex understands the truth and mythopoeia of Art. He would never default on your promise to keep our community alive.

"What Aaron and Jeffrey offer is a vibrant paradigm that most people can't understand without the definite parameters of a brand, so even if *we* understand their dynamism outside four walls and a sign, Alex really does believe that sharing their ideals requires we restore the gallery.

"He wouldn't simply abandon you in the face of such an important shared value."

"What shared value, Erica? What is this super-important thing Aaron and Jeffrey offer, anyway?" I say.

"Honey," Dani murmurs to me.

"Well, I know you guys don't want to believe me, but they represent the true self as it must stand amongst others. They set the gallery on fire to show that nothing is truly necessary except the self. Other creatures don't matter once their relationship to you is severed."

I stare at her, dumbfounded.

"C'mon," Dani says quietly.

"So you're saying what Aaron and Jeffrey offer is the lesson that all creatures are worthless?

"If no one is worth anything when they aren't in front of a given subject, then no one can possibly realize his or her full meaning except when he or she is alone, only at that point in time, he or she provides no value outside the self . . . and, therefore, value no one can perceive except the self, which, for utilitarian purposes, is as good as no value at all."

Erica looks at me with pity still, her eyes dilated. She's breathing heavily, "It's why I don't think you should throw them a party. It undermines what they tried to teach at Art."

"You bitches are crazy," says Chrissy quietly.

"Wow, for once, you're fucking right," I say to Erica, but Chrissy's face crinkles in pain.

"Holy shit, guys, maybe we shouldn't have this party after all," says Dani. "I mean, maybe Alex's painting, you know, I mean, I know it's not, like, ominous or anything, but, like, the Gulf isn't really that great, anymore.

"It's pretty, but they're always burning stuff and dumping chemicals in it. I don't want us to fight. Maybe we could just, like, bring them food on a schedule or something—or do something here."

"No one will come if we do it here," I say. "Here?"

Chrissy picks up one of the privacy curtains and makes a face. We crack up again, our heads leaning in towards each other, and, again, everything is fine.

"Listen, don't sweat Alex," says Dani.

"I'm not," I say.

"You are talkative tonight, though," she says. "It's nice."

"Well, the coke is good," I say.

We are back at the bar. Sweat dribbles down the back of my dress into the crevice of my ass cheeks.

Andrej and his friends buy us another round, even though we are barely talking to them. We dance somewhat lazily around them. They are grateful for this. They know we have coke.

Andrej asks Chrissy if he can have some. She tells him no, that we're all out, even though we leave *en masse* every twenty-five minutes or so and huddle in our futon palace for ten, coming out blank-eyed and re-amped for shitty techno.

The night feels interminable. The chemical scent from the Gulf still coats everything.

Andrej and his friends buy more drinks. They hope if they buy enough, we'll tumble into a fantastic orgy with them, but the coke has us too wired to even consider it. Andrej moves on from me to talk to Chrissy. He has his fingers in her hair. He pulls on her curls.

His friend, a boring meathead from South Pasadena, takes over at my elbow. He tells me if I know where to get more coke, he'll buy. I can't decide if I want this or not. He has an incredible body, but I don't care about talking to him.

"C'mon," he pesters. "You know where to get some."

I close my eyes for a moment. My phone rings. I open my eyes and walk away from the meathead.

"Hello?" I say.

"Hi," says Alex.

"Hi," I say.

"You sound like you're somewhere loud."

"I'm out. At House," I say.

"Oh."

We say nothing for a moment.

"So, I have good news! I got a commission in Naples. I have to drive down there on Sunday. Do you want to come with me? I could drop you off on Fifth Avenue downtown and you could go shopping or check out some of the galleries for two or three hours and then we could have lunch in Tin City or something. No, how about Marco Island?"

"Oh, that sounds nice," I say.

"I haven't seen you in awhile," he interrupts.

"I know, it sounds nice, but I can't. I have—I can't," I say.

"Oh . . . OK, no big deal. Well, some other time, then."

"Sure. Alex?"

"Yeah?" his voice brightens as if I've given him good news just by saying his name. My facial cavity feels dry and stuffed.

"Are we still doing that fundraiser thing for Aaron and Jeffrey?" I say it as if I'm only vaguely familiar with it. I feel as if I am only vaguely familiar with it.

"Yeah! Yeah, we are! Of course we are!" he says, and, again, he sounds as if the question were some kind of present for him. "I'll talk to you really soon about that. I'll come right back on Sunday from Naples, and since you can't come with me, we'll have dinner. We'll talk about it at dinner."

"OK," I say. "That sounds fine."

He starts to say something else, but I hang up and go back to the meathead.

"I totally know a guy," I say to him, because the truth is I have absolutely nothing to do between now, Wednesday, and dinner with Alex on Sunday.

12.

I text him at 8:30, "Hi, can't wait to see you tonight," but he doesn't text back by 8:33, 8:39, 8:41, 8:46, or 9:12, at which point, I think about bailing, except I feel on the lowest part of my spine that if I do, I just won't see him again for days or maybe ever again.

Wisps of dust swirl into my brain. I see slideshow images of black water, a girl with something in her hand. I shut the visions out. This is why I came here. To shut this out. I take half a Klonopin from my grandmother's medicine cabinet. Half is not so bad. I can't believe this is coming back. I know why my mother sits in front of the TV with a bottle all the time now.

At 9:13, I tell him, "I have a lil surprise for you. ;)," but I don't. I just want a response. I watch the rise and fall of my ribcage in the mirror. I take smooth, sustained breaths until I absolutely believe that he has responded, because I am supposed to see him in less than two hours.

I check my phone again, only nothing, and it seems rude at this point, but then I remember that sometimes other people just don't care.

At 9:38, he still hasn't responded, which means I have been waiting for him to confirm our plans like a normal person for over an hour. I text him again, "Hello? Are we still on?" and then go to take a shower, content that, by the time I get out, he will have texted back that we are.

I am sitting in the tub with the shower running over the crown of my head and down my forehead. I want to put my hands between my legs, but I don't want to pass out. My eyes are shimmying shut, anyway. My lungs feel soft and weak. My pores are open. My clit is so hot and covered in thick lubrication. I suck on my fingers, and the tile is cool on my cheek, and everything feels so good for a moment, and then I wake up, startled and disoriented.

The water is freezing. I haven't shaved my legs. I scrape at my calves and get out. I look bluish in the mirror.

My nipples are a little swollen. I lift them to my mouth and bend my neck to lick them and feel my pussy tighten up again and lubricate. My neck hurts when I do this, but I do it again, and leave the bathroom, rolling my wet nipples in my fingers.

Alex still hasn't fucking texted back, so I check every online account I have until I finally find a message, "In my studio tonight," at 9:38, exactly the same time I sent him a text. I feel myself shivering that he was thinking of me just as I was thinking of him.

I text him, "I'm on the way!" and rush into my lingerie. I accidentally rip a ladder up the leg of one sheer stocking, but I like how my sweat beads through the net around my thighs. I look flushed. I'm cold from the shower still, but I'm sweating from the Klonopin.

The door is open for me. He sits at his computer, wearing the intense look people have when they're online, even though they're doing nothing. I put my hand on his shoulder, and he turns.

"Oh my God. Hi," he says. This is what I have been waiting to hear, that catch in his voice. It feels like I have been waiting forever to hear someone sound like that when they see me.

"Hi," I say.

He leans back in his chair, his eyes wide, his mouth loose with heat and surprise as I straddle him, one leg lifted high in the air, so that he can see the rip in my stocking. He looks down at it, looks up at me. I smile.

"What are you doing?" I ask him.

He puts a hand on my hip, nervous.

"I was watching oil burns out in the Gulf."

"Oh yeah?"

"Yeah, my friend sent me a link. They just constantly set the water on fire. It's crazy."

"Yeah, it's a cool idea."

"Well, it's not really an idea. It's a real thing."

"No, I know. I mean . . ."

"What?"

"I don't know. What?"

I try to smile, but he just stares at me.

"It was a good idea. It's not anymore."

"Why not?"

"Why? Why is it a good idea?"

"I don't know. Maybe it'll all work out," I say, but suddenly I'm terrified. I don't know what we're talking about.

He says nothing. The monitor behind him flickers with plumes of smoke over a raft of fire in the water.

"What about, like, when you paint? Sometimes, you don't know how it'll turn out. You have a vision—"

He is staring at me intently now. I take a deep breath, but it feels like I'm sucking black water into my throat, the same black water I saw when he didn't text me.

"Not a vision," I falter. "I mean, a vision, but you don't know . . . the full panorama. You don't know everything. But then it all works out and it's really good."

"When did you see my work?"

"The night you took me to that art show you were in."

His face goes blank. "You didn't look at any of the art. The black lights were off by the time you got there, and then everyone left, because of the fire."

I blush. He nods. I look down at his crotch and up at him again with wide eyes, but he just looks at me like I'm pathetic. He tilts his head sideways and, finally, peers into my eyes, but I'm nervous now and I can't look at him.

"Either way, they're burning where we live," he says.

I'm still straddling him, and it's almost awkward, so I rub his hair. "No, they aren't. You don't live in the Gulf. You live on land. This is where you live." I try to cradle his head, but he pulls away.

"Right. Please. Things have been falling apart for years. My friends can't survive like this. I can't survive like this. We all just party and hope we don't run out of money."

I slide off his lap, lifting my leg again for him. I want him to touch my pussy. I want my pussy to distract him and comfort him. I stay crouched over him, ready to mount him again.

"Every beach north of Sand Key is closed for the rest of the summer," he says. "That's twenty miles from here."

"Well, we don't ever go there," I say. "And it's only another month or so."

"What?" he says. "Lots of people go there."

He pushes me away from him and stands, "Lots of people *are* there."

"You're worried about your party, aren't you?"

"How did you hear about that?" he asks.

"This girl Erica recommended a hairdresser to me. She invited me to an audition to model, so I went to the gallery and saw your name on the flier."

"Erica invited you to audition?"

"No, the girl who cut my hair. It sounds fun," I say.

"How do you know Erica?" he asks.

I look at his face, but I stumble anyway, "I met her the night of your art show."

"Listen, I didn't have any art there. You just thought I did. My art doesn't exhibit with those guys. That was my friends' art show." His voice is deep and angry.

"OK," I say quietly. "That's how I met Erica."

"And then Vanessa cut your hair?"

"Yes."

I wait for his next question. I can feel his next question simmering at the top of his head, but I don't know what it is, and it doesn't come.

Instead, he nods slowly. The room hangs with silence, and I think about the rest of that night, scan my brain to make sure I'm not missing any details that will ruin this even more.

"OK," he says finally.

He walks into the kitchen and gets himself a beer. He doesn't offer me one.

"Can I have one?" I say.

He looks at me carefully, his eyes running up and down my body. He can see my puffy nipples through my lace top. He lingers on my hips.

He pauses. "Yeah. Sure."

He is pensive, looking out the window at nothing, at the future. I am sweating underneath all this lace. The straps of my bra cut my shoulders. I want to roll down my stockings. Alex drinks his beer at the window. Suddenly, I understand something new.

"Is that girl who did my hair . . . someone you used to date?"

"Yes," he says.

"OK," I say. "OK."

I step toward him, so that I can stand next to him and put my head on his shoulder, but I stumble again. I want to tell him that it's not that important.

"I'm tired," he says.

"Me, too," I say, honestly.

He looks at me expectantly. I am wrapped in lace and gauze, the film of oncoming slumber. I wait for him.

"I'll call you a cab," he says.

I blink, trying to press tears back into my eyes. He leaves the room for a moment. I lay down on the couch. I don't open my eyes when he returns.

"Did you get my message?" he says.

"Yes."

"Why are you over, then?" he asks.

"I only got one that said you were in your studio. Did you send me another text?"

I feel a surge of hope, like the night might turn around, because we've discovered his role in tonight's failure, too. He had something else to say to me.

"No, that was the text I sent, but why did you come over if you knew I was working?"

"I thought . . . you were just telling me what we were doing tonight?"

"I'm working when I'm in my studio."

"But . . . it's just over there," I sit up and point to the back of the room.

"It's still my work," he says.

"I know," I begin, but I can't think of what to say, so I stand

and walk over to him and I think he is accepting me, finally, but, instead, he walks me out the door and puts me in the cab.

I am in the front of my grandmother's house, still in the back of the cab, but I just don't want to go in there, so I grab my phone instead.

The cabbie clears his throat.

"Turn the meter back on," I say, and then, "Hello?"

"Hi."

"Hi. Do you want to hang out?"

He pauses and then says, "Yeah, I'll come over. What's your address again?"

"No, I'll come to you this time," I say.

"Hey, why don't we go to Tradewinds?" he says. "You're new here. We should make sure you get to as many places as possible."

"Really?" I say. "I'm in a cab."

"Tell the cab to take you there," he says.

"OK!"

"Hey, the only thing is I have to hightail it out of there at, like, five. You stay and sleep, but I have to get down to the marina to work with my buddy, Ray."

"OK, no problem."

"See ya there, babe," he says and hangs up.

"Let's go to Tradewinds," I say to the driver.

He pulls away from my grandmother's dark house, where it always smells like her, even though she does nothing but sleep and watch TV. I feel so much better, having somewhere to go in the hot night breeze with the cab window open.

It's suddenly obvious that if you're dating two people casually, and one drives to new restaurants all over the county and does spontaneous, romantic things like rent a beachfront hotel room last minute, he's a better guy than the one who messages you to say he'd rather work than chill.

13.

I wake up and my head is thumping, gently, behind my eyebrows. My sinuses are dry. Lactic acid burns my muscles. My throat won't swallow. I need water, but I cannot figure out how to get some without getting out of bed. I don't feel bad. I just don't feel like anything.

I can recognize that my body is in a particular state, but the hallway and the kitchen and the sink seem like they are on another dimension. I just cannot be bothered at this moment. Perhaps, in another moment, I will care that I am extremely dehydrated, but, right now, I don't even remember what I did last night or yesterday.

I have the impression I have not seen people for many days, but this may not be true. My tongue feels fat from disuse, but I am comforted by its sluggish existence in my dry mouth. I have a tongue; therefore I am, and I decide to get out of bed, because I have just confirmed something is real.

The floor is hot, not comforting. I consider returning to bed, but my own stickiness in the sheets will disturb me. My feet must stay on the ground now. I walk as if I am ancient, slowly, so as to maintain my posture, which seems difficult. I could collapse at any moment. I could always collapse at any moment. Anyone could.

I touch my stomach. My core is solid, a bit tender, weak in the lower portion. I cannot remember the last time I ate. I cannot remember much of anything.

I haven't worked in a long time. There hasn't been any reason to work. No one calls. I spent a lot of money in a club recently. I can't remember how much or why, just that the night became wet and vicious before anything aired out and I blew away.

The insides of my thighs are sore, as if I have been masturbating for many hours, with my knees straightened and spread. I suppose this is possible. I touch my breasts. They feel a little tender, too, but I think I was sleeping on them for several hours. My face feels relaxed. I am as lucid as possible.

I am slipping away, slowly, from other people and the things that matter to them, and I know that other people—what other people?—will think this is bad, but, actually, it feels just fine.

I turn on the tap, and the sound of water alerts me to my dry, empty bladder. I am not sure what is inside me, really. I drink a glass of water and then another and then another and then another, until the fourth glass spills down the sides of my cheeks. I must be thirsty, after all.

This seems fine, too, not quite as comforting as my slug tongue, though. This is need, not just existence. I was stronger just existing, but then I am just existing again, once the water is inside me.

I turn around, back down the hall, and see that it is covered in taped-up pieces of paper, under the garlands of paper dolls that line the hallway. I didn't notice this on the way to the kitchen, but, now, the pieces of paper are fluttering. Their bottom edges are waving gentle reminders at me, trying to brush me, like ferns that need petting or music or something unexpectedly human like that.

The pieces of paper have pictures of disembodied heads, sketched in navy blue pencil. The necks spread out like tree trunks with roots that snake downward. The balls of foliage above are tangled and tied into spirals and spikes. Thin braids dangle giant beads at the bottom, like tire swings that make the striations of the tree-trunk necks bulge.

Monstrositrees, I think, and squint, because I can't remember the real word. I take a deep breath and look up at the paper dolls overhead. Girls. The drawings on the sheets of paper lining the walls are girls. I knew that word, though.

I consider laying back down again, but the phone rings. I look in the kitchen for it, but I cannot find it. Whoever it is calls again. I look in the bedroom. If I can't find it this time, the caller will just go to voicemail forever and ever and ever, until I decide to use the phone myself. Eventually, everyone—who, though? I am having trouble remembering who—will go to voice mail, and the phone will cease to ring altogether.

This is an interesting idea, that the phone knows I am slipping away, before those other people do, but, then, I find it and say hello, feeling giddy and a little dizzy.

"Where are you?!"

I look around. "I'm in the hallway, near my bedroom."

"Why aren't you here?"

"Who is this?"

"It's Jeffrey!"

"Oh, hello, Jeffrey."

"We have our open call today, remember? There are girls here who want to be models. Aaron is freaking out that you aren't here . . ." He is trailing off, becoming quieter. "You have to pick whose hair you want . . . don't you . . . need to be here? You said you were going to be here."

I blink in the hallway, looking at the curling edges of the paper, thinking that on another astroplane, these girl-trees exist. Everything exists somehow, unless it doesn't, but that just means it doesn't *anymore*, because reference is proof of existence at some point in time or space.

I look out the window. The sun is low, but it is still so bright out. I pull the phone away from my ear. It is almost eight. They have been waiting for me for almost two hours.

"Oh. Jeffrey. I forgot. That's all. I just forgot. I'll come down right now," and, suddenly, I'm not slipping away anymore, and I'm sad.

The gallery teems with so much absurdity that everything normalizes upon a full scan of the room. I expected a sense of decay, of hanging on, but then I realize I am just projecting—other people progress the best they can, because they are vivacious in a way that I have lost.

The walls have been replaced with an intricate wire pattern, so that everything is shiny and cool and futuristic. I wonder if perhaps Erica is right, that Aaron and Jeffrey do not need a fundraiser. This feels cold and expensive, as if it emanates from something that has no beginning or end. It feels like it will just wrap around and around, warping as it needs, shimmering, prominent, then evanescent, and then I see what it is.

It is a cage. They have re-imagined the entire room as Snuggles' cage.

No one else seems to notice that this is not particularly useful for an art gallery. The girls—and there are so many of them; who are all these girls?—do not care that textured, silver walls do not showcase paintings with any purity. I am confused. Aaron and Jeffrey know that the walls compete with anything near them.

I want to mention that renovating the gallery twice is not exactly the purpose of a fundraiser, but then I remember they didn't actually ask anyone for a fundraiser. This was Chrissy's idea. Where is she? Where is Alex? Why am I here? Nothing makes sense. I sit down on a wooden cube. The walls throb.

"You're here," Jeffrey says.

"I'm here," I say.

He looks gray against the cage he's built.

"The walls . . ." I say.

"Yes," he says. "Do you like them?"

"No," I exhale. I look up at him. "I'm sorry. They're . . . overwhelming."

"It's all right. I don't like them, either."

"Were they your idea?"

"Yes," he says.

"Well . . . these things take time," I say.

"We have time. We also have . . . girls." He says this last word distastefully.

"We have to pick our favorites? Where is everyone?"

He sweeps his hand grandly. His neck wobbles along the same arc of his hand. "Where is everyone," he intones.

I find this intensely difficult already.

"Is anyone . . ."

"Yes. Aaron," he says. He sounds melancholy and hateful at once. He is confusing me even more.

"Jeffrey, are you . . ." I trail off. Something is wrong with me. I have no idea what is wrong with me. I cannot see in here. I don't understand how other people can see in here.

"I'm fine," he says sadly.

"OK," I say.

He stands and nods toward Aaron. We walk over to him. He makes a distressed, whimpering noise as if my arrival is a reminder of my lateness.

His broken arm hangs inside another kimono. He has only just begun wearing these. He is a little heavier through the face, and his eyelashes are gone. They are neither of them as well recovered as I initially thought.

"How on the brink of something are we!" he says. "What glory shall we discover by revealing the vulnerability of woman, that vessel of all mankind, against the raging tragedy of nature, upon a boiling, black sea that we must cross to explore in recompense for suffering the horror of masculine fire! Are you prepared to pick the next icons of Art!"

Nothing is a question, which works, since no one knows what he's talking about.

The girls are a swarm of cicadas, five-eyed flies looking all around at each other and us, singing indifferently, thronging in thongs and crop tops, rubbing their wings. Who has told them to come looking like this? Aaron blows a whistle. The girls startle and then suddenly fall into awkward, crooked rows, standing still and gawping. I realize they are not looking at each other anymore. They are looking at the wall behind us.

I turn around. The wall is the only one to remain smooth and white. Aaron and Jeffrey are streaming a live feed of the burning oil in the Gulf, a mystical blaze atop diamond ripples of water in the sun.

A black cloud bounces in place over the flame. Its density is incredible, so plush it's almost welcoming. Its existence is incredible. It is a floating miasma, but made of oil smoke, burning molten rock from millions of years ago. It is raised like a cushion from which a gritty, sensuous god might lounge and entertain. Under it, bridges and trellises of fire laugh and puff and crackle in the water.

The fire is the orange of hell, a painful, faceted orange that smothers any gentle, rhythmic blue that should be there. It is a bacchanalian ring, full of single licks that undulate into a dangerous, cavorting circle.

The water rolls the fire across its waves, so that the mass of flame and smoke blurps and slides across the coordinates of the Gulf. The sun begins its final drop behind everything, flashing harshly.

The room is entirely silent. Even Aaron is standing with his face raised to the screen, as if he were sunning himself in the rays of light that hop into the camera lens, blinding out portions of the video.

"What the fuck is this?" I say.

"It's just a feed of the burn. This environmental group streams it online. They showed it to me the other day." It's Alex. He is next to me. I don't even know how he came to stand next to me.

I turn to Jeffrey.

"Why is this playing?" I ask him.

The wall to my left makes me immediately dizzy. Jeffrey shrugs.

"Who knows? Aaron is obsessed with fire these days," he says.

He is languorous. His *s*'s are soft, hissing. The low *a*'s are open and rounded. His lids and shoulders hang low.

"We watch this all the time now. It's like watching the Yule Log, only it's real."

"We should start picking girls," I say.

I turn away from the video to face the room. Everyone is still in formation. I can't possibly pick anyone, though. They are all so entirely average looking. Not ugly or even unattractive, but just not attractive, either. There is nothing compelling in these rows of women who want to be chosen for their physical beauty.

I don't know what to do with any of them. I can't see them as people. I have no way of knowing whether any of them are worth anything. They are just rows of cutouts. It is impossible to pick.

I look at Alex. He is looking at me with a tenderness I have never seen before, as if there is something about me that requires grave concern. I feel my eyes water, because I am almost sure he has finally seen how I see people. I cannot excuse this or hide this. No one connects to me. I am a fluttering scrap in front of an army of paper dolls. I look down, but I cannot bear to be here any more and I need him to pick who he wants.

I am intensely interested in which handful of soon-to-be giggling girls appeals to him as personable or pretty, because I know he sees people. He feels them as people, and they reciprocate. Whoever he picks will be right and, suddenly, I realize why my eyes are watering.

I am about to cry, because he can never pick me, because I know I will die with a certainty that eludes these light-hearted, hopeful models, who are able to trick themselves into all manners of stupidity, including the idea that they are pretty and that if someone recognizes them as pretty, they will transcend their personalities.

Other people connect because they do not consistently bear the gravity of their impending death. They let it trail behind them or over them, like the sleeve on a kimono or a plume of smoke from sweet crude oil.

The unobtrusive veils of all their deaths surround them in one net, the catacomb of life, ready to unfurl them into an abyss, one by one, all of them unaware, until, momentarily, they notice and then forget again as the veil trails behind or overhead once more.

Alex is so unaware of these details that darken life. His absent-mindedness is the same as his kindness. He only sees what allows him and everyone else to walk through life pleasantly. Anyone he picks, I know I will hate, but I know they will be good, and that their goodness is why I will hate them. They are not burdened with death and so they are as vibrant as can be.

But, then, that isn't it—I won't really hate his choices. I will be jealous that they recognize each other within the safety net of a life that cannot fathom death. I always see death approaching everywhere and I always will until it's mine. I can't claim this focus or vision for achievements in art or career. I cannot say it for romantic dreams, only for dying.

Life just seems like death's troublemaking godchild, a silly girl-sprite who lacks the serious glamour of her spiritual mentor.

I turn back from the crowd of women, skinny and fat and tall and short and rounded and sharp, all such similar humans, and I whisper to Alex, "Which ones should we pick?"

Jeffrey leans over to us. His eyes are bright. "You don't have to pick. Aaron picked them an hour ago. He's just putting on a show, giving them what they expect now. Everyone he picked is totally meh, but we both thought neither of you would be here."

"What about Dani?" I ask.

"Aaron vetoed her for some other girl with a similar body type, but sort of bronze-ish hair. Aaron says her vulnerability is the perfect backdrop for your masochism."

I feel my stomach drop as I realize who Aaron picked and I want to tell Jeffrey to shut the fuck up, because he just told Alex that girl's desperation is a perfect fit for his shitty artwork, but then I realize he might have meant me, that I'm the masochist, and I blink rapidly, curling forward just a little bit, because I know even Jeffrey doesn't see Aaron's ludicrous, pointless spitefulness, and Alex just looks confused.

"Who?" Alex asks.

"You've seen her in here before. She was here the same night."

He calls it this now, the night of the fire, "the same night," as if it's the only night we might ever discuss.

"I know who that is," I say.

"Right, I've seen her around with Jason, too," Jeffrey says. "She's OK."

Alex frowns a little, as if trying to place her.

"You know her," I say.

"I don't know," he says.

"You do. I've seen you talking to her."

They both look at me, surprised.

"I have," I say simply, and they both look away.

"Anyway," Jeffrey continues, "he picked the prettiest ones he could. We don't have a good-looking town, it turns out."

"Yes, we do," Alex says in surprise.

"No, we have a town on the beach, Al. It's different."

"Let's put Dani in, anyway," Alex says.

"Instead of the other girl?" Jeffrey asks.

"I don't think it's right to exclude Dani."

"I suppose it's the same body type. It's not like it'll fuck you up," says Jeffrey.

"Don't all models have the same body type?" I ask. "Why would anyone buy a ticket to look at short, fat people?"

We all look at each other again.

"This is a weird idea," Alex says.

"Wasn't it yours?" Jeffrey says.

Alex rubs his face. "Yeah, it was."

"You should have picked the girls yourself," I say.

"How were you going to do their hair?" he says. "I thought we were picking together."

"I don't care. I decide what to do to people's hair the minute I see them all the time. It doesn't matter."

"I thought we were going to collaborate."

"How? You put them in an outfit. I do their hair."

"It's not just a pretty pony show," he says indignantly. "We're supposed to be creating actual art with this."

"People aren't art, Alex."

"Yes, they are! That was the point."

"I thought that was the point, too," says Jeffrey quietly.

"No, you thought what you were going to *do* to them would make them art. You don't think they're art by themselves."

"No, that's what *you* think."

I sigh. "Yes, that is what I think."

"Are we OK?" Jeffrey asks. He looks worn down.

"Yeah, you should have picked the girls yourself is all," I say to Alex. "It's too late now."

"Why should I have picked them?" Alex says. He is angry. I have never seen him angry. "Maybe we don't get to pick people. Maybe they just show up, and those are the people that are there, and we aren't unhappy about it. In fact, we're kind of into it and we want to keep those people there."

"OK, you're traveling," I say. "You can see the beauty in everyone or whatever. I get it, but it doesn't mean that you have to be thrilled that Aaron picked some ragtag army just to make him feel like he has his circus freaks to herd when you're the one who needs to do the actual creation around these people."

Alex is near sputtering. His mouth opens and closes and opens and closes again. The cage around us throbs more closely to my skin. I feel clammy and almost nauseous.

"Where is Chrissy, anyway?" I say.

"She's standing over there with the other models," Jeffrey says.

"They're not all models," I say. I feel like I am going to pass out. "And shouldn't she be over here with us?"

And, then, a wide, toneless roar detonates in my eardrums and the back of my skull. A flickering light jags across my eye. I reach out for something, Alex or Jeffrey or anything solid, anything that isn't metallic and latticed or burning, and then I see what's happened. The video has stopped.

Girls begin humming. They are cicadas discarding their shells. There is nothing to see on the wall and, not that they have quite forgotten, but, with nothing to look at, they are reminded that they are here to be seen.

Aaron has propagated the worst kind of myth—that simply wanting something and showing up for it is as valid as being qualified for it.

He is enraged, though.

"What happened to the feed?" he bellows.

Everyone looks at him. He is a ball of heat in the center of the cold room. The girls are startled.

"Oh no," Jeffrey murmurs.

Aaron pushes through the room, his kimono lifting up behind him. He bends over the computer. He lifts the laptop with one arm and frantically begins checking wires and looking around the room. The harsh lights have not dimmed. The set-up is nearly entirely wireless, but, still, someone has managed to step on a projector cord somewhere. Aaron is livid, one arm flailing.

"Jeffrrreeyyy!" he calls.

Jeffrey shakes his head sadly. "Stay there," he says to us.

He goes over to Aaron, and they inspect the laptop and projector. Aaron leans inward, towering over the cowering

Jeffrey. Frozen, staring at the disloyal projection system, they are in repose exactly as they were the night of the fire before Snuggles started barking.

Jeffrey looks up at Aaron and shakes his head. Aaron's shoulders puff out. If his arm weren't broken, he would look like he were about to hit Jeffrey. Jeffrey just shakes his head sadly again. Aaron looks up at the wall in agony and rage. Jeffrey stays low and continues to look sad. He is staring at the point in the cage where they have woven metal around an outlet. The cord is plugged in. The router is blinking a healthy, happy blue. Nothing is wrong with the Internet or the projection system.

"What is happening out there?!" Aaron screams, but, suddenly, it becomes obvious what happened out there.

The controlled burn became uncontrolled. The wall holds nothing but a juddering black square.

Aaron hits a button. The control bar for the video module appears. He slams the mouse on the play arrow over and over and over, but nothing happens.

"What the fuck?!" he says. His face twists in tortured disbelief.

The room is agog. People instantly understand what has happened, that something very bad has happened, that even if it is not as catastrophic as the millions of gallons of oil constantly gushing into the Gulf, and even if it doesn't kill millions of more birds and sea creatures, what just happened is very bad. It made part of the Internet stop working.

Phones latch to ears immediately. No one has a single care for the person next to them. It is the person far away and unknown that matters now. The person next to anyone is fine. They are right there, here, standing, sitting, making phone calls, alive, existing.

There is comfort in existence.

I look at Alex. Neither of us have anyone to call. We look away from each other.

Jeffrey is pounding on the laptop, dumb and ineffectual. Aaron has sunk into his kimono. His good arm rises over his head, so that he is inside a tent of threaded polyester-silk. People are now on the phone, and it seems obvious that everyone on land is fine, that it's just another explosion out in the Gulf, but people are unnerved by the destruction of the web page and Aaron's failure to control the video feed. They clamor to leave.

They pull together articles of clothing and bags. No one cares if they are a model anymore. They need to go home and check their Internet. They look up at the wall in the silly hope that the feed will return. The devilish burn seems, in retrospect, modest and necessary.

Aaron stands up and proclaims to the room, "Go if you must! But the show will go on!"

"Things aren't going well," I say to Alex under the rising volume of the room. "I forgot about tonight."

"I didn't. I was just scared to see you, actually."

He looks forlorn and hopeful at once, as if his admission will save something, and I think I might tell him something that is different, but then I know I can't, because I don't even know if he really has anything to do with it.

People depart, barely looking at us.

14.

I am in the park across from the gallery and I don't know how I got here. Aaron flipped out. I said something to Alex, but I don't remember walking out of the gallery. I am bleeding, crouched over on my haunches, next to the fountain. Black chunks of blood run down my legs and over my wrists and up my arms, from where I've tried to mop it up with the translucent soppage of my palms.

I am sobbing in the thick, nighttime heat. It is so fucking hot still, even at night, and I am not going to stop fucking bleeding and I think this is about right, this is about fucking right.

Air is trapped in my lungs, pushes out through my throat, and I cough as I cry. I bend over more tightly into myself, seeing the blue tile on the side of the fountain. I think that this might be the last thing I see, this perfect blue tile. I reach out to touch it, crying in soft whimpers of pain now. I leave a bloody red palm print on the tile and know if there ever was a God, it has passed over me and isn't coming back.

I have the idea that if I can stand, I can flush out all the blood somehow, even though I know, very clearly and consciously, that isn't true. It will stop soon and start again in a few hours and then it will stop completely, and I'll be alone again, but none of this matters right now. The impulse is to stand and release everything from my fucking body and be done.

I do, and blood gushes in amounts that I hadn't imagined before, a pure, rushing, maroon river, and I seep my hands into it again. I feel the force with which it expels—steady, gentle, unrelenting—and I am dizzy and fall back to the ground again, breathing a sigh of relief as my head hits the fountain hard enough that I feel the concrete graze my cheek, but not so hard to knock me out.

Erica is at my side. "Oh my God, what happened?"

"Nothing," I say. I sound like a ghost already.

"What happened?" she says again. Her voice rises in panic.

I say nothing. My head rolls to the side.

She looks back at the gallery, at me again.

"Don't," I say.

"OK, what happened?" she says. She is urgent, quiet.

"Nothing. I'm going to fucking die," I say. "Don't you get I am going to fucking die?"

"I'm calling an ambulance," she says.

"Don't," I say.

"Don't what?"

She sees my arms, my thighs.

"Oh my God. Oh my God. Oh my God."

She grabs her phone and begins dialing.

"Do you see now?! I am going to fucking die. I told you. Just let me fucking die."

I speak this last part, but, then, I am screaming, as if there is nothing to me but black and red dust and pale yellow bile. My throat burns with bubbles of hot spit. Erica is on the phone.

"Please don't," I say. I am so weak again. The sky is at eye level. The ground is so rough under my blood.

Erica is looking back at the gallery.

"I should get Alex," she says.

"No, don't get Alex," I beg. "Please, don't get anyone."

Her eyes are discs of fear. "I won't. Oh my God, OK, I won't."

I am suddenly furious. I punch myself in the face, but I don't feel a fucking thing, so I do it again.

"No! No! Stop!" Erica says.

She reaches out to grab my wrist, but she stops, because she doesn't want to get blood on herself. I laugh at this. She doesn't care. No one really cares. Everyone is trained to respond in certain ways to certain things, but no one *cares*. She has to go into Art and she doesn't want to have blood on her. She can think that she can't keep her word if she has blood on her, but, really, no one gives a fuck about anything but themselves.

I see the ambulance on the other side of the park, so I get up and run toward it, coughing, stopping to bend over and cough more. I straighten up and run again, until I fall into the sharp grass, blood everywhere now, on my face, on my hands and wrists and arms, in the crooks of my knees, and I am laughing like a total fucking maniac, because, of course, I am, now. I am a total fucking maniac.

A man in a uniform runs across the park to meet me and crouches down next to me, asking me what happened, what happened, what happened, and I try to sit up, just to look for Erica, but she's gone, and I look at the man in the uniform and punch myself in the face again, as hard as I can, and this time, my cheek rattles a bit under my eye, and I lay back down on the grass while he hollers for a gangbang of uniforms who pick me up, tie me up, and want to just fuck me raw with no regard for warmth or anything I might want, but they won't let me die.

The world will kill me someday, but it just won't let me fucking die.

Two cops scream at each other in the doorway to the property intake room. A sloppy, nappy black man stands to their side, spitting out a pathetic, disjointed, meandering attempt at a rap about his money.

"I ain't wanna take this cash from him. If it goes stolen, I'm the last one to touch it. I ain't tryin'a go out like that," says the Puerto Rican cop.

"You have to take his money! You have to count it and take it in an envelope! These are the rules, man! You have to!"

"You ain't lettin' me do my thing. I let you do your thing."

"You bag the money."

"You do it, then."

The islander cop looks away and steps over to the metal detector.

The man with the nappy hair says, "I got three hundred twenty-two dollars. 'Cause I'm a baller, shotcaller, three hundred twenty-two dollars.'

"I know, man. Sit down," says the Puerto Rican cop.

He sits down next to me. I am in a soft blue pajama set, over-washed, pilled, with snaps down the front. He laughs at me and then growls to himself, staring at me intently. I stare straight ahead. He continues to stare at me while I count to five hundred, slowly, and, still, he is staring at me, with his face turned to my profile, his neck leaned into my face, breathing heavily, his hands in his lap.

When I reach five hundred, I turn my face towards him and look deep into his eyes. They are caverns. Their depths hold nothing redeeming. The only evidence of untrustworthiness, danger, damnation is absence. This person is nothing. I turn my face from his deliberately. There is nothing possible to prove to this person. I stand up, walk over by the metal detector, stand next to it.

"Get over there!" yelps the black cop.

"No," I say. "I'm not sitting by a man with a staring problem like that."

"I am not staring at you! Sit down!"

"I didn't say you were. I'm talking about him." I gesture to the nappy-headed man.

The cop looks at my hands and arms, still covered in dried blood. They brought me, when I arrived, to a bathroom with no doorknob so I could change, but the sink was smeared with shit. The blood is crusting along my legs, too, and chipping off as I move, flaking inside the over-washed pajamas.

"Sit down," the cop squeals. He sounds like a hyena. I realize it may be more likely that I can defend myself against my fellow patient than this officer.

I sit down next to the nappy-headed man again. His body smells of shit. He exhales a long, gruff, vibrating breath of rotted air. He turns his face to stare at me again. I look back at him, full of hate this time, only to find something in his eyes now.

He is excited that I left, that I was commanded back. He takes off his shorts, his breath coming in shorter huffs. No one has offered him a blue uniform yet. He pulls his shorts over his sneakers. I stand up again and begin to cross the room.

"I said sit down!" shrieks the hyena. His note of hysteria vibrates, too, like the nappy-headed man's breath.

"He's jerking off," I say. I sound the sanest of everyone in the room.

The nappy-headed man is tugging at himself. The cop looks at my arms again and grabs me by the elbow. He pushes a pass into a metal plate by the door and hauls me through it once it beeps. He goose-steps down a hallway. It's the same hallway they dragged me down to change my outfit, only now, fresh blood splatters it, because this place gets worse and worse. Everything always gets worse, and then he hurls me into a narrow room with a hospital bed and a flickering fluorescent light, before swinging the door shut and walking away the same way he came.

They, a series of bored tech-school graduates, tell me I'm next to see the emergency psychiatrist. They say this at three in the morning, at four forty-five in the morning, at five-thirty, at eight, at nine forty, and at eleven.

I continue to ask, "How many patients are ahead of me?" even though I know they will tell me the same careless lie.

The three o'clock attendant tells me, "You're a legal issue now. You just a legal issue and can't nobody change that right now."

The five-thirty attendant tells me, "You're just like everyone else here."

This is expected in a way. They all look alike to me, too.

After I have lost track of time, I try to sleep. This place is timeless. The only punctuation is the constant staccato of harsh lighting, but even that is perpetual. I am still caked in blood. New blood is seeping though the blue outfit and into the hospital bed. I curl into a ball on my side. I have been in this hospital for at least twenty hours, and no one has come to see me.

As far as I know, no one but Erica and the ambulance men and these attendants know I am here. Even Erica may not know where I am, only that I am not where I was before, which was nowhere, really.

My stomach hurts. I refuse to eat the food—processed yogurt made with gelatin, the ground bones and melted fascia of farm animals, a bagel wrapped in cellophane, a variety of other obligations. Everything lists high-fructose corn syrup as either the first or second ingredient.

I am bleeding profusely now. If anyone ever comes in to see

me, the blood may complicate things. Or it may not. I am surprisingly lucid, because I have something on which to focus, the expulsion of blood coming out of my body. I would not mind if I bled to death here, but I don't think that is possible. The only thing I mind is the continuation of time here in this particular place.

From the next room, a commotion arises, the broad hills and valleys of black women, at first, being loud, then calling out in angry urgency.

"She shit on the floor! Yo, somebody get in here! She shit on the floor!"

The voices carry over and through each other. There are four or five women in the room next to me, and I realize, suddenly, that I have been given a partiality, that the hyena gave me a private suite.

The women fall silent as a rasping shout overwhelms them. "The fuck you motherfuckin' bitches want? I been motherfuckin' in here askin' for motherfuckin' water for two motherfuckin' days! Ain't nobody bring me no motherfuckin' water. Only way to get a motherfucker in here is to shit on the motherfuckin' floor!"

The same voice begins sobbing, choking, gasping for air. "Get me a motherfuckin' glass of motherfuckin' water. You have to motherfuckin' come in here now, 'cause I shit on the motherfuckin' floor!" Her words are punctuated with sobs and jagged, dehydrated catches.

The other women in the room begin keening and complaining around her, a medley of curses and cries, a dark, sickening, cascading, feline orchestra of several women in an orgy, careening towards orgasm at once.

Police officers rush past my room and into the next. None of them carry water. They hold someone down. Two large male attendants or nurses pass next. No water. I realize I am thirsty, too. I am still bleeding, though—calling attention to this will prolong my stay.

I curl into myself more tightly and stare at the floor. Rice Krispies and bagel crumbs and tight curls of hair cover the linoleum, a fine and consistent layer of debris. None of this came from me, and I am saddened that I will have to pad over it in soft socks, that the Krispies will crunch underfoot, and the hair and bagel crumbs will stick to the traction grips on the soles of the socks, the most expensive socks I will ever have, when I consider what the bill for this sort of thing probably looks like.

The shitting woman is subdued by drugs and handcuffs. I fall asleep. I am still bleeding.

There is no way to know how much time has passed anymore. I go out to the nurse's station to ask if I can read the copy of *Ebony* they shared when I arrived. The amount of dried blood on my pajamas has caked the fabric's softness into layers of earth and rust, but I don't even worry about them acting upon it anymore.

As long as I don't raise my voice, no one will notice that I have lost so much volume. Even if anyone does notice, no one will care. The smell would be troublesome anywhere else—rich and metallic and urgent—but I don't mind right now. The cramping is gone and, in its place, is a hollow feeling between my hips and a mask-like feeling across my cheeks. I may have blood on my face, but I have no way to know for sure.

A woman with a shock of lye-destroyed hair is at the bulletproof window that protects the tech-school graduates. They idly check for text messages or post updates on their phones.

I lean my mouth towards slats that are supposed to be at face level, but, instead, just blur out the attendants' stupid, lowered eyes.

"Excuse me. Do you have any reading material?" I ask.

No one stops what they are doing. No one is doing anything.

"Excuse me," I say more loudly. "Do you have any reading material, please?"

The woman next to me bangs her fist on the glass. "I know y'all got some marijuana back there. I don't want y'all givin' me that Ativan. That shit ain't natural and that ain't what God put me on this earth to do for, but if you give me some of that natural shit, that shit that came from the earth, then I'll be straight, and y'all won't need to give me that Ativan no more."

The attendants continue in their prison, and the woman pours out in a tumult, "That shit ain't right. It don't mess with me right. I don't mess with it right. I ain't takin' that shit no more. It ain't right. Y'all get to get outta here and do whatever you want.

"I know you be smokin' that green when you get outta here, but I can't get outta nowhere. I don't know why you even keep me here. I ain't got no family. I ain't got no house. I ain't got no car. I ain't got no man. I ain't got nothin' so what the fuck I wanna live for? And y'all won't let me die! Y'all just wanna keep me alive, and I can't never leave and I can't never do nothin' and I wish I was dead. Don't you get I wish I was dead?! Why can't I be dead?!"

I can see the copy of *Ebony* on the desk, next to an obese woman with a bright yellow weave in her bangs. The weave looks up as the ashy woman continues to wail, more and more loudly, "Why can't I be dead?! I wish I was dead!"

The fat weave stands and waddles slowly to the door of the attendants' bulletproof pen. She stops at a cart and positions her heft so that we cannot see her and then she opens the door and walks, the fat rippling in flapping wings at her sides.

She puts one arm on the shoulder of the ashy woman and says, "Now, honey, why would you get yourself all upset like that?"

The ashy woman says, "I just wish I was dead, and y'all won't let me outta here, but y'all won't give me nothin' to make me happy, neither."

The obese woman hushes her and extends the ashy woman's arm so gently, I don't even realize what is happening until she has stabbed a needle into the woman's arm, no permission needed. The woman smiles up at her, half shameful and half relieved.

The weave turns to me, "Did you need something?"

"Do you have anything I could read, please?"

"No, we don't."

I go back to my private suite and wonder if the same fate will befall me. They will not let me die. I am a legal issue. I have free roam of the ward—and, although I am weighed down with the armor of my own or maybe technically someone else's dried blood, I cannot interest myself in the hallways that lead to the blood- and shit-smeared bathroom. The ward itself is locked by magnets within heavy steel doors that require a pass from the other side of the attendants' station.

I consider taking off the thick, stiff pajamas. The front of the top remains unstained. I look back out at the attendants' station. Still, no one notices anything. I look up at the hot, buzzing light and begin to calculate how to position the bed in order to remove the plastic cover from the light, so that if an attendant were to accidentally look up, no one would see me. I scratch at the worn fabric of the top. The weft easily thins.

I stand to swing my door open lightly to check for hallway interlopers, and I am about to move the bed, remove the light cover, remove my fraying shirt, and see if I cannot set this whole place on fire, when a white man in his 60s come to my door and smiles at me broadly.

"Ah, here you are!" he says. "Come with me."

I follow him to the other side of the ward. We pass a room that looks like the intake room, only it has a television and a sign that says, "Patient Lounge." Dirty men jabber to themselves, convulsing on chairs underneath daytime talk shows. The smell of shit is strong.

The doctor opens his office door and almost bows, indicating I should sit. He settles himself comfortably in front of me. He is trained in Austin, then New York, and each diploma shows narrower and narrower concentrations, ending with a clinic on addiction and the thalamus, so that he necessarily works in hyper-niches or horror shows no one else wants.

He smiles again and sighs. "It can be hard for people like you and I to find appropriate psychiatric care," he begins.

I realize that all I must do now is sit in a straight, but relaxed posture, nod occasionally, and speak clearly at few intervals. I know now, too, that I do not have blood on my face.

The time is still irrelevant.

Out in the sun, I squint and turn on my phone. It is 9:42AM

on Saturday, August 18, just under thirty-two hours from the time of my commitment. I do not see a sign for the name of the hospital and I do not want to look at the discharge paperwork. I am somewhere in the northern part of the county. I consider walking the perimeter of the hospital to get my exact whereabouts. There are only two places I could be. Neither are very close to home.

Whatever happened that killed the video at Art on Thursday night was probably not so bad or there would be more commotion here, a TV crew, at least, so I search the news for "Sand Key explosion" on my phone and find an article. Five dead, none hurt. Burn crews back at work this morning. Just another explosion.

I walk up a stretch of ramp onto a four-lane county road that I am almost positive is Route 19 and head in the direction of a gas station, so that I can ask where I am and sit in the sweltering heat to wait for a taxi.

I have a text message from Erica, "Please call me when you get home. I haven't said anything to Alex. XO."

I press and hold her message, and the phone dials her.

She answers immediately, "Are you OK?"

"I'm fine," I say.

"But what happened?" she asks.

"OK, thanks," I say, as if she has said something else. "I'll talk to you soon."

"But, wait—what happened? Where were you?"

I look ahead at the gas station sign. The sun is pale yellow.

"Oh, they had to run some routine medical tests on me and make sure I didn't get too hysterical. I was pretty crazy for a minute there—probably from blood loss or something. But I'm OK."

"I was so worried!"

"I have to go now, but I'll call you soon."

"But, wait, Vanessa, what actually happened?"

I look directly into the sun, and it hurts, the first time looking at it directly has hurt in years. I have been away from daylight for too many days.

"I'll call you in a few days," I say.

"OK, please do."

We hang up. I continue walking toward the gas station, knowing full well that I have no intention of discussing any version of this with her. I feel a simmering exultation that I cannot quite identify, except that I finally know, with the same certainty that I felt the future slide from my body—humanity is fucked.

15.

I am in the middle of nowhere again, driving close to 95 miles an hour. The van doesn't really go faster, but I am shoving the pedal to the floor, watching the needle strain higher on the dash, anyway. There is no traffic. Old people don't go out in heat like this.

The only signs of life in Charlotte County are the billboards—signs for Cracker Barrel or gated communities near golf courses. Even the trailers with their low ceilings and 8x16-inch windows look lifeless. For the next sixty miles, it's all pedophiles and Midwestern Jews who can't face who they are, people who will rarely see their grandchildren. The only time the temperature drops below ninety from May to September is if there's a hurricane.

The houses, where there aren't sun burnt fields of trailers, are all the same—one-story, block concrete with flat roofs. The occasional cross-hipped addition, a garage or workshop done in mismatching materials, abuts a driveway, but the cars all stay outside, fading and rusting in the sun, with decals of praying hands or tributes to dead teenagers across the back windshields.

On the other side of this hodgepodge of trash is Naples, a gaggle of multi-million dollar homes owned by East Coast Jews, who claim their heritage and preserve their middle age with facelifts and caps.

This is where I'm going, and, even though it is a terrifyingly unreal place, it is no less surreal than anything else in this state, and they are buying a sculpture from me—the Jankowitzes, Harry and Jan, who tells me Harry used to be a former captain of industry, although she failed to mention which one, and I didn't think to ask.

I don't care, though. This is my first metal commission. The timing is amazing. The wife found my website after someone told her about the show in Athens. She saw a shot of me and Ray by the scrap sculpture at the marina, the same one to inspire my idea for Aaron and Jeffrey. I can't help but think this means something.

I push the van over the Myakka River. The water is like a mirror in the heat. There is no breeze, no disturbance under its surface. Its current is invisible at these temperatures. The van rattles and smells like rust and rubber and sweat. My dripping human stench and the reflection of the blinding sun on the skinny, winding river all seem like portents. Everything smells or tastes like blood, a sensual component.

I wanted to crush Jeffrey's head when he told me what Aaron said at the open call, but, in the end, I have to recognize that I haven't proven myself to either of them. Today changes that. The show will change that, too, even though I haven't actually started anything yet.

The gallery as a cage is just so perfect, in tribute and symbolism and craft. I feel like a fucking asshole thinking my art could help their situation. Even Ray killed me the other day at The Bait Bucket, drawing an absurd portrait of Luke, on a bar napkin, with coke bags for eyes that somehow still managed to look like his bombastic, round eyeballs inside his hollow face.

I may never command the respect of a serious underground art community, but the Jankowitzes and this show are a beginning, a chance for me to get away from these easy paintings and show people that, despite having a fairly common style and not nearly as much imagination as my friends, I really do have a message that is unique.

I think, too, that when Vanessa sees my work, she'll understand our argument in the gallery and rethink her comment that people are not art. I think I can impress her, which is fucked up, because she impresses me most with her complete containment.

She is the only person I have ever met who never tries to hurt people, but it means she almost always hurts me. She makes me feel like an idiot, because she is so self-centered, but it impresses me, too, and if I impress her than I know I am really impressive.

The Jankowitz' house is so pristine, it's almost unbearable. The front is pure white siding with bougainvillea trailing from the top windows in between tropical green shutters. The house has a double front door, twelve feet high, made of gleaming wood and glass insets, etched with a palm tree in each.

I have a moment of wanting to get back in the van. I don't even own pants. I don't even own shorts that don't have paint on them. My face is caked in sweat. I picture Harry in a golf shirt, pleated shorts, crisp, cool, a well-preserved, healthy look of never counting money and standing in the air conditioning with a gin and tonic.

I look around for something to rescue me. A majestic banyan is the only thing in the yard that could provide an excuse. If I stood under it, touched it, pretended to admire its grandiosity, that could explain why my hands are gritty, why my face is blotchy from the sun.

"Hello," says a voice, a cool growl. A woman has been sitting in a corner, in a leather chair with some sort of slim, wooden legs, shaded by a linen curtain that drops from a high porch roof. She stands and glides toward me. I wipe my hands on my shorts and feel my face flush.

"Hello," I say.

"You must be Alex. I'm Jan."

Her voice is the rehearsed warmth of women who do nothing but meet important people who are only indirectly important to them. She reaches to shake my hand. I give her mine.

"I'm sorry. I don't have any air conditioning in the van. I'm a little dirty from the ride."

She laughs as if she is gargling. "Please come in. It's cool inside."

She walks me inside, and her ass cheeks wiggle under a long skirt, like puppies wrestling under a blanket. We enter a giant kitchen, and she takes out two glasses. She reaches for a bottle of gin. I feel a surge of hope when I see this. My instincts were right. I feel the cool hum of metal inside me, the light strength of a finished work in the future. The bottle is intimidating. The label says that it's Bombay, but it looks heavy and it has a giant blue gemstone in the cap. Jan's grip strains at the bottle's weight.

"What is that bottle made of?" I ask her. I am suddenly

comfortable. My questions are the polite inquisition of an artist hoping to learn her taste in material. Any feeling that I may be a rube in the midst of all this cold, carefree wealth has boiled into a liquid sense of creation.

"It's crystal," she says, "with a sapphire centerpiece in the stopper. It's Baccarat for Bombay. They only made five."

"It's beautiful," I say, although I am queasy at how gauche it is. "I'll be sure to savor this."

She laughs again, that deep-throat gargle, and hands me my drink. "The girl has refilled the bottle a thousand times at least—with Bombay, but still."

I laugh with her. The grime on my hands melts into the cold glass, but the drink is perfect, and I stay relaxed.

"Why don't you show me where you'd like the work to go?"

I never talk like this, but I like how I sound in this cold kitchen with its gleaming wood and glass cabinets that match the front door, a hundred yards away. I sound like someone who drinks gin that comes in a bottle only four other people own.

She nods and leads me out of the kitchen, through a sitting room and a casual dining room and then down a hall that has an entire glass wall, and, finally, I can see the Gulf. It looks tremendous and gentle, as if it were some mother-god source of the entire world, deserving of glass shrines through which simple humans could stand and gaze, mesmerized at its distance and color.

Even from inside, with the sun streaming into the hallway, so that the temperature is substantially higher, uncomfortable even, I can sense its current, the thick, invisible rope that moves it, lulling my eyelids toward my cheeks, so that I hold the glass away from me in a comfortable and proprietary stance. From this view, even inside a stranger's home, the water looks like it belongs to everyone, but, also, like everyone belongs to it. I feel Jan looking at me and I turn to her.

"I apologize. Let's go. You were going to show me where the work will live," and, again, I don't sound like myself. I apologize? I have never . . . apologized.

"It's all right. I'm only tired of it, because we can't seem to keep it cool in here. It's as if we just can't control the sunlight, no matter what we do. There's only one vent in the hallway here—" she points toward the floor, "and it's a stupid place for it, really. It's always an oven in this hall. I can't enjoy the Gulf at all from here. It's very unfortunate."

"You could go outside," I say.

"It's even hotter out there," she says. "I go out to color sometimes, but I stay by the pool most days. The pool is beautiful. Cleaner than out there, too."

"I understand," I say.

"No, you really can't. This was supposed to be an oasis for me and Harry—a place where we could connect when he isn't working, where I would be able to enjoy women friends and a community that lives the same lifestyle we do, but, now, it's all ruined by the Gulf. You'll see in a moment."

We walk into an atrium that is bigger than my studio. The ceiling is three stories high and domed. Trees and flowers jockey in a lush array for space, pushed together in sensuous bundles. The air is perfumed with greenery, a warm scent of chlorophyll and dirt and fertilizer, tinged with a lasting note of heavy flowers. I gasp and am embarrassed at the sound. Jan has put her glass down somewhere, but I still have mine. The ice is melted from standing in the hallway. I sip at it, but it no longer tastes as good.

"Look," she says, flatly.

She looks, too, out another glass wall that shows a porch with more linen shades rolled up under the roof. Beyond the porch is a line of people, men and women and children, holding hands across the sand. They remind me of the paper dolls that line Vanessa's hallways.

"What are they doing?" I ask.

"They're protesting."

"Protesting?"

"The spill. They're protesting the spill. They've been out there every day for a year, holding hands, chanting, as if it will do something."

The water looks perfect and clear from here.

"Is there tar on the shore?" I ask.

"No, they're just . . . hippies or something, and the police are useless," she says. "That's why we want a large piece to display here. We're sick of looking at them, but we still want something large and cool to view. We're thinking of a long, rectangular piece to run the length of the property. You could do waves at the top, so that it were the same as the Gulf and perhaps those cuts that reflect light the same way water reflects light. The metal should look like water."

I look at her and sip my drink. It is flat now and warming. She tilts her head at me.

"Shall I refresh your cocktail?" she says. She cups her breasts lightly, a nurturing offer of a drink, and pulls her hands away. This, too, is practiced, like her greeting.

"No, thank you," I say.

"How long would it take you to create something like that?"

"A fence, you mean?" I say.

Her face loses its studied welcome. She pauses and holds her breasts again, pushing them upward just slightly. "I think we've started off wrong. Maybe you could tell us your vision."

I look out at the protestors. They're blocking the view of the water, but that's it. They don't have signs. They aren't loud. They're just standing there, holding hands. They are unnerving, but I realize with a sudden, nauseous feeling that this isn't a chance to prove anything at all. This is the same fucking mistake I always make. I think I'm an artist, because I hang out with artists, but all anyone wants from me are dull paintings and uninspired metal rectangles.

Jan is staring at me incredulously, becoming angry.

"I have no vision," I say flatly.

"So you don't want to sculpt something for us," she says. She is impatient, disgusted. "You don't want to sculpt something for Harry Jankowitz." She pauses before she says their last name, as if she were making another sentence, as if that would make any of this more understandable.

"I'm sorry," I say. "I don't know who Harry Jankowitz is."

She laughs. "He's my husband. My father invented the non-slip decking on commercial boats. Harry is the operations manager for the company. He's my husband."

The job is lost. The chance to prove myself is lost, except it never existed, and I still don't know who Harry Jankowitz is, but I can't accept it, somehow.

I look at Jan as humbly as I can, even though there is something now distinctly unattractive about her, and I say in this voice that is still an amazing surprise to me, "I would need to know you in a more organic sense in order to create something meaningful for you," and all I mean is that I can't truly create art when the work is commissioned, that I don't want to be a monkey with a paintbrush. I want to be an artist.

She smiles. She looks like a cat on its deathbed.

"Of course you would," she says. "Come here."

She takes my hand and leads me to a tall tree and pushes me up against it. I don't know how to say no. She has my zipper undone in a flash and pulls my cock out without unbuttoning the waistband. She starts to suck it, but I'm flaccid, so she pulls her big, fake volleyball tits out of her dress and starts moaning on my cock. Her tits look hard. I have no desire to touch them. Her face doesn't move as she sucks on me, and I get hard only through sheer willpower, because I think maybe it will save this job. I want to sculpt something for Harry Jankowitz after all, it seems.

She knows she isn't really arousing me, though, so she stands up and unbuttons my pants, smiling like a hag, and turns around, gathering her dress. "Fuck me," she says, in a horrible, infantilized voice, and the grating, pathetic sound of it drains any attempt at an erection I had.

"I can't," I say.

"Yes, you can. C'mon, big boy, Harry isn't home."

"No, I can't. I have a girlfriend."

She drops her dress and turns around to look at me, all the seduction gone from her face. She laughs.

"You mean it," she says.

"Yeah, I mean it," I say.

Her face hardens again, then relaxes. She rolls her eyes, trying to remain composed.

"OK," she says. "You're as bad as them." She nods toward

the people standing on the sand, and I know she means I'm useless, full of impossible dreams, unable to understand reality and conform to it so that what I want actually works.

I hand her the glass of gin and tonic and water, but she turns away, so I walk past her and down the stairs of the atrium and through the burning hot hallway and through the casual dining room and through the sitting room and put the glass in the sink in the kitchen.

"Please leave it," she says. I hadn't realized she was behind me.

"I was going to," I say.

I walk past her again and out the door and out the gate. I am glad I parked on the street. The van is sweltering, but I start it up immediately and gun it hard, so that it jerks its way down Vanderbilt Beach Drive as I try to unroll the windows and stop shaking.

I feel like a complete and utter failure of a human being.

I have to pull off the interstate on Route 41 and then I have to pull off Route 41 in Punta Gorda, because I am filled with such rage and sadness that I can't drive. I stop at a crab shack on the Charlotte Harbor and order two beers at once and stare at the water.

By the time I finish the first, the waitress thinks a date has ditched me and she brings me another on the house. I try to remind myself that only eight years ago, this whole county was flattened, blown away by Hurricane Charley, that martial law was in effect for weeks, and no one had homes or food or money.

The sense that things are falling apart is not new. The world has not ended yet, so there is no reason to think it will end because the economy is bad and a few beaches are closed. There is nothing to indicate that life as I know it will collapse, just because some cougar bitch tried to suck me off after she thought I propositioned her.

But, then, I realize I have stopped here because I don't want to go home. I don't want Aaron and Jeffrey to patronize me. I don't want Vanessa to look through me like I'm nobody.

It feels like nothing will ever amount to anything. I slam through the third beer in no time and order another two, but the waitress asks me if I'm driving.

"No, ma'am, I'm sitting here," I tell her, and she clucks her tongue at me and puts the order through, anyway.

I stare at the harbor and breathe in its scent of algae. A cold, sweaty panic hits me. Just because we've recovered before doesn't mean we'll recover again.

It is entirely possible the world is going to end soon. In fact, it probably is going to end very soon. Our one main resource has been leaking into our second main resource for years now. Oil and water. The classic bad combination. It's still profitable for some people, but the rest of us are just choking on it as it gushes non-stop and over half of it burns.

The water is burning. Animals are dead and dying. We're running out of money. All of us, who used to have plenty even five years ago, are losing everything. The world is ending, and no one sees it.

I cannot fathom the finality of this, but it sends a sudden, dull pain through my head that makes me shut my eyes.

I open them again as the waitress puts down my beer. She gently slides a menu on the edge of the table. I can't look at its garish yellow background, its logo of smiling crabs scuttling across the top.

I tip my fifth beer into my mouth, and I realize that if the world ends—it could be within the month or the year—it either won't matter if I finally create a masterpiece of sculpture or it will be the most important thing in the world, the thing that allows me to savor that moment of the world ripping away from me and everything else—if I am even aware of it happening.

And, then, with the clarity that rings from beer and sun and days of uncertainty and loneliness, I realize that I love Vanessa. The painting I made is a mess. It barely looks like her, but I can see now that all along I've wanted to succeed this weekend to impress her.

Our sudden distance and our argument yesterday, that bitch's assault and insult to me today, oil everywhere, no money left—I can see so plainly, staring into the clear, pungent harbor, that the world is on its way out, and the only thing left to do—of course—is steal the show and get the girl.

I am about to laugh when Jeffrey calls.

"Jeff!" I crow.

"Al," he says. He is congested, dull.

"What's wrong? Is Aaron's arm OK?"

"Aaron's arm is fine. It's everything else, though. Alex, we can't do the show." I can hear, suddenly, too, that he's been crying.

"Nooo, Jeff, no. What's wrong?"

"Aaron is going bananas. He's been taking way too much Oxycontin. He insists that we continue."

"Why don't we? What's wrong? Have you been meeting with Chrissy?"

"Yes, she's fine. Everything is fine with her, but—Alex, where are you?"

"I'm in Punta Gorda. I had a commission in Naples, but it fell through."

He doesn't react to my failure, and I feel a stab of sadness again.

"They shut down some of the coastline from Crystal River to Belleair. I know it's kind of far from us, and they say it's just for this week, but Aaron is flipping out."

I stand up and begin fumbling for cash.

"That's . . . not so bad," I say, but it is.

"No, Alex, Aaron is going, like, psychotic. He says the execution of the show within the arc of the Art story will result in a true art-life paradigm and that the complete enactment of the paradigm will be his ultimate work."

"Huh? Jeff, it'll be OK," I say, but I only think it's OK because now I know for sure the world is about to end, so I can act. I have to make sure I complete my life the way I want. "Jeffrey, everyone will be OK."

"How is everyone going to be OK?!" Jeffrey yells into the phone. "Everything is falling apart, and Aaron thinks this show is going to be some redeeming masterpiece in the face of apocalypse!"

He is hysterical, sobbing, but I still have that heady sense of clarity and I agree with Aaron. We are facing apocalypse.

"Jeffrey, I have to go. I have to drive home now, but everything will be OK, I promise."

"He's got a fitting tomorrow. You have to come to look at the girls tomorrow. Please just tell him you can't. You can't do it."

He is swallowing his own words, choking on tears, but I have to go and I rush out to the van. The waitress stops me and offers me change.

"No, no, keep it," I say. I am choking, too.

She coos and smiles. "Thank you, sweetest. Whoever missed you here missed out," she says.

I get back in the van and think of Vanessa, of Jeffrey, of what I am going to create, and I put my head down on the steering wheel and cry, too, shoulders shaking, breath coming in gasps, because I am just as common as everyone else. I want to have made my masterpiece, but I still want my greatest creation ahead of me.

I don't want the world to end.

16.

Luke is DJing tonight, so I am in the bathroom at House. It's early. I'm tired already. I have not worked in almost a week now, but I'm not too worried yet.

I told Chrissy I would take care of her drinks tonight, but as the afternoon waned from blistering, yellow heat to sunset's pink exhaustion, I changed my mind. There is no way to tell her this, though, so, I slithered past Luke and am in a bathroom stall at ten-thirty, a full half-hour before I should meet Chrissy.

I have a straw buried in a bag of coke, resting on top of a shelf thoughtfully provided for my purse, but since the coke is there, my purse hangs on the hook on the door. I sit on the closed toilet with a mirror in my hand, applying lipstick and generally hyperventilating through the first few breaths of coke I took as soon as I got in the stall.

The plan is to down two vodka tonics before Chrissy arrives and be just fucked up enough to deal with her puppyish gratefulness and not so fucked up that she notices that I am annoyed by it, that I find her sticky and unseemly when she is so thankful. Dancing would add to the appearance of normalcy, too, so I need to be carefree enough to dance and, right now, I am vicious more than anything.

Today is the two-year anniversary of my parents' death, a private anniversary that was in all the papers. No matter, though.

I line my lips softly with feathery strokes that are easier to make when I have coke in my system. Daub, daub, daub, daub, daub. The repetition helps me get a handle on the coke, too. I exhale loudly and then check that an impossible cross-breeze didn't somehow ruffle the bag of coke. It is still there.

I gather up my things. I need to have my second drink down to an eighth-inch of liquid and an ice cube when Chrissy arrives, but the door swings inward, and I freeze, paralyzed by a sudden, stiff paranoia. Two girls enter, and I can sense their weight, the closeness of their short, round bodies, the aroma of hairspray captured in their hair.

"She was bleeding everywhere by the fountain across the street. I didn't know what to do."

"Holy shit, girl, are you serious?"

"No, there was blood, like, *everywhere*. She had a miscarriage. It was really obvious. There was blood all over her legs. I just couldn't see it at first, because she was kneeling by the fountain."

"*What?!*"

"She was just out there. We were leaving the open call, and she was just out there, talking to herself about how everyone dies and nothing matters, and I thought she was just . . . you know how she gets. She was fine at the open call. She was late, but Alex was, too, and everything seemed . . . fine, but, then, she had all this blood coming from . . . you know. And it was on her hands, too. She had been trying to stop it—or keep it going. I don't know. She was acting crazy. She didn't want me to get Alex."

"Oh my God. We have to tell him."

"Oh God, no! Please don't say anything."

I tuck my feet up in the stall. My heart is beating like a cornered animal. Droning, the sound of shock, fills my ears. All I can think is, why is Erica saying this? Why is she saying this? But, in a rush of humiliation, I know why she is saying it, and I know, too, that I could not bear for them to find me in here.

"Oh my God, so Alex doesn't know?"

"No, he'll find out soon enough, I'm sure. We can't say anything to him right now. He is so dedicated to creating art that satisfies the same standard Aaron and Jeffrey have. I mean, think of why they set the fire. They wanted to teach us that all you need is the exact moment of the present and the anticipation of art. Anything else, no matter how horrible it may seem, is unimportant."

"Doesn't that mean we should tell him, then?" asks Dani "Like to prove their point?"

"No," Erica says. "Alex isn't that strong of an artist. The loss he feels from the fire is enough for now."

"Are you sure?"

"Dani, I told her I wouldn't tell!"

"That is fucked up," Dani says.

"I know," Erica says, "but shut up about it. I only told you because it freaked me out. I needed to tell someone."

She approaches my stall and pushes on the door, while Dani washes her hands. My whole body is buzzing. The door sticks, and she shoves it.

"Erica, honey," Dani says, "it's out of order. Now, look, use the other one. You're getting all upset."

She sighs deeply. "Ugh, you're right. I am upset. Don't say anything, though, OK? I said I wouldn't say anything."

"All right, no, I feel you. I won't say anything."

I cannot keep breathing this shallowly for much longer. My heart is going to explode through my dress like this. I am sure my heart is audible. Finally, Erica finishes in the stall next to me and washes her hands, so that they re-enter the stall together to do some coke, and, just as I am about to collapse in tears, clanging against the door, they leave.

I drop my feet to the floor, and my head falls into my lap, cradling the mirror and my lip liner. I sit up again. My bags are still fine. The coke is on the ledge. My purse is on the hook of the door. Everything is the same as before they entered.

I breathe heavily and then slowly. I tie up the coke and put it in the back flap of my wallet and leave the stall and wash my hands slowly and thoroughly, including the tops, looking at myself in the mirror while I do.

My eyes are large, but my jaw is somehow relaxed, if only from all the tension just previously. I look pretty, even.

Erica and Dani are with Kim and Chrissy, standing in front of the speakers. I go to the bar first, but Luke sees me and throws his hands up and points at me and then waves his hands in the air, another person who does not care, who cannot think outside himself for just a moment that maybe I just wanted thirty minutes to—I cannot think of anything I wanted to do, after all.

I order my drink and go over to them. They squeal and hug me and smile and ask me how I am and ask me about the show and about Alex and if I can take the boat up to Sand Key or have I even tried and why not, and I can barely say anything, I am so coked up, except that I like Kim's eye shadow. I offer Chrissy a drink without considering that I just made it obvious she's broke, but no one notices or they pretend not to notice, and she says yes, anyway, so I can walk away.

The drinks go down quickly after this, and I dance with such abandon that Kim and Erica start slapping my hips to make me wiggle faster. My disinhibition inspires the whole club, and Luke puts me on his tab. I hand Chrissy fifty bucks and I just mean for her to go get herself a drink and bring me back the change, but she thinks, somehow, that it is a gift, and she hugs me so tightly, my ears buzz.

Of course they do. Everyone is talking about me.

I am on my way out of the club and I look at my phone. Alex has called four times and texted, "Hey, please call me, I have some bad news."

I put the phone back in my bag as it rings again and, then, drunkenly, in a buzz of cocaine, I pick up, anyway.

"Hello?"

"Hi. Listen, I'm sorry to call you so late, but I needed to tell you this as soon as I found out." He is drunk, too. "I have a little bit of bad news, but I think it will be OK, you know? I think it can be OK."

"I don't care about your bad news," I say. I hang up, surprised at the roiling anger in me. Today is the day my parents died. I had forgotten once I had started drinking, but, now I think I may cry.

He calls back, twice, three times, four times. He texts, "I'm sorry. Please talk to me," and I remember we were supposed to have dinner tonight, too, and I turn off my phone and walk home.

17.

This girl has two cocks shoved in her pussy. She doesn't look like she's enjoying it or not enjoying it. Jason is entranced, though. His dick is in his hand, but it's only semi-hard. He looks down at it and then at me.

"Suck it," he says.

I climb in front of him and put it in my mouth. It tastes like salt and vinegar. I love that he wants to be hard again right after he finishes fucking me. He pushes my head down on the shaft.

"Don't block the TV," he says. The girl with two cocks in her squeals. I gag on him. He hardens.

I take as much of him as I can each time I drop down around him. He groans and, another few seconds later, begins panting. My cheeks run along the sides of his cock. His head hits the back of my throat. I race my tongue up and down him as fast as I can.

I reach my hand under his balls to massage the root of his cock through his ball sac. He feels so strong, but, as his cock jerks in my mouth from the sensation of my fingertips so low on his body, I see a tree in my mind.

It's a mangrove, full of knotted cords, thrusting from bony roots. The tree is in pain. But, no, that doesn't make sense. I push the vision out of my mind and gag myself on his cock again. He growls. His hips buck. His balls pulse in my palm. The tree flares in my mind again. Its branches scream. That doesn't make sense, either. I bounce off his cock and look at him, kneeling in front of him, gasping.

"You're so good, baby. That's why I'm trying to make you my baby," he says. "Get back on it."

I put my hand to my head, my thumb and middle finger each on a temple. The porno moans behind us. I can see the room. The wallpaper is pale pink with white baby's ear seashells. I can touch the popcorn ceiling if I raise my arms. The tan plastic phone is next to the bed. The steel door to my right leads outside to a pool with a bar and the beach behind it. Everything is here, where it should be.

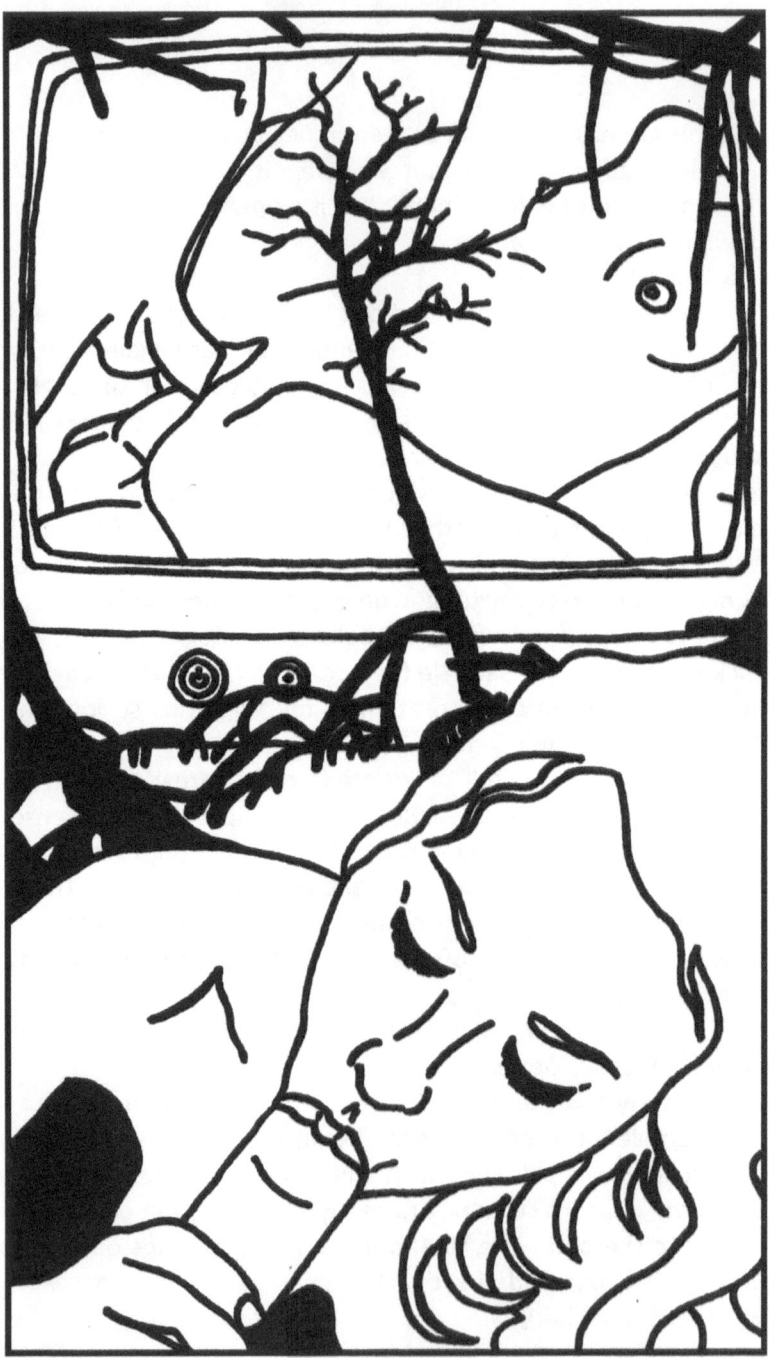

"Get back on it," he says.

I dive onto his cock again, fucking my face with it hard. He slams his hips toward my head and pushes on the back of my skull. The mangrove tree explodes in my mind again. This time, its branches burst forth as if expelled from some vortex. I can see inside the branches of the tree from above. Something with gray wings folded into its back sits in the curling nest of branches. It is both lonely and gleeful, and then the tree snarls around it, and I cannot see it anymore.

My head twists around Jason's cock. His palm pushes harder, and I begin to choke and struggle.

"Yeah, c'mon, girl, c'mon," he says, but I am burning up, sweating, choking, as if I am trapped, suspended, lowering over a fire. I cannot breathe. I rear up, coughing and crying.

He sees my face. The look of lust falls from his. His eyes dart to the television, where the same girl as before is still squealing, but I don't turn around to see why. He looks at me again, bewildered.

"Baby. Babe. I thought you liked it," he says.

My mouth opens and closes again. I can't think of anything to say that won't make me sound like a complete freak show. My phone rings. I look at it, next to the tan bedside phone. I am scared for some reason that I will hear those gray wings flapping hot, dusty pollution into my ear if I answer, but that's ridiculous. I have never confused worlds like this before.

"Get the phone, baby," Jason says. He sounds scared, which scares me more, until I realize that he thinks he scared me with his sexual aggression.

I pick up the phone and grab a robe on the chair.

"Hello?" I say. I nod to Jason that I'm going outside.

"Hey girl," Kim says.

"Hi, how are you?"

"I'm doing the makeup for the show for Art! Aaron just called me!"

"Oh, that's great," I say.

It's after midnight, but the night is still hot. The pool glows aquamarine. A father and daughter play at its edge. Old people,

151

locals, dot the bar. The pool flickers too brightly to see stars or the Gulf.

"Did you hear from them yet?"

"No, I don't think they're going to pick me," I say.

I think of standing there while Alex and Vanessa stood next to each other in the front of the room. When that same video Alex was watching the day he dumped me went black, we were the only three in the room who didn't need to call anyone. They had each other. I was alone.

"Julie, that's insane. You're beautiful."

"Thanks, girl," I say.

The father wraps the little girl in a towel. I pull the robe more tightly around me.

"Well, if they don't pick you, come on the boat with me. Aaron said I could have a plus-one. There'll be drinks and stuff."

I think about this, if it just means I'm making the same mistake I made with Alex, trying too hard to do too many things with his friends without him knowing. But I want them to be my friends, and I owe it to Jason to just fit in and be cool. I gaze into the glowing pool. I want things to work with Jason. I am going to try harder to make this work.

"OK," I say to Kim. I sound happy. "Hey, I'm in the middle of something, though. Can I call you tomorrow?"

"Def," she says. We hang up.

Jason is watching the same porno when I come back into the room, but he is soft and he is not trying to get hard. The girl who had two cocks inside her now has one in her mouth while another girl in a black patent leather corset fists her. I see in the mirror that my mascara is streaked down my face.

"Hey, babe," Jason says carefully.

"Hey," I say. "Sorry about that."

"It's OK."

"Can I tell you something?"

He shifts. "OK."

"I liked what you were doing before. Sometimes, this thing happens to me, though, where I get these ideas about things that might be happening at another time or in a different place. It can be distracting."

"Oh, yeah, that happens to everyone. Hey, sometimes, I do it on purpose, so I don't cum so fast."

"This is something that happens even when I'm not having sex. It's something that's happened my whole life, really."

"What do you normally do?" he asks.

I look around the room. My eyes rest on my bag.

"Since I got here, I've been taking my grandmother's Klonopin."

He grins at me, relieved, and reaches his arm out to pull me toward him. He tucks me into his chest and grabs my breast with the other hand and kisses my hair. The motel bedspread is stiff under us, but he feels so good holding me.

"Babe," he says, as if it were the simplest thing in the world. "Just take another Klonopin, then."

18.

I call him, anyway, the next day, on my way to the marina, around noon.

The sun is at its highest, but there are still at least two hours before its rays become painful. There is just white light everywhere that makes my eyes feel bright and my head feel dry, but I am limber in the heat. My stomach no longer has the sick, acid feeling I felt last night from overhearing Erica.

Alex will be in bed still, although maybe awake, but, then, on the second ring, I feel a slice of insecurity in my gut that he is wide awake, but will not pick up at all, because he is with that girl whose hair I cut or some other girl, but he picks up on the third ring, and I'm fucking scared by the time he says hello, because I am so far away from anything I used to be.

"Hi. I hope I didn't wake you," I say. This is already too formal.

"No. What are you doing?"

"I'm almost at the marina. I went out with Chrissy and a few people last night, but I thought maybe we could head out to the Key and talk out what we're going to do. You know, take a look at the place. I mean, I know Ray and Chrissy have been going out there, but we probably should, too. At the very least, we should make sure nothing unexpected is happening after that explosion at Sand Key."

"Right. Like Hands Across the Sand."

"What?"

"Hands Across the Sand. They're, like, a grassroots awareness group. They were in Naples when I went down to see that lady. They hold hands in the sand."

"An awareness group? Because people don't know that there's oil all over the Gulf yet?"

He laughs. The sound is natural, and I feel better than I have in weeks.

"Do you want to meet me at the marina?"

He pauses. I feel equally weak and exhilarated that I want

him there and that he might come.

"OK, I'll come. Give me twenty minutes."

"OK," I say, and we hang up. Everything seems slightly ridiculous. I am not even sure why I have decided to see him suddenly, except I want to and I am not interested in faux tourists or friends of his friends or sundry others and I miss him and I cannot imagine that whatever Erica said last night will turn out that badly when I think of how hot it is today and that the sunshine might stop suffocating me when he arrives.

Ray sits a few slips away, just staring at the water. Alex still isn't here, and I'm not as excited about seeing him once he's a half-hour late, so I decide I will invite Ray instead or too, depending on if Alex makes it.

Ray is entirely still at the edge of the dock and he doesn't feel me walk up behind him.

"Hey," I say softly. I put my hand on his shoulder.

He turns around slowly. His face is puffed with sleeplessness, creased from crashing on a deck or a floor somewhere for an hour or two when the sun rose. His pores are oily, and his hair is chuffed together. His teeth look bad, something I had never noticed under his shiny yellow hair and round, prominent cheekbones.

"Hi," he says.

"You wanna come for a ride with me? I'm going out to Egmont Key to make sure it doesn't stink like oil for our big show."

"I don't have any gas left here," he says.

"That's OK," I say. "I have enough right now. Maybe you can hook it up again when I pay this month's rent. You're not gonna make the loan payment, anyway."

He looks up at me and inhales, as though he is about to laugh at himself, but he just exhales loudly instead, and looks back down at the water.

I sit down next to him. The marina is nearly empty, a ghost town of weathered wood and glassy water. "No one told me. I can just tell."

He looks over at me and drops his head. I put my hand on his shoulder.

"Fuck it," I say. "Worse has happened. Worse will happen. Come with me."

He starts to stand up, creaking and exhausted. "Yeah, fuck it. Let's go."

We walk over to the boat and are already in the harbor, my stomach chained to my heart as I try to maintain no wake and build a breeze, when Ray spots Alex waving from the dock.

I circle back to get him. He will not be angry that we left without him.

We are along Tierra Shores, and everything looks fine. The turquoise water is full of dark green glints. We cannot see fish, but there are no longer fish close to the surface at mid-day here, anyway. They are deeper, further out, somewhere else. This seems OK, is reassuring, even, and I realize that we are used to the idea that we have changed the Gulf for our lifetime.

Ray is laid out on the bow. He needs sleep badly, but I can tell from his stillness in the sun, punctuated by fidgeting, that this won't happen soon. Alex is grinning, dopey, standing and leaning into the bow next to Ray. I have a sick reverberation from last night that I am in the bathroom stall again, hearing Erica's dramatic, "Oh my God," and I push it away. I am soaked in sweat and already dehydrated.

These things don't matter when I look at the Key. It floats in the water, white and green and shimmering in the heat. There has been little wind this summer. This is our savior, this windlessness. Today is Monday, August 20, and the season's tropical storms have all stayed in the Caribbean or south of Cuba or east of the Florida peninsula. Containing or burning oil in a hurricane is impossible, and when I think of the expanse of water that may be saved from this strange lack of storms, I cannot make myself care about Alex fucking that girl who came into the salon.

The sun is shining. The water is clear beneath the boat. These things are larger than I will ever be and only show the weakness of private pain. When I am dead a hundred years, the

Gulf will still be at the mercy of microbes eating away drops of indispersible oil. We tell ourselves that everything is entirely under control, but we just mean that nothing has killed us yet.

"So you said you had some bad news?" I say to Alex. "Are you OK now?"

I don't want to hear his bad news, but I don't want to talk about the show, either. I know why he's doing it.

"Oh, yeah, well, Naples was pretty retarded," he says. "And Aaron and Jeffrey flipped out. That was mostly what I wanted to tell you, but they're OK now."

"Oh . . . that's too bad."

"The woman wanted me to build a wall so she didn't have to see demonstrators on her private beach. She kept trying to make it sound like she wanted it to look like the water, but it was stupid. The water was right there. She just wanted a wall."

"You're not doing it? She probably would have paid you an insane amount of money."

I am thinking I have not worked in a week, that Chrissy took the last fifty dollars I would have made last until next time we hit a bar.

"I don't just create artwork for money," he says.

I don't say anything. Ray doesn't move.

"I'm not going to spend the next month of my life working on some ugly slab of steel for her," he continues. "It's stupid."

Ray sits up and rubs his eyes, laughing. "Rich people are fucking retards."

"Hey, you used to have a little bundle over there, buddy," says Alex.

"Yeah, and I blew it all on coke and boats and shit."

They laugh. I smile, but then Ray's not laughing anymore.

"What were Aaron and Jeffrey flipping out about?" he asks.

"Aaron took a bunch of Oxys and lost it. He told Jeffrey that we're all on the path to apocalypse or something, but they're OK now."

Ray stares out at the Key.

"Why are we doing this, anyway?" he finally asks.

Again, we fall silent.

"Right," he says. "We're doing this, because my woman had a hysterical idea after Aaron and Jeffrey blew up their gallery. She thought it would save the marina or some shit, didn't she? It's not going to, though. The boats are gone. Everyone sold their boats for so little, they couldn't pay off the remainder of their contracts.

"What the fuck is a party where we give all the money to Aaron and Jeffrey going to do for the marina? She's out of her mind sometimes. It's like she can't deal if we don't have ten grand sitting in the bank.

"Do you know how long it's been since I've even had a savings account? She's crazy."

"Hey, Ray, c'mon, there are a lot of people who have put a lot of work into this," Alex says. "Don't talk like that."

"Yeah? Who?" he says. "You mean Chrissy, dude. She's planning this big shindig for a couple of people who don't even care. They've already rebuilt. You've seen that cage they built. It's a freak show. You can't hang any art on those walls. I need her working in the marina. If she can come up with ideas like this to generate money for other people, I need her to be doing it for us."

"Have you said that?" I ask.

He cranes his neck as if he can look past the Key somehow. The ruthless sun shows the lines and folds on his cheeks and around his eyes.

"Well, I'm excited about it," Alex says. "I think we need to show a little more empathy for Aaron and Jeffrey, too. Sure, Ray, your situation is bad, but we can do something together to help you, too. This happened to get our attention first, because a fire is so dramatic, and Aaron was in the hospital. It was more sudden, so it got more attention."

Ray still says nothing, just hums tunelessly, standing transfixed by his own tiredness and the glassiness of the water in front of us. Alex looks down uncomfortably.

"Have you even started making anything yet?" Ray asks Alex. "Or is it just Chrissy running errands and sending a million emails for Art while Aaron bosses her around like a douchebag?"

"Yeah," Alex says slowly, looking up. "But it's not going as quickly as I thought."

He looks at me, then down at the deck again, and I realize he is sad that I haven't been there, that his sadness is why his progress is so slow. He looks up once more and, this time, he looks fine.

"Do you know what you're doing with everyone's hair?" he asks me.

"No," I say, grinning. I don't even know who is supposed to be in this stupid show. "I do people's hair on the fly all the time, remember? They show up. We figure it out. I won't make you look bad."

He hugs me. His body radiates nervousness. The Gulf is so vast around us, and we are so powerless, and this is so important to him for all the wrong reasons.

Ray continues to stare straight ahead, humming. Alex goes over to him and puts his hand on his shoulder, exactly as I did earlier. Something about his posture seems to require this sort of comfort. We don't know what else to do with him.

"You all right, man?"

He doesn't move, though, just stands there without acknowledging Alex's hand on his shoulder.

His voice drones, "I should just set the fucking marina on fire."

"Ray! No, you shouldn't!"

I laugh. I can't help it. Alex is so horrified, but it is so obvious this isn't the first time Ray has thought this. He just stares as we approach the Key.

"Look at all this! We're here. We made it just fine," Alex says to him. "That means boats will come back, Ray. People overreact. They make stupid decisions. People will find new boats to buy or repair or rebuild, and you'll bounce back."

Alex leans his face into Ray's. He looks like he might cry. He is so agitated by his friend's hopelessness, but hopelessness is nothing new to us anymore. The water remains hopeless, too, but that doesn't mean there is anything permanently broken about it—a paradox, but the truth. Transcending hope requires its absence, but, more importantly, it is an overrated virtue.

Survival does not require hope.

"Alex, can you grab the anchor for me?" I ask. He looks up at me, understands, and leaves Ray's shoulder. Ray doesn't move from his post or even seem to respond to the Key's white sand, its lonely, lush huddle of palm trees in front of the ruins of the old Fort. There is no one else on the island. The oil has indeed scared people away.

Ray says, "You don't even see it, do you?"

"Ray, I know things have been difficult," I say. "Alex is right. Aaron and Jeffrey just had a more dramatic situation. It's why we reacted to them instead."

"Oh, yeah, my own fucking girl reacted to someone else instead. Don't remind me."

"Do you want to go back?" I ask. "We only came out here because of that accident on Thursday night. We just needed to make sure everything is OK here."

"You know what people are saying?" Ray says. His teeth grind as he finishes his sentence. "People are saying that they did it on purpose. That they burnt my paintings and everyone else's paintings. That they set fire to their own gallery full of people on purpose. Did you notice how Snuggles' cage was in the corner farthest from the door? That's not where they used to keep her. They set fire to their own fucking gallery and ruined all of our artwork and killed their fucking dog on purpose, and we're throwing them a party."

Alex drops the anchor into the water. "Why would you say that?"

"Erica told me," Ray says. "Aaron had some stupid fucking idea that we needed a central inspiration as a group, that we would question our attachment to each other after witnessing death and experiencing the fear of it, and that it would make us better artists, and that if we're better artists, we're a stronger community."

"Who is this community, anyway?" I ask. "Does it just mean, like . . . us?"

"Exactly!" Ray says and he begins to shout. "Not only did they kill their dog, they burnt all my paintings, so I could paint better paintings for them?!"

"OK, stop it," Alex cuts him off. "If you don't want to help Aaron and Jeffrey because you have your own problems, that's fine, and I'll still do everything I can to help you however you want, but you can't go around talking shit about them, either."

"Alex, you're not helping Aaron and Jeffrey," he says.

He lets his words hang for a moment. I look at Alex. He looks miserable. Ray chuckles. He still has not moved.

"Whatever, Alex. There's nothing anyone can do about the things that have already happened. The marina is fucked, so, sure, you want me to haul a bunch of shit out here in coolers and stand on the sand and greet people while my girl spends the last of our money on those fuckheads? Sure, I'll do it. Who cares? It's not going to fix my God damned marina. What fixes my God damned marina is money. Why shouldn't I burn it down? I won't be able to renew the policy for as much as it's insured now."

"Ray, seriously, man. Stop it now."

"OK, fine," Ray says. He looks up at Alex. "You still just don't fucking see it, do you?"

"What?!" Alex shouts and, finally, he has lost it. "What do you want me to see?! So what if maybe I wouldn't mind if they asked me to show with you guys just once. But that never happens, does it? So this is a way I can gain some respect from people I admire and help them. What do you care? Just because no one is doing anything for you?!"

I want to stop him. I want to tell him he is giving himself away, but I say nothing, because I see it, too. I see it so clearly, I cannot believe I did not see it before. The whole time, Ray was humming like the sun disintegrated his soul, never moving, and I didn't see it.

"No, fuckhead," Ray says. "Look in the water. Look at the reflection in the fucking water."

We look together. The dark turquoise is a mirror, and, reflecting back in the mirror, is a panel of black with scalloped edges. Smoke, thick, velvet smoke, rises on the other side of the island. The Fort blocks a fire vortex, a wide burn blowing away from us, so that we never noticed its perfect reflection in the flat, calm, hot water.

"Alex, can you pull the anchor back up, please?" I ask.

He does so defeatedly, and Ray lies down again on the bench. His breathing finally deepens into sleep.

As we cross the mouth of the bay, I say to Alex, "It's OK. We can still come out next weekend. They'll be done here by then. We don't want anyone to see us is all. They'll keep coming back and they'll bust up the party if they see us now."

He nods. He moves almost imperceptibly, and I realize he wants to put his arm around me, but he doesn't.

19.

I am both awful at this and have not given myself enough time to learn how to do it properly.

The sheets of stainless steel basically bankrupted me, which I didn't even consider. I can't find anyone with mannequins I can borrow, either—another thing I didn't consider. I sort of know the approximate sizes of most of the girls Aaron picked, but if I do, it's exclusively because I've drunkenly hooked up with them, which is not a reliable resource for measurements.

I keep pushing back the suspicion that Aaron is setting me up to fail. Why didn't he email me the measurements or tell the girls to email their measurements or something? Why don't I have anyone's email address? I can't help but picture Aaron malicious and satisfied that I have to message everyone and hope they find me in a ticker of shitty party directions and drunken rants.

But, then, I know I'm being stupid. If I wanted measurements or email addresses, I could have asked for them.

I have no idea what to do. Chrissy has already sold over sixty tickets. I don't even know if I can pull this off now, but I know I have to show up with something.

It is totally possible that I am looking at a long, hot day of most people half-heartedly pretending these chicks look fine, while Aaron prances around demanding attention and insisting everything is fantastic when it obviously isn't.

The worst part is the acetylene torch freaks me the fuck out inside my studio by myself.

I was so sure of what I was going to show. The warmth and beauty of humanity can make everything around it just as warm and beautiful as we are. This is the ultimate gift both to and from the universe, but everything I've done so far is just an unflattering mess.

The guys are going to be here any minute. I cannot have them see this stupid, clunky garbage. Normally, I don't care if they see what I'm doing. My art isn't that private, which is, in itself, a failure, but this isn't exactly private, either. It's just embarrassing.

I am going to have a complete fucking panic attack if I can't get this shit put away before my friends get here. I do not want them to see this work. I do not want anyone to see this work, but it doesn't actually fit anywhere it would be invisible.

I think about smashing it and haplessly admitting my failure to them when they see the crinkled metal. Destruction would be manly and honest and would indicate I have hope that I can do this, even though I totally fucking don't—plus, they would be distracted from my failure by the viciousness of the crushed metal, and we would talk about how I'm a monster, instead of a failure.

And then I have no choice but to rip my sheets off the bed and throw towels over everything and pretend as though things are going just fucking swell, as if showing them the work would ruin its impact when I unveil it.

The real problem is that now I am probably going to look like a totally arrogant, talentless douchebag this weekend and if I look like one—well, I might just actually be one.

"Heeyyyy," I say when I open the door.

I sound fine, totally normal and casual and ready for whatever. We don't have plans. I don't think we have plans. I think we're just deciding what to do now. I am losing track of everything, it seems.

They file into my studio, slapping hands and pushing each other. I cannot breathe. My stomach is filled with acidic cramping. Nothing is working.

They crack beers. I have one in my hand now, too. I drink it quickly. My stomach relaxes and then refills with acid. I open another beer while Ray and Jason talk about whether Dani looks better in red or pink. Ray likes her in red. Jason likes her in pink. I don't know why the fuck they're talking about this. Vanessa looks good in gray and purple, but all girls look good in pink. Pink is nothing but pussy. I feel nauseous, agitated. I wish they would change the subject.

"I dunno, man, you haven't seen her in this pink shit she has with, like, holes in her bra, so that her nipples stick out, and then there's this pink ribbon that ties the holes up, so her nipples can stick through the ribbon, like, real tight or just part of her tits can stick out, too, when the hole is untied. It's fucking . . ." Jason shakes his head. "I'm not breaking up with her as long as she wears that kind of shit. Just trust me, she looks better in pink."

Luke slaps him on the back and hands him a beer, "Yo, dog, I know you got pictures. Let me see your phone."

Jason pulls out his phone and pulls up the picture. He looks at it for a minute, shaking his head slowly, clucking his tongue.

"Yo, let me see that shit," Luke says and grabs the phone from Jason.

Jason punches him in the face and takes the phone back.

"Yo, what the fuck!" says Luke.

"Don't be trying to look at my fucking girl," Jason says.

The acid in my stomach roils, and I chug the rest of the beer, while Luke stands in front of Jason trying to act like he isn't stunned and hurt, both by the physical impact and the insult of the blow.

I am aware of my silence, that they have been here less than ten minutes, and I have already drank two beers without saying a word, that I do not react as Jason and Luke continue to stare at each other.

"You wanna see a picture of Chrissy?" Ray says.

Jason grunts. "All right, man."

Luke fakes at him. Jason flinches, and Luke fakes again. Jason hooks him this time, hard, with the other fist, and his ring breaks the skin.

"Yo, fuck you, you need to stop bein' so aggro. You don't even know when people are playin', you pussy bitch," Luke cries out, but he's upset this time, and we can hear it. His hand is on his face.

"Yo, whatever, you fuckin' swung at me."

"I didn't fuckin' swing at you. I was playin'. You 'roidhead fuck."

"Why you talkin' shit? Fuckin' bitch. You talkin' shit?"

"Yeah, I fuckin' am now, motherfucker."

I realize that Jason is jacked, and Luke is scared, and Ray is just looking at the wall behind me.

We all know that I am the one who can stop this, by asserting dominance in my kingdom. The art. My studio. My lair. If I don't want them to fight here, I just have to say so, but I don't care, either. I am having difficulty focusing. I need a crescendo of some sort. Through the warm fuzz of the beer, I wonder if this would be the thing to snap me out of my ineffectiveness, if watching my friends pummel the shit out of each other would make it so that I stop beating myself up over things I can't control.

I am not a good artist. Maybe if Jason knocked the shit out of Luke, just laid him out, this would relieve my constant anxiety and growing suspicion that the world just fucking hates me, that some people are just bad luck and will never fulfill their dreams.

Ray opens another beer, and its hiss sucks something out of the room. Jason's 'roid rage simmers down. Luke regains his ground. The silence is booming through my ears and nose and throat, filling my lungs with black wind. Someone needs to say something before I hyperventilate. They have not noticed my failed artwork.

Now. I need to say something now, or they will naturally turn their attention to anything else, and the obvious thing is that my mattress and pillows are exposed, stark and yellowed. My sheets and dank, unwashed towels are over what is clearly unfinished work.

I feel like I am standing too close to the wall and I try to put the back of my head against it, so that its cool stucco calms me down, but I stumble instead, and realize I am nowhere near the wall. I am trapped inside my own fucking head. The walls are nowhere near me. There is plenty of space around me. I just cannot do anything with it.

I have to say something. Jason is starting to smirk, and Luke is beginning to blush. Ray stares at the wall behind me, drinking his beer in long, quiet gulps.

"Yo, did you know I hit that chick we met at the beach a few months ago, like, five times now?"

I say this just as Ray crushes his beer can in his hand, and the room spins, because I didn't have to say it. I could have made the same comment I had imagined them saying to me, amongst a sea of crushed metal, something about how Ray is a monster, a fuckin' animal, that it looks like he needs to bang something out, acting like that, crushing things.

The world just . . . it fuckin' hates me.

"What?!" Jason says.

He knows who I mean instantly. He grins, like a canine, with his lips pulled back, and the whites of his eyes showing around the irises.

Ray snorts and shakes his head at me. I realize suddenly that we did the same thing. We both tried to make some kind of stupid, fucking noise, but he was cooler about it, and he knows I know I gave myself away for nothing again.

Jason laughs like a sea monster. He is too high, hitting the juice too often. I haven't seen him in almost three weeks, and he is suddenly shredded.

Luke looks back and forth between us, "Wait, who?"

Jason puts his hands behind his head and chuckles. "Dude. I hit that shit, too. I thought you were done with it."

"Who?!" Luke asks, more insistently.

I feel my spine tighten between the shoulder blades.

"You got that?" I say to Jason.

"Dude, I pounded that shit to oblivion. That chick is a freak."

Ray laughs and opens another beer. I gesture at him to hand me one.

"What do you mean?"

I hate tonight. I hate my life.

"You know what I mean. That chick is a fucking dog-faced freak."

"She's not dog-faced," I say.

"You didn't get the fuckin' paws in her mouth, then," he says. He makes two claws with his hands and motions as if he is spreading something. "That bitch will let you hold her open every which way and just shove shit in her."

My fist tightens around my beer. The soft crinkle of aluminum rains in my head. I force myself to relax my grip, but the can pops back into shape. Its sound is cheerful, mocking. Jason has been fucking Julie. Luke looks as though his eyes are about to fall out of his head. Ray looks sorry for me.

I think of her at my house for the last time, how stressed out I was by how much she was circling me. She pretended she knew my art. She made friends with Erica. She went to Vanessa for a haircut. Aaron picked her to model. And it hits me that Aaron knew. Julie only isn't modeling because I told Jeffrey I didn't want her there, but Aaron did want her there, because he knew Jason is fucking her while he still lives with Dani.

Time stops. I suddenly feel as if everything that has ever happened to me is happening at once, has always been happening, and I am too fucking stupid to get it.

Julie wasn't circling me. She was fucking Jason, too.

The room snaps back, like someone has shot me in the face with a rubber band.

"Whatever, asshole," I say to Jason. "Don't chase after my shit. Get your own piece."

"Who are you talking about?" Luke asks. The cut on his face is drying. He looks and sounds innocent. He has lost his swaggering speech after taking the clock from Jason.

I am too aware of the fact, too, that, normally, I like him the least of all my friends. I dislike his affected speech. I can't stand how he drops all bravado in front of Erica. I resent his inane DJing, but I resent even more that the only reason I resent it is because he has earned some inauthentic artistic credibility through a discipline I don't admire. I normally like him the least of all my friends, because he wields this credibility so obviously, when it is equally obvious he is just a suburban white kid who splits with his rent with his girlfriend, so he can afford a ton of equipment to play other people's music.

In other words, I'm fucking jealous.

"He's talking about this phat-ass chick we met at the beach a few months ago. You've seen her. She was there the night Art burned down, like, all jockin' up on us."

"You got her that night?" I ask.

Jason grins.

"You fucking asshole."

"Whatever, dude, you left her outside. She was scared. She almost died. The place almost burned down."

"She didn't almost die," I say. I walked her the fuck out. That fucking prick. That bitch. I am so filled with hate for myself and everyone else, I cannot stand it.

"She could have died," Ray says tersely, and I know he isn't defending Jason. He's maligning Aaron and Jeffrey.

"No, she couldn't have," I say.

"Yo! Just shut the fuck up for a minute," Luke shouts.

"Oh, you're back," I say. I feel like a fucking tool.

"Could one of you have got her pregnant?" Luke asks me.

The room goes silent, as if someone put a sheet over the world, too. No one looks at anyone. I no longer hate Jason or resent Luke. Jason's shoulders drop. Ray seems to stand up straighter. We have all neutralized, tumbled away from the evil weighing on us to become nothing in the wake of his question.

"Did you?" he asks again.

"I . . . I don't think so. She didn't tell me that," I say.

"When's the last time you talked to her?"

"It's been awhile."

"One of you fuckers got her pregnant. Either that, or you got Vanessa pregnant," he says to me.

"How do you know that shit?" Jason spits. "My shit swims, but I didn't knock that fucking bitch up."

Luke puts his hand to the cut on his face, unintentionally. "I overheard Erica on the phone. She was talking to Dani. She was talking about how she promised she wouldn't tell you," he says to me, "that 'she'—I thought, you know . . . Vanessa—was pregnant. She tried to commit suicide or some shit? Erica said there was a bunch of blood and that when she called the hospital, they told her they had to put her in the psych ward, and I . . . fuckin' a, dog, I'm sorry. I thought you must have known. I mean, fuck, I don't know.

"Vanessa's been crazy since her parents died, anyway, you

know, the way she's all spooky half the time and doesn't give a shit about anything. I just thought you knew, but maybe . . . maybe she meant that other chick. Erica and her are friends."

"How are they friends?" I ask.

Luke looks at Jason.

"You fucking assholes," I say to both of them and, then, to Luke, "Dude, you have to ask her!"

"I can't. She'll freak out if she knew I overheard her."

"No, she won't."

"Listen, yes, she will. We had this dumb fight about how I stay out every night, and she's always there for me, and she goes to all my nights when I spin, but I never get involved in any of that Art shit unless they ask me to DJ. She really wants me hang out with Aaron and Jeffrey, but I don't . . . whatever, man, they're her friends. They're fucking cool. I'm just not into talking about stuff like that, you know?"

"Dude, you have to ask her," I repeat.

"Listen, last weekend, at House, her and Dani were all whispery, and I just thought it was girl shit, but then Erica wouldn't talk to me, so I asked Dani if she was mad at me. She said that they were just worried because Vanessa was acting fucking crazy, but, like, also, of course she was—it was the anniversary of her parents' death, too, so who knows?"

"Wait. It was?" I ask. "How do you know this?"

"Because I'm her friend, douchebag," Luke says. "You don't remember her mumbling about how August 19 is eight plus one equals nine and shit when it happened? She thought it meant something. She was real hung up on the date."

"I forgot," I say.

"Whatever, dude, it was in the paper last week. 'On this day' with a picture of them and shit," Jason says. He turns to Luke, "You're such a bitch, anyway."

"Why? Because I don't think violence is the right reaction to a fucking joke? Or because I actually love my girlfriend and want to keep her happy and think you guys are shitheads to yours?"

"Guys," I say.

I put my head in my hands. The vacillation of Luke's speech is disturbing me. I feel empathy for him in direct correlation to the way he speaks. Nothing about this is OK. Nothing about anything is OK.

"Dude," he continues, and I can hear he is freaking out, too. "I just thought, like, if Vanessa was suicidal, you would know, and I didn't need to get my face all up in it. But, yo, you didn't know anything about this?"

"I don't know, man."

"When's the last time you saw her?" he asks.

"Yesterday. She was fine. We took the boat out to Egmont Key to make sure everything goes well this weekend," and then, finally, panic overwhelms me, and I am hyperventilating in giant gulps of air.

Ray comes over to me and hands me another beer. I cannot even see it, though. It's just a swimming mess of silver rings in front of my face.

"I think I fucking love her, actually. I didn't want to leave her when we got back. She's all I think about. Nothing I do is good enough anymore, because of her."

I can hear myself as if I am someone else and I can hear that I am very drunk. I am about to start blubbering.

"But she was fine," I say. "She was fine."

"When did you see her before that?" Ray asks.

"A couple weeks," I say. My voice is hollow. "She . . . she got upset about something. I didn't know what to do. Like, some girl thing. She didn't care at all when I went to Athens and then I didn't know what to do and then I went to Naples and I invited her, but she didn't want to come, so I gave her some space and then she called me yesterday . . . and— and—and it was . . . it was fucking awesome to see her." I am sobbing now, for the second time in two weeks.

This summer is fucking killing me. I want to blame it on the heat. It really is so fucking hot. It has been for days. But I am fucking bawling over a girl in front of my friends.

"God dammit," Jason says. "When did all my fucking friends become pussies?"

"Grow the fuck up, Jason," Ray says. "All you do is follow

other people around waiting for them to drop girls or cash. Who the fuck are you?"

"No. Stop," I say. "He's right. I'm being a fucking bitch."

"Dude," Jason says, as if I've come to my senses.

"No, dude, maybe *you* got her pregnant," I say.

"No fucking way."

"We only know what Luke heard Erica say," Ray says. "Which is that someone got pregnant."

I look at him, selfishness filling me with gratefulness for how dull he has been in the face of his financial failures. His conviction sounds so trustworthy against his usual apathy.

"That's either Vanessa or this other chick, and that means it's either you or you or someone else," Luke says.

"Fuckin' a," Jason says. "They're both fucking crazy."

"What do we do? You can't just ask Erica?" I say.

I hear the hysteria rising in my voice again. I see Vanessa in the boat. I smell the sugary scent of her perfume. I feel nauseous and rabid all at once, like I want to run out of my studio and see her, kick down her door, hold her down on her bed, tell her I love her, tell I heard something awful, tell her I won't care about anything else in the world ever again, if she will just tell me anything to make me feel better.

"I can't ask Erica," Luke says flatly.

"I can," Jason says.

"Jason, you need to fucking chill," Ray says. "We all need to fucking chill." He begins pacing.

Jason opens another beer. Luke rubs his face where Jason hit him. I stare at nothing, feeling gashed open.

"Nothing is going right for anyone anymore," Ray says quietly. "We all just need to chill."

He sounds eerie, like he's talking to himself, like he's planning something dreadful.

"I need to know if Vanessa's pregnant," I say.

"What if it's that other chick?" Luke asks. "And, seriously, you douchebag," he says to Jason, "it could be yours, if it is."

"Yo, if some chick gets knocked up and doesn't tell me and doesn't tell anyone and then tries to fucking kill herself, there's not much I can do for her," he says.

"You realize you might be talking about Vanessa, you fucking asshole," Ray says.

"That's different, dude."

"How is that fucking different? Just—Jason, just shut the fuck up for awhile," he says.

We are all silent again. Ray throws beers at each of us, and the only noise in the room is our slurping, until Ray stands still and faces us.

"An orgy," he says.

"What?" I say.

"Have an orgy. The four of you."

"Um, what about Dani?" I ask.

Jason looks at me aggressively.

"Dude, I have to ask," I say, because I see exactly where Ray is going.

"I don't know. You guys decide if you can pull it off. The four of you would be best. One of the girls will give herself away at some point, whether you can actually go through with it or not. Shit, you probably won't pull it off. Somebody will get mad or start crying, but just trying will tell you. And if you do go through with it, no one can be angry over any pregnancy."

"Except Dani," Jason says. "My fucking girl? I gotta live with her, remember?"

"Maybe you should have thought of that when you fucked somebody else raw," Ray says.

"But, also, the only reason Dani would have to know, then, is if it really is yours, in which case, she would eventually know, anyway," I tell him.

"Holy shit," Luke says.

"Just fucking ask Erica," I say.

"No," says Jason. He is grinning again. "Let's do it. C'mon, man, it'll be fucking bad-ass. If he asks Erica, his pussy ass gets in trouble with his girlfriend, and she might not even fucking tell him or tell him the truth, anyway. We have to find out for ourselves."

His teeth are glassy in his smile. His eyes are black on black. Sweat beads at his forehead.

"It is kind of a hot idea," I say, faking a smile until I realize how fucking hot the idea really is, and then my smile is huge. I think of the two of them on each other and nearly go blind right then and there.

I love Vanessa. She might even be into the idea. She is about as easygoing and undemanding as possible and never deflects my advances. And I need to know for certain, so that I don't hurt anyone I don't have to hurt.

This is how I can be with Vanessa for good, I realize. Fuck Jason. I feel sorry for Dani, but I can't handle everything all at once.

This is the right thing to do. I am already getting hard and I have to blink repeatedly and think of my dank towels over my cock to soften it, because we still have a six-pack left. I feel giddy and nauseous and scared, but, strangely enough, this seems like the best thing to do.

I smile gratefully at Ray. He looks at us with a stark mix of pity and resignation.

20.

I have butterflies in my stomach. I haven't felt butterflies in my stomach in years, but I've never been on a double date, either.

I didn't even know people did things like that, the way he called this morning and told me to wear something hot tonight, because he wanted to take me somewhere nice, he wanted me to meet a few of his friends.

I have to fight a strange giddiness that could be really embarrassing if I don't watch it. The possibilities of four people at dinner seems nasty before it seems sweet, like we could all be rubbing the wrong people under the table, and I feel all bubbly and curious about how the night will actually unravel.

When the doorbell rings, I literally jump as it tra-la-la's throughout the house. I run by my grandmother's door to see if she stirs, but her room is dead quiet as always. I feel my insides tighten in anticipation. I feel goofy and happy all at once again, but, this time, happiness washes over any tinge of embarrassment I feel about the goofiness.

He looks insane when I open the door, dark almost, as if he has something dangerous to show me, a vicious animal on a chain that I could tie up in my room or a snake behind his back that he plans on wrapping around me in some test to see who can squeeze the tightest.

"Hi," I say.

My voice is low and warm from my grandmother's Klonopin. Its slow ring reflects in his giant, inky pupils. My throat and his eyes ripple from how much we already want to be on top of each other, even in these four seconds of opening the door. The Klonopin feels good, too. It really helps my mind stay focused on the present.

I kiss him on the cheek. He smells fiery. I step outside.

"It's nice to see you."

"It's nice to see you, too," he says. "You look fucking amazing."

I look down. I don't want him to see how much I want him

yet.

"Are you ready to go?"

"I'm ready," he says. "Let's go."

He turns around, and my hips pull me after him, a strange sensation I have never felt before, even after having fucked easily a hundred guys just like him since I lost my virginity, as a twelve year old at the Volusia County Fair in Deland, bent over a fence and not understanding what was happening.

I liked it anyway. There was a pack of little lambs that hopped and brayed inside the pen, and the early morning sun made me squint with every thrust.

The restaurant is beautiful. The scent of rosemary dances between us, and the tablecloths shimmer with metallic thread. I like the lighting. Its radiance warms the tile and unfurls into the dining room.

We sit, and I feel the gentle tickle of fingertips at my ass, a secret caress and a gentlemanly offer of a seat. I feel my ass cheeks spread fully atop the chair and I am completely primed to rock on top of something hard and warm, letting my hips roll out like the seeping light over us. He is being so romantic tonight.

I haven't spoken yet, because I want him to speak first. I scan the menu. The paper is smooth and heavy in my hands. I can already taste a pear martini, but, suddenly, I feel a little thrill at the back of my neck. I hear Alex.

"Hey!" he drawls.

He and Jason slap hands. We are now on our double date. I almost panic. I thought we were meeting Erica and Luke, and it hits me that Jason might not know I fucked Alex, even that first day at the beach, that this means Alex never mentioned me, but of course he didn't. He has a girlfriend.

I look up, eyes wide, ready to say something or nothing, depending on what he wants to do. I shouldn't like him, but I do. He leans over to kiss me on the cheek. He makes me warm.

"Hi," he says. "This is Vanessa."

He gestures at her next to him. She looks sad and distant and pretty.

"You cut my hair!" I say. "You're the girl who told me to go to that art show thing at that gallery that burned down."

Alex turns his head to her sharply. But I don't care. He knows I met her.

"Oh, right," she says softly. "It's nice to see you again. Did you go?"

"I didn't notice you there," Alex says quickly.

"So, it looks like we all know each other, then. Awesome," says Jason.

I turn to him and then look at Alex and Vanessa. They all seem full to me somehow, as if they are about to burst with things I can't possibly know, but, then, I think that perhaps I smell this on them, instead, even though that makes no sense. I am glad they are here, even though Alex was so horrible to me. I still think we can be friends.

"Pear martinis?" I say.

"Nice!" says Jason. His jaw only moves slightly when he says this, and I want to run my thumb under his chin and press on his Adam's apple because of it.

Alex and Vanessa nod. No one says anything while we wait for the bartender to arrive. Jason orders, and Alex says, "When's the last time you had one of those, buddy?"

"Fuck you," he says and, then, to me, "Sorry."

We laugh, and I smile at Vanessa. She was serious when she cut my hair, too. I can't really imagine Alex and his playful smiles and big, white teeth and swimming eyes being with this girl, even though I liked her when I met her. I want her to like me, too.

I saw her the night I met Jason, too, standing alone. I just didn't know who she was. I think if she were my friend, I would make lots of other friends here, too, and that Jason would start taking me places with all their friends together. Even now, she's so quiet while Alex and Jason joke and talk about their friends at the gallery.

It's like she is alone, no matter who else is around, and it makes me want to be like that, too. She doesn't smile back, but does something in my direction with her eyes. Even her eyes are unsettlingly quiet, gray irises crackling against the whites.

"Did you go check out the gallery?" she says to me.

"Yeah, it seemed cool. Not really my usual scene, but it was still cool."

"What's your usual scene?"

"Bars?" I say and I grin at her, because I've never had a scene before, but she just nods back and continues to hold my eyes with hers. I'm pretty sure she doesn't know that I fucked Alex, but she suspects it, which is worse for her, really, because, at least, if she knew, she could relax or leave or demand something from him. But, like this, I can show her we can be friends.

Alex's shoulder is open toward her even as he talks to Jason. His head tilts toward her. His hip shifts toward her. If he isn't her boyfriend, he is something close to it or he wants to be.

I have been here for a whole summer now, and even though I didn't know anyone but Kim for the first two months, I have been here long enough now to be friends with someone I dated and to make friends with his girlfriend. It feels weird, but it feels good, like I finally belong here a bit.

Jason pulses with testosterone, and my attention flows back to him. I let my shoulders fall back to let him into my body the same way Alex does for Vanessa. Her posture is perfect, the spine curved and suspended in all the right places. Her head hangs above her neck like a weighted balloon within a shiny blanket of dark dirty blonde. Everything about her suggests composure. I decide I'm going to be like this, too, now.

This will reassure her, too, that I am not a threat, that I am open to whatever evil pleasures Jason has to offer tonight. I wait for her to grin back, but she doesn't. She still hasn't answered me, either, and it takes me a minute to understand that she isn't going to.

I still want her to like me. She is like a giant iceberg, traveling coolly, totally indifferent to anything she might smash during her careless float to the other side of the world.

I try to remember the last time I felt shy around someone and cannot think of when. Neither of us are saying anything. Only Jason and Alex are talking. Vanessa is looking at the rows of liquor behind the bar, scanning them for the sake of scanning them. I get the crazy feeling she could recite the order in which they appear once we get to the table and that she would just report the sequence from her memory like it were nothing.

There is something inhuman about her. The humming sounds that surround everyone else do not surround her. She doesn't need anything to exist, and I remember Alex's violence in bed, his deep and thorough need to pull a reaction from me, and I realize, suddenly, that he is hers if she wants him, because he could spend forever looking for different ways to get the responses from her that he got from me in a matter of minutes. She does not respond to need. I am awed by this.

The sweat on the back of Jason's neck, the thick bulge of his shoulders under his thin, linen shirt, are suddenly irresistible to me. The hostess calls us to our table, and, as we depart the bar, I let my hand rest on the side of Jason's ass. Vanessa and Alex see it, and Jason adds a bit of a strut to his walk. I smile at Vanessa again. She smiles back, vaguely, placidly, and I shiver a little bit, ashamed at how exposed my own need is. I'm always so incapable of hiding it.

They keep talking as if I'm not here.

My salad is like nothing I've ever seen before, a pile of almonds, some chopped and some whole, heaped over an asymmetrical hill of lettuce. The menu calls it "European." It is slightly slick and pungent and beaded with cold tap water and a few wrinkled cherry tomatoes.

I try to appear pleased with it, but I don't really understand what I ordered and I want Alex's lollipop chops. They are growing cold on his plate, because, while I sit here poking at the blistered skins of tomatoes, the three of them just talk about people I don't know.

"All I know is last time I went over there with Ray, the place looked fucking killer, but there was no one inside. So, I don't know what that means. They're open, but they don't have any art in there anymore? They just need some time, maybe. Ray is freakin' out, because he doesn't want Chrissy working for someone else, but, you know what? Fuck him. Those guys deserve our help, too. Plus, I mean, like, we're already going out there, too. We're leaving from there, you know?" Jason turns to me, "You ever lose a pet?"

"No," I say.

"Well, these guys, they're not doing real well, like, up here." He points to his head.

"That's too bad," I say.

No one is mentioning that I was there that night, standing with them, talking to them. Jason seems to have forgotten that was the night we got together, that he used a fishhook on my mouth and spit on my tongue and told me I was the greatest girl he had ever met. My eyelids feel heavy knowing that the moment made nearly no impression on him. The intensity of his fingers spreading me so many ways stayed with me. I poke at the lettuce, flip it over.

"Jeffrey doesn't know what he needs right now," Alex says. "He says he wants to call it off, but then, like, he's crying. How can you cancel an event that's meant to help him when he's crying? He's not crying because we're throwing him a benefit."

"Maybe he is," Vanessa says.

"Why?" Alex asks her.

"Maybe he's sad, because he doesn't want a benefit," she says.

She is sitting across from me, but she hasn't looked at me again. I flip the lettuce back over again and expose a dark green tangle of rotted plant. I put my fork down and put my hands in my lap.

"He's just confused, babe," Alex says. "They're proud, you know? I mean, think about it, they owned the best gallery around here and then it caught on fire. Because of their own show. And, I mean, Snuggles . . ."

"God dammit, man, seriously," Jason says. His voice is low and thick and raspy.

I put my hand on my inner thigh, and they continue to talk about how the dog yelled, as if I wasn't there that night or this. Jason's voice is mesmerizing. Vanessa describes in a dreamy cadence the sound Snuggles made after we left. My Klonopin is wearing off. My drink is empty. I pull the edge of my skirt up and rub the insides of my thighs. My finger flicks my panties while Jason talks. I pay attention to my elbow, making sure I don't move it next to my body as my middle finger runs over my pussy like a feather.

I don't mind if Jason sees me. I want the attention. I'm a little drunk, but not enough to stay focused. He won't give me away, or he will, because he's surprised, but he'll joke about it, and it will feel good. I stare at Vanessa dumbly. I think about kissing her. The little hood of my clit retracts, so that I stroke the most sensitive nerve ending, and my pussy gets wetter.

They continue to talk as if I were never there.

"Are you ready, by the way?" Vanessa says.

Alex looks at me, alarmed, for some reason I don't understand. I am still half playing with myself, but I know he doesn't know. The gentle light from the bar hurts my eyes. I am crashing off the Klonopin.

"Oh, yeah," he says. "A thing or two here and there, but, mostly, sure, I'm ready."

"Who did you pick?" Jason asks.

I don't know where to look for a moment, because he didn't pick me.

Alex laughs. "I didn't pick anyone. Aaron did."

"Who'd Aaron pick?" Jason asks.

Alex laughs again. He sounds mechanical. "Oh, you know Aaron," he says.

"So, a bunch of out-of-shape art groupies who think he's the Second Coming," Jason says.

I strap on a smile. This means it's a compliment no one picked me. Alex didn't even look at me that night. I stood in the back of the room and waited for him to notice me, but no one said a word to me all night.

"Nice," Vanessa says. She sighs. "Ray might be right. Why are we doing this again?"

"Because you and Chrissy said so, and then she sold a bunch of tickets, and I want to go to a party where no one dies," Jason says.

"No one died," I say.

They look at me. Finally.

"No one died, right?"

"Well, Snuggles did," Alex says.

"Oh, right," I say. I take my hands from my lap and twist the fork in my salad. My index and middle fingers are tingling with pins and needles, which makes no sense since I was just wiggling them.

"Poor dog," I say.

I sound confused. I look up, and Vanessa is looking right at me, her gray eyes boring holes into my face.

"Hey, enough of this. We're going to do whatever we have to do, right?" Jason says to Alex. "If we need each other, we're here for each other, but, tonight, I got a little something for the ladies."

Alex smiles broadly at him, the same smile that nearly drowned me when I first saw him.

"Word up," he says.

Jason reaches in his pocket and pulls out a little baggie. He dumps out a handful of pills and hands four of them to Alex. The two of them each swallow two immediately and smile.

"What is that?" Vanessa says. She is looking at Alex without a smile, but her eyes are brighter than before.

"A little Ecstasy," he says and hands her a pill. She grins at him, the first time I have ever seen her smile. She looks like a wolf as she swallows it.

I turn to Jason, waiting to see if he gives me one. I don't want to ask. I don't even know if I want this, but I want to stay with them tonight, so when Jason puts one in my hand with a devilish grin that blacks out his entire face and makes his irises disappear, I smile, too, and swallow what he offers.

We slam against the wall of a hallway, and my arm goes up over my head, and my ribs twist with the wet tingle of kisses, and my throat contracts against thick, masculine fingers that squeeze around my neck.

I am breathing heavily, more heavily than I would be by now from kissing. The Ecstasy has me sucking in air and blowing out

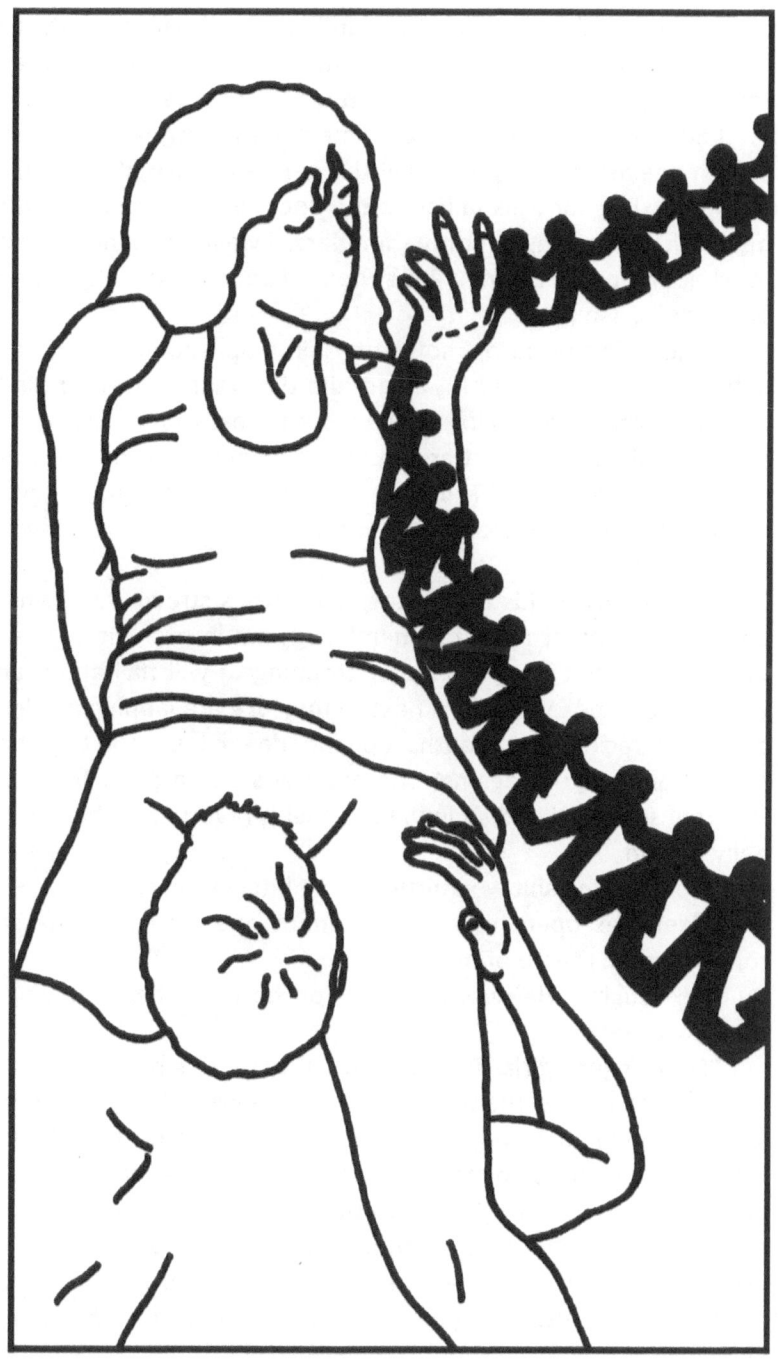

deep breaths like a locomotive, and my body shivers with the pressure around my throat. I go limp against the wall and, as I release any resistance, the hand around my neck releases, too.

I hear rough breathing next to me and the soft, husking sound of skin against wallpaper. I feel the gentle release of something above me, like corn silk falling to the floor. Something is brushing my forehead, trailing over my shoulders. I wave my hand at it and touch it and pull it off me. Paper dolls. I am covered in a chain of paper dolls. I laugh.

Either Alex or Jason hoists my skirt up and puts his head between my knees, and my head hits the wallpaper and rolls to the side with my eyes closed. Vanessa is next to me, kissing me, and she pulls up her shirt and puts one of my hands on the front of both her boobs, and I rub her nipples with one hand, splaying my fingers out, while we all moan softly.

I am on my hands and knees, my clothes strewn somewhere else at some point I don't remember. I am in excruciating pain, but I also cannot imagine it ever stopping. I will flail about and expire if it stops. Vanessa is next to me. We are lapping at Alex's balls and racing our mouths up and down his cock together, flicking our tongues against one another's and around his shaft. He groans so hard and so low, I can feel it reverberate behind his belly button.

"Holy fucking shit, you dirty fucking bitches," Jason says.

I feel Alex open his eyes. I cannot open mine. Vanessa's tongue teases the tip of mine.

Alex laughs. He puts his hands on both our heads, lovingly. He is so sweet.

"Four fingers, girls. Both of you. Dirty fucking bitches."

Vanessa laughs, the first time I have heard her laugh. She has a deep, melodious laugh that makes my nipples hard. Alex shudders, a whole-body reaction, at her laughter vibrating around his cock. I want to ask Jason to put his whole fist in my ass, but I can't imagine requesting anything from these people who don't give anything away and then are all over the place.

Something suspends time. It's the idea that if I ask Jason to fist me, he will hurt me.

I am riding Jason at a full gallop, tearing the skin off my knees on a rug in a room with high ceilings and double doors that open to a lanai, the same layout as my grandmother's house. My brain is hot, sizzling in its own liquid.

Alex is fucking Vanessa on her back, his arms hooked under her knees. She has her hands on his stomach. I have my hands on Jason's stomach. He is so solid and strong, and his cock feels so perfect and hard inside me. His arms are behind his head, and I can barely breathe I am so enchanted by how handsome he looks. Alex and Vanessa are locked on each other's eyes, their rhythm exact. I can feel that they love each other.

They are one, whereas Jason and I are two acting as one, but, still, I bounce on top of him like a loopy, sprung jack-in-the box and I cum all over his lower abdomen and balls, so that Vanessa and Alex slow their rhythm without losing it to watch the back of my head touch my spine, and Jason pulls his hand out from behind his head and strokes my throat, so that my cries sound like a warbler, as my shoulders jerk and flap above my hands, the palms still pulsing on Jason's abs, and Alex nestles himself deep into Vanessa, so that they can watch me, and when I am through, Jason says to Alex, "Switch with me."

"Really, Jason?" Vanessa says, smiling, that same deep laughter in her voice.

"Fuck yes, really. What do you think we're doing here?" he says and, through the waning heat of my post-orgasmic mind, I realize they have never done anything like this before, that they are just friends with no prior chemistry. I feel a thrill of anticipation that Vanessa will see Alex fucking me. The Ecstasy chugs through my heart, pumping my lungs. We are friends now. Her earlier coolness feels like another day. Everything is hot and pliable now.

Alex pulls out of her, and she puts her hand on her pussy, a shocked reaction to the feeling of him leaving her. I swing my leg over Jason, so that he can get up, and they switch positions. I roll on my back, so that I am lying next to Vanessa on my side. She faces me, and we kiss, our hands running over our stomachs, grabbing at the cocks that are already thrusting between each other's legs, guiding them into each other.

They both start off slow, letting us suck on each other's nipples while they grind into us, but it takes too long. We both want them deep inside us and we push against each other and them to take more of their cocks, harder and faster and deeper, until I am pinching Vanessa's nipples, and her face is buried in my neck, and our clits touch once, so that electricity burns between us, and then she cums, breathing in my ear, a hot, soft panting that rolls into wet purring, so that my pussy clenches around Alex. He has to pull out, and he sprays his thick, salty cum all over us.

Vanessa licks it off my face as Jason pounds her and cums a second later, pulling out and spraying all over us, too.

We twist into a pretzel on a bed, lashing our tongues into each other's cunts and massaging each other's assholes while Jason and Alex watch. She puts her finger into my pussy and swirls it around, getting it as wet as she can, and then she circles my asshole with my own juices before dipping into my ass and rubbing the inside of it with more finesse than Jason could ever understand.

I buck my hips into her to tell her that I love it, that I want more, and I kiss her pussy, slurping crazed licks into her lips as I make out with her dripping cunt. She knows I am about to cum, but she stops, anyway, and the cry I emit is like a baby bird tumbling from its nest.

She rolls me on my back, though, and mounts me and we scissor our pussies together.

"Holy shit," Jason says again, just as Alex says, "Oh my God."

I cum when I hear their voices, and she grinds her cunt into mine, but she doesn't cum this time. She just looks down at my tits and back up at my face and back down at my tits and back up at my face as I cum alone. When I finish, she untangles her legs from mine and lets me breathe, laying back on the bed with such regal entitlement, it takes me a minute to realize we are in her bed and not some palatial heaven as I had imagined.

We leave as the sun rises, nearly sober, or if not nearly sober, at least lucid once more. Alex and Vanessa are both cool. From Vanessa, I expected this, but I don't understand Alex's darting eyes and lowered chin. He seems furtive, as if he isn't sure how to process what happened and needs privacy for his feelings. I am surprised at this good-bye, devoid of the heat we shared. I still feel incredible from the Ecstasy, anyway.

In the car, Jason pats my knee. "Did you have fun?" he asks.

I laugh. "Oh my God! Yes!"

"Good. Me, too."

"Maybe we can do it again," I say idly.

He chuckles. "I don't know—but it was still fun."

I spend the rest of the drive home fantasizing that we are all best friends, even though I know that once I sober up, I'll be shy around Vanessa and Alex.

I'm nervous about Jason suddenly, too. It's almost like he's too cool, too smooth for me, but then I remember that's why I came here—to have a better life.

21.

My first thought upon waking is an old superstition my father read to me from a book about personality and compatibility.

Two people who sleep in the same position are more likely to fight than two people who sleep in different, complementary positions, unless those two people sleep on their backs, because such vulnerable slumber is the realm of kings and queens. Kings and queens don't need to struggle for power. Their benevolence lets them sleep fearlessly. No one will stab you in your sleep if you are good.

Alex sleeps on his back. I curl into his side. I am a side sleeper, private and prone to paranoia when I feel exposed. He mumbles contentedly as I run my hand across his stomach. I wonder if he is dreaming of last night. We are still covered in the residue of each other, of Jason and Julie.

I slip out of bed and put on a bathing suit in front of the mirror. Alex doesn't move. I gather together a bag. I leave and walk down to the beach. The air is warm from the day's heat, but we have slept through the worst of the sun. The temperature hovers comfortably around me. The scent of frangipani fills the air with sweetness, the flavor of cupcake icing.

The sun is about to set. I haven't checked a swimming advisory in weeks. The beach is empty. This isn't necessarily an answer. After an entire summer of warnings, people stop checking altogether. There is a sign a quarter-mile down, but I can't be bothered to walk to it. The water looks fine, welcoming even, dotted with golden points of light, as it shushes and rocks toward low tide. I consider stepping into it, anyway, but I know that's foolish. If there isn't a clear advisory, I'll only screw myself with coughing that will last the weekend from odorless dispersants in the water.

My phone rings, jarring me. No one has called me for days. It's all just texts all the time. No one calls anymore. Today is Thursday, August 23, and I haven't worked in ten days. It's only Dani.

"Hello?"

"Hi, Vanessa."

"Hi."

"So, how's it going?"

It's feeding time, but there are no birds nearby.

"I'm at the beach."

"Yeah, I can barely hear you from the wind. Can you go somewhere else?"

I look around at the sand, the water, the sky.

"No."

"Oh . . . huh, OK, well, I won't keep you, then, but I need your help with something."

She pauses, waiting for me.

"OK, what?"

"Do you know where Jason is?"

"No."

The water licks my toes. Sand pits under my feet.

"Oh . . . OK . . . because we got into this giant fight last night, and I told him not to come back until he has a job. I just meant, like, he was pissing me off, and I want him to get a job. I didn't mean don't really come home until he has a job, but that's sort of what happened. He didn't come home all last night or all day today and, now, you know, I'm worried."

"Worried about what? That he OD'ed or something? Did you call him?"

"Oh my God, girl, no, I don't think he OD'ed. Do you think he OD'ed?"

"I don't know, Dani."

"I think . . . ugh, I have to tell you something that, like, isn't a big deal now, but you don't know about it or part of it, anyway, and, like, maybe it matters now."

Her voice makes me dizzy. The sand feels cool under my feet, though, and the sun is still a foot over the horizon. I have a strong sense, suddenly, that the past is not so important, except when it is the future, and that Dani is quite incapable of understanding the elegance of time right now, because she has been waiting for Jason for so long.

"What's wrong?" I ask.

"So, there's this girl in town, Julie, she's new. She's just here for another couple of weeks, I think, but Erica is kind of friends with her now, but I didn't want to be friends with her, because Erica told me—"

"Dani, I know who Julie is."

She pauses, flustered, before continuing, "She told me she knows her because Alex was banging her, and I just knew I couldn't be friends with her without you finding out, but, listen, it's not as bad as it sounds. For you, anyway, because, well, I think Jason is the one banging her, not Alex. She lied to me, Vanessa. I think Erica lied to me."

The waves refuse to run up to my ankles. The sun hangs like an orange beach ball, threatening to bounce away.

"How do you know?" I ask.

"Remember at House when she kept going on about that painting? I told her, like, shut up, that it was obvious you knew about Julie, and she was going to make you feel bad, but she said she was wrong about that. She said she didn't think Julie was fucking Alex after all."

"So?"

"So, how does she know her, then? I think Jason has been hanging out with her. Not Alex. Jason."

"Wait, Dani, you thought Alex was fucking this girl, but you acted like you thought that painting was some beautiful gesture, anyway?"

"Well, sure, but that doesn't matter now, because Alex isn't fucking her, but I think Jason is!"

I say nothing. The sun begins to fall rapidly, turning hot orange and then pink. The sky behind it becomes a fantastic lavender and then a liquid, fluorescent purple. Gold twinkles on the waves, and then the whole sky is fire, a majestic blaze without smoke or death that sends the Gulf toward sleep, a lullaby sunset. The last crooning notes bring a flash of lime green, a halo around the solar disk, a beautiful, unpredictable phenomenon of color and light unseen anywhere else at any other time, just before the ball drops into the water.

"Vanessa?"

"Yes?"

"Are you mad?"

"What?"

"Don't be mad. It doesn't matter now, but I needed to know how serious you were, you know? At House? You didn't think the painting was you. You thought it was Julie, didn't you? So, if you were totally sure Alex was sleeping with her, then it means Jason isn't."

I think of Alex, in my bed, his muscular thighs turned outward in sleep, his chin in the air as he dreams, reveling in memories of last night. I know he hasn't awakened, that he won't unless I go back and wake him. I watch the last licks of pink fade into the mauve horizon. I blink hard, trying to recapture the gift of green from the sky.

I realize with a jolt that everyone last night—Jason, Alex, and Julie—spoke of the night of the fire as if Julie wasn't there, when we all know she was. I saw the three of them in conversation. Julie told me she was there when I cut her hair. She didn't understand why Jason and Alex were acting like she wasn't there.

No—she understood why Alex was acting like she wasn't there. She didn't understand why Jason was. She said, "No one died, right?"

I feel as if someone is laughing too loudly in my ear.

"That's not what it means, Dani."

"What?" she says.

"That's not what it means," I repeat. "I have to go."

I hang up. I am suddenly cold in my bathing suit.

I stare at the water for a long time. Everything floats in front of me. The momentary betrayal of my body by the fountain after the open call. Erica in the bathroom at House. Alex and Jason wanting to double date. They both fucked Julie. They didn't know who was pregnant or how. They don't know I'm not anymore. Erica told Luke, but she didn't know what to tell, and Luke told Alex.

There are squiggling sea worms inside me that will not stop screeching at me until I see every kind of loss in the world, every lie my friends tell me.

I walk home in the dark. I know with a vast finality that bad and hurtful things will always happen to me and that I won't control them.

My phone goes off just as I reach my corner, a text from Jeffrey that says, "Girl, this weekend means so much to me! I'm really excited to get everybody together in such an important spot!"

This most recent dishonesty, at least, is immediately obvious.

22.

I am dripping in sweat. Beads race down the valleys of my temples and over the cliffs of my cheekbones. I am so physically attuned to my work right now that it looks alive. The metal forms hang from large hooks in my ceiling around the perimeter of my studio. They shimmy with vitality, dancing just slightly in the air. There is something innately feminine about them. They are teasing me, beckoning me to finish them, so that they can fill with the bodies of the models.

It is 11PM on Saturday, August 25, and I have twelve hours to finish. I have not slept for more than a few hours at a time since our little conviviality. I fell into an hour in a chair, accidentally, while sitting and gazing upon my progress. I slipped a couple of hours on the floor, after stretching and looking at the ceiling, letting its popcorn surface tell me what should come next. I snagged a few long blinks with my head on the counter or the table here or there. Each time I wake, I am sweating, either again or still, and I have new inspiration.

I've been alone this whole time. My only contact has been incoming. Chrissy sends emails that are too dense to read. Aaron and Jeffrey send a rash of grateful texts, moments of double beeping on my phone when they clearly have finished some private lovers' talk and don't realize the other is sending the same emotional missive.

I keep seeing words like "so much" and "unimaginable" and "wanted to let" in my notification bar. I don't need to catalog the exact words of my friends right now. I am moving in image and feeling. I am drinking from a reservoir of exceptional clarity that is nothing more or less than how much I love Vanessa. Any other concerns have fallen away.

She was so beautiful when I left. She was quiet, as usual, but her skin was radiant, and she seemed stronger somehow. We recognized some new truth in each other, some new understanding of the world and what we are able to do in it. She kissed me so wistfully when I left, her lips holding onto mine as if she were a flower lowering its petals in the mid-day sun around my lips. When I looked at her, I couldn't imagine ever looking into a mirror again without seeing the melancholy peace of her gray eyes reflected back within mine.

I am almost sure neither she nor Julie is pregnant. I am almost positive it isn't true. Erica gossips constantly. She could have been talking about anything.

They were too comfortable with each other and with us. If one of them were pregnant, she would have protected her body somehow from the Ecstasy, pulled back a little from the brutality Jason and I served up.

Only then, it occurs to me with a stupid, thunking sound in my skull that echoes in my throat. An orgy is the perfect cover for them, too. If we are all depraved, no one is responsible for anything.

This last thought exhausts me. I think about ordering a bag of coke, giving myself one final jolt, even if it is artificial, to fully churn out every last iota of creativity inside me. Then, afterwards, I can sleep for at least a few hours, dreamlessly, without moving. My head is already nodding gently toward my arms, like a feather drifting toward a cloud. I am almost in blackness when my doorbell shrills and yanks me up as if I am a marionette for some demanding muse that requires more art.

Aaron and Jeffrey are leaning into each other, heart-shaped faces agog and touching, with their arms around each other, at the door. They are wavery to me. The doorframe is a bit wobbly around them. They are grinning and brimming with announcement.

"My God, what took you so long?" exhales Aaron. "We thought you might be dead in there!"

I rub my head. I can feel my mouth stretch into a smile that matches theirs. "I've been working."

"Yes! Yes, you have! Let us in!" says Aaron.

I step back, and they bustle inside, jostling each other in the doorway. Aaron pushes Jeffrey playfully. Jeffrey curls into his shoulder.

The bench table is horizontal across the room, dividing it so that I have a private section cordoned off for working. Nothing stops anyone from walking around the table, but almost no one ever does. Aaron and Jeffrey stop at its edge and put their elbows down on it together, cupping their hands in their chins to look at the work, these hanging outfits, suspended off the ground, cold and glistening, but somehow lively, like cows in a butcher's refrigerator.

"Oh my," says Jeffrey.

"Alex!" says Aaron. "These are dirty!"

"You look exhausted," says Jeffrey.

"I've been at it for two days straight," I tell them. I can't help it. I'm proud.

They nod knowingly. Jeffrey puts his thumb to his nostril and snorts loudly, running his face over an imaginary line. Aaron gapes at him mockingly.

"No," I laugh, "but I was thinking about getting a bag just now. Kind of burn the last of my energy off and then pass out."

"That makes perfect sense," Aaron says.

Jeffrey slithers his hand up Aaron's voluminous butterfly sleeve and wiggles his fingers around. Aaron yelps. Jeffrey gives him the same mocking gape Aaron just gave him, as he pulls out a little baggie, half full of yellowish coke, from somewhere near Aaron's elbow.

"So, you're really into these kimono things now, huh?" I say to Aaron.

"There is a part of that night that is still with me," he says dramatically.

No one says anything for a moment. Jeffrey taps the bag out onto the table.

They look at my art behind me. They smile at each other, then at me. Jeffrey rolls a dollar bill perfunctorily.

"Ooh, no, wait!" I say. I give them an open, unfinished finial that I decided not to attach to a vest.

"A whatsit from whosit! You are in a mood, my dear!" says Aaron.

"Yeah, you guys, too," I say. We're all smiling. We haven't

smiled in a long time. "You seem really . . . lovey," I say.

Aaron nods his head and raises his eyebrows toward Jeffrey, who is bent over. Jeffrey stands up again, sniffing back a line.

"I had an idea," he says, almost shyly.

Aaron stands by him like a proud father.

"What is it?" I say.

"Well, we've had some trouble, you know. Trouble we didn't want to admit. Emotionally. This is embarrassing for us in a way, but you've all been so amazing. You and Chrissy, especially. She comes to see us almost every day, too, and she talks. She's having a hard time with Ray, because the marina is failing, and it's affecting their love."

He looks at Aaron when he says the word, "love." Aaron nods at him, urging him.

"And, well, we know that you, too, must have suffered financially when you were unable to create a meaningful relationship with that awful woman in Naples . . ."

I blush. I had forgotten about her, that horrible day, how she made me feel like a complete fraud, how Vanessa wouldn't talk to me, and the two seemed so inextricable.

"But don't feel bad, Al. I'm sorry, I didn't mean to embarrass you. Just that we want to open an Art annex at the marina, while we continue to rebuild, and we thought you could do a solo show for us. We could all use the money, and you have the draw."

I look up again. This is not what I expected. I have to bend down and take a line to hide how much this hurts me. When I stand, I inhale deeply. I try to focus on what I told Ray, that we could do something to help him next.

"That sounds nice," I say. I sound tired, shaky, like I don't mean it. I summon every scrap of will I have to make my voice sound casual. "So, maybe we could hang this stuff I'm making for tomorrow over there. They look pretty cool suspended from the ceiling like this, right? Like they're puppets or like they come to life when no one is looking, right? I bet we could do something cool with some old weathered wood like what's on the docks. Oh! Maybe set them up as an old hangman game!"

Aaron and Jeffrey look at each other.

"What about some of those paintings?" says Jeffrey. "Like of sailboats and that sort of thing?"

I pause. "Sailboats? Oh, because it's a marina? Well, paintings can't stay outside all the time, and the marina is outside, so something else would be better."

They pause, too. The coke drip hits my stomach. Aaron holds perfectly still. I have never seen him so still. Jeffrey shuffles a bit.

"We thought we'd do it inside. People like air conditioning this time of year," Aaron says. "And, you know, what if it rained?"

"We wouldn't have to leave them out all the time. We could have exhibit hours. Chrissy could prep the place, so that people think about coming back, or we could even just keep doing shows there if it's successful enough that they can keep things going."

"Oh, well, sure . . . that's a good idea," says Jeffrey unconvincingly. "But would you like to do a series of paintings for us?"

"I'm trying to create work with inspiration behind it these days, you know? I'm not as excited about painting just for sales and deadlines anymore," I say. My voice is firm.

Jeffrey bends down to take a line and passes the little metal bat to Aaron who bends down to take his line, too. We are all panting.

"That's very lovely. We appreciate what you're doing for us, Alex, really we do," Aaron says quickly. "But how will these pieces sell?"

"I wasn't planning on selling these until you mentioned it for the marina just now."

The room is getting too hot again. I force myself to focus on the cool that emanates from the metal behind me.

"We didn't mention that," Aaron says. "We would like you to paint a series for us."

"You don't sound like you're asking anymore," I say. They say nothing.

"I'm sorry," I retract. "I'm tired. I've been working for two days straight. The coke has me a little reactionary."

They relax. They have won something I didn't know was at stake.

197

"That makes perfect sense," Jeffrey says, but something isn't right when he says it. It's because Aaron just said the same thing to me.

"We're all probably a little bit tense," he continues. "This is a big weekend. We're completely out of money. We're just tired, too—but we know how easy it is for you to sell a few paintings to regular America. It's a gift you have, really, a different gift than ours, but a very reliable gift. We just thought that sort of help may be more practical."

"Chrissy has sold over sixty tickets," I say. I am trying so hard to keep my voice light. A dark sleepiness is creeping into it, though.

"This is pretty successful already, from a practical perspective," I tell them.

"She what?" Aaron says.

"What?" I say.

"Chrissy sold sixty tickets?" Aaron says.

"Yeah," I say. I can feel my empty girls swaying behind me.

"Well, I . . . oh my! I had no idea!" he says. There is a desperate chirp to his voice.

I furrow my brow at him. "Well, sure. We can't have an event with no people," I say.

Aaron and Jeffrey don't look at each other as much as vibe something to each other, something private that changes how they have decided to treat me.

"We haven't paid attention to the numbers, really. We're not numbers people. We're artists, for heaven's sake!"

I stare at them. The coke is powerful, and I am already ziplining off my first rail. I shake my head slightly and bend down to take my last huff. When I rise again, they are leaning into each other once more, damp this time with clammy coke sweat beading at their foreheads.

"That's a real relief," says Jeffrey. "I didn't think to ask Chrissy about if this was actually making money." He laughs. "I think we were so wrapped up in everyone's good energy that we were just enchanted by the fun of it all!"

He and Aaron laugh in exact unison, the highs and lows of

their *ha ha ha*'s swooping up and down like an old, wooden roller coaster.

"No, you guys are good," I say. "We should still do something for Ray and Chrissy, though. You're right that Chrissy has put in a ton of work, and I told Ray that we would do something together for his place next, too, so this is a good idea."

"Oh, OK, great, then," says Jeffrey. His syllables are a glandular, coked-out monotone.

"So, tomorrow will be fantastic! Has anyone checked the weather?" Aaron asks.

"It's going to be hot."

We laugh. Their laughter still matches. Mine is a thick bass to their complicated, high-pitch synthesizer. Aaron wiggles a bit, and Jeffrey gives him a cloying look.

"All this S&M stuff should be fun, too!" Aaron says.

"S&M stuff?" I say.

"Yeah, your whole . . ." he waves his hands behind me. "Your S&M costumes back there. They're, like, all sexed out and stuff."

They laugh. Jeffrey leans his head on Aaron's shoulder.

"You're such a good friend doing this for us," he says. "You've put all this amazing work into this event, just so our supporters can feel included and still be part of the Art brand while we rebuild. It's a good thing you're so good at selling paintings, Al. You'll be able to sell just fine."

He smiles broadly at me. His teeth are very white. His eyes crinkle affectionately. I can't figure out what they think I'll be selling.

Aaron rolls his head into Jeffrey's sweaty egghead on his shoulder and laughs with him.

"It's true," Aaron says. "We love you, Al. You're, like, the only other guy in the world who could convince our fans all this medieval S&M club stuff is art. People are just crazy, aren't they? They'll fork over a buck for anything you tell them is art. But you're, like, the nicest guy ever, too. When we create our little art jokes, we sometimes wonder how much our people recognize the farce.

"Like, maybe we're not getting away with anything after all—

you know, like, is it a joke if no one gets it? But you really mean it, and that's convincing, too, in a different way."

"You mean, it's art if you just want it to be art badly enough?" I say.

"Exactly! That's what you bring to the table!" Aaron exclaims.

I think I might cry if I can't go to sleep now.

"I don't know, guys. It just really matters to me that everyone is happy," but, even as I say it, I know it hasn't been my motivation at all.

"It's so special. We really do love you," Aaron says.

They stand up and come around to hug me. I dip my head between their shoulders and feel my face crumple a bit. I hug them tightly for several seconds, so that I can calm my crinkling eyebrows and tightening cheeks, but when they leave, two hot tears fall from each eye and hug the curve of my jaw, so that they can dry on my neck, salty trails of my undeniable failure.

I look at my work hanging from the ceiling. The pieces barely move now. They look heavy. They may be too heavy for the girls to wear comfortably all day, but no one will say anything. They will just wear them and suffer, because no one will want to tell me the truth.

I stare at the pieces until my eyes unfocus and all I can see is the hardness of the lines, the gleam of steel. I try to see the pieces as Aaron and Jeffrey saw them—a joke to show the true nature of art, because what I've done isn't art to them at all—but I can't see it.

It's a joke I don't understand, and I feel foolish, because I still like them. Art and people. I still like them.

23.

I lift a key to my face and inhale a giant pile of coke, while Aaron stands in the shade and Jeffrey and Alex load Ray's boat.

Jeffrey sweats through his clothes, but he and Aaron smirk at each other in quiet satisfaction each time Jeffrey passes. They are smirking at Alex's work.

Every now and then, Aaron barks out an excited, useless command, insisting he would help if he weren't in a cast. I take another bump and wash it down with a split of cava.

They finish loading, and Jeffrey disembarks to help Aaron aboard. I stare into the kapok tree overhead and kill the split. My swallowing drowns the sound of Aaron's neediness.

When I look ahead again, I am dizzy from craning my neck at the wide arcs of the branches, and the boat, with Aaron, Jeffrey, and Ray, is gone.

I am patting my hips absent-mindedly—I want more coke; I cannot remember where I put the bag—when I see Alex on the ground, asleep, nestled into the kapok's long, fibrous roots.

I try to imagine what he must have thought, sitting there, exhausted, waiting for me to notice him right next to me, while I stared into the branches, but I can't think of anything.

It seems more likely he just sat down and passed out and is next to me out of habit.

Ray returns. He bounces the bow into a dock post and throws a rope around it. He turns off the engine and legs over his boat, storming into the blinding sunshine, stamping across the dock, his face furious.

We are under the kapok still. He walks past us without a word and heads for Chrissy. He pushes her with both hands on her shoulders and walks her backwards, roughly. Her gangly legs trip and hop. She looks over her shoulder at the tree and then again at Ray, and then her back is against the kapok's trunk.

He leans into her face and says something dark and angry. He pushes her against the tree again, harder than before, and stares at her, his face close to hers, and then he turns and walks away, looking only at the ground a few seconds ahead of him.

Chrissy straightens her skirt and walks behind him, looking at the ground ahead with the same focus. Her face is stricken.

Alex is awake. He tries to roll toward me, but the kapok's root keeps him where he is.

"What the fuck?" he says and, suddenly, I know what happened.

"We're supposed to be over there by one," I say. "What time is it?"

I step out of the kapok's shade and look at the sky. The sun is a finger's width past noon in a cloudless stretch of blue. There are not enough people here.

"What?" Alex says. He rubs his face.

"Nothing," I say. "We need to get moving."

I walk to the boat. Alex follows me. I crouch on the passenger seat and jump high into the air and slam into the deck. The boat sloshes back and forth.

"Don't rock the boat," Alex laughs.

"I won't," I say.

Alex's grin dwindles and, suddenly, he understands what I am doing. He stands on the chair, too, and looks out over the harbor to the other side of the marina, where Ray hides his boat. There are at least thirty people there, next to a bouquet of balloons.

"Get your shoes off the leather," I say.

He jumps down.

The wind lifts my hair. Alex wants to say something, but he doesn't know what.

"These things happen," I tell him.

24.

He walks right past me, a dense cloud of smooth, tanned skin and the scent of sweat melting through a cheap, beachy fragrance—cucumber, wood, wet sand.

"Hi!" I say, startled by his brush off, knowing he brushed me off. I really mean, instead, "Why?"

He turns around and looks forward again and turns back to me, his eyes wide with some sort of alarm or warning. His eyebrows raise up and down, the mimic of surprise, a second too late to be real.

"Hi," he says in a stilted voice and turns and walks away.

He sits on a low wall near the marina entrance, next to a girl with shiny bangs and heavy makeup. She has beautiful, strong features, black wings for eyebrows and a square chin with a pretty dimple. Her hair is a staircase of flat, shiny layers that tickle her cheekbones and jaw line.

Jason puts his arm around her and kisses her cheek. She looks at him peevishly and swipes at his mouth. She is telling him to wipe the sweat off his face before he kisses her next time. Her mouth is set like a long, dead fish in her face.

Of course he has a girlfriend.

For some reason, that never occurred to me. He was so attentive on the phone, so polite and romantic when we went out. I knew we were moving quickly, but I thought that was because we were right together. He was there when I needed someone. Each time Alex blew me off, he was there, until he was just who was there. He made all those big gestures.

He wasn't letting things move quickly because we were right for each other. He was letting things move quickly because he knew they'd be over quickly.

He has a girlfriend.

Even the first day I met them at the beach, I wanted Jason, but he and Alex figured something out without me, and, after a few drinks, it didn't matter to me which one of them I had.

I had a dirty, drunk fantasy of both of them at once, but I've never been able to say things like that. They either happen or they don't. The guys have to decide.

But when he found me again, the night Alex disappeared with his friends after the fire, the first time Alex ditched me—even though I didn't get he was ditching me at the time—I thought it meant he felt it that first day, too.

We are on the wrong side of the inlet, almost thirty of us. Chrissy runs across the parking lot and stops short in front of the waiting crowd.

"You shouldn't be here," she wheezes, "There was a mistake . . . I don't know . . . this isn't where you should be."

She reminds me of a broomstick, her voice scratchy with anxiety, her hands sweeping us to the opposite side of the inlet. The crowd begins to groan, but it's too hot to do anything but follow. No one speaks as we walk. I look for anyone I might know, but I can't find anyone, because I don't really know anyone.

It hits me with a sad finality that Alex and Vanessa won't talk to me today. It will be easy for them to excuse themselves. They are the party. I'm just someone they fucked.

I text Kim as we march, "I'm at the wrong marina. Meet me in front."

Kim is drunk, loping up to the far corner of the wall. I can see Jason and his girlfriend if I look to my right, but I only look straight ahead.

"I'm late," she says. "Where were you?"

"Over there," I point across the water.

"What were you doing over there?"

"There were people there."

"Ooh, I heard Ray hides his boat over there, so it doesn't get repossessed. People have probably seen it there, that's why."

Her knees buckle, and she catches herself.

"Shit, let me sit down. Look, I brought something," she says and hands me a flask.

I take a sip. It's strong and sweet.

"Whiskey with honey and green tea," she says.

I laugh and take another sip and feel better.

"Oh! Hey, Erica!" Kim calls out.

She turns and smiles at us.

"Hi," she says, coming over.

She hugs us hello. I tip her the flask.

"Yes, please," she says and sips. "I'm nervous."

"Why?" Kim asks.

"Oh . . . everything. I've been saying it for weeks now, but I just don't think this is the right way to fix things. Aaron and Jeffrey were making a point and now they're backtracking from it, because their insurance company is giving them a hard time."

"A point?" Kim says.

"They set the fire on purpose," Erica says seriously. "They were working on a great arc of artistry, art as life, life integrating the ideals of art, transcending the whole what imitates what question.

"We spent so much time talking about it, talking about the risks and how to make sure the worst didn't happen and, now, they're acting as if it were just another stroke of bad luck in our group."

She trails off and takes another sip and then another, staring at the empty docks.

"I'm hurt. They hurt me," she admits. She blinks rapidly. "I committed to them. I feel like something is going to go wrong now, because they've forsaken their path."

Kim takes back the flask and smiles at her blankly.

"Erica!" Jason's girlfriend stands on the wall and shouts at her.

"I have to go," she says to me. "We'll talk more, maybe tomorrow."

She hustles over to Jason and his girlfriend, bumping into people on her way. Jason's girlfriend sits down and peers at me with narrowed eyes as Erica sits next to them on the concrete wall. The girl leans her face into Erica's to ask her something and looks at me again. I realize she is asking Erica who I am. Erica says something quickly, and the girl asks her something more pointed with a sharp shake of the head. Her aggressive haircut twists around her cheekbones.

Jason reaches across Erica and taps the girl on the leg. She looks at him like she hates him and then asks Erica the same question again.

Kim puts her hand on my arm. "That girl is crazy. Don't listen to her. They're all fucking crazy. What bullshit. Why would you even say that about your friends?"

Chrissy stands up on the wall next to Jason and Erica and Jason's girlfriend. I turn my body away from them, toward the sun.

"Hello, everyone!" she shouts. The scratchy anxiety in her voice echoes through a microphone.

The crowd cheers back at her.

"Thank you for coming—and for helping our dear friends and important community artists, Aaron and Jeffrey from Art!"

The crowd claps and cheers. Someone whistles. A girl up front whoops.

"This is our boarding call for artists and models. I know everyone can't wait to see Aaron and Jeffrey, so we're going to drop off the beautiful people and come right back for you, the party animals!"

The crowd erupts. I take another swig from Kim's flask. I am not a beautiful person or a party animal. I am just here accidentally.

Chrissy's voice scratches over the microphone again, "Now, before we bring out the girls, let's hear it for our captains, Vanessa and Ray!"

She gestures grandly at the two boats behind her and pauses to let the crowd applaud. Vanessa looks up and waves, but Ray just stands and wavers, staring at Chrissy, looking dumbfounded and clumsy in the sun.

"Yeah!" Chrissy shouts. "And now, just to get you warmed up, let's get a peek at our models!"

She continues to shout, her vocal chords straining, as she names each girl. The crowd roars back at her, hollering, clapping, whistling, jumping up and down. Everyone strains to look at Ray's boat. The girls wave like Miss Americas on the way down the dock. Vanessa looks out at the crowd and smiles, that same vague smile she wore at dinner. Ray still stands there.

"C'mon," Kim says to me. "It's time to go!" Her eyes glint like bright olives in the sun.

I look at Vanessa's boat and see Jason and Alex and Erica and Jason's girlfriend head toward it. Chrissy does not announce the artists, and I realize there are no artists to announce, only Alex. The crowd doesn't notice.

I have a sudden image of birds molting, their feathers drifting to the ground, and a memory of my grandmother telling me as a child, while my mother sat drunk in front of the television, that I should never touch feathers, that they carried invisible parasites that would burrow into my skin.

After that, I felt the same mesmerizing attraction to them as always, but they scared me. I knew how sinister and full of disease they were, but I wanted to be near them, anyway.

25.

The water is exceptional, turquoise and bright. Far off, I can see a viscous polish, a layer of film on an iridescent soap sliver—oil, but it's light, and we aren't heading toward it.

The small cruelties we have dealt each other recently are almost meaningless out here. The sun is hot and white and scorches away what weaker beings might call pain. We mug, haute and cold, behind sunglasses none of us can afford to replace anymore.

I study Julie. She is undeniably pretty, buxom, and softer than I usually like, but alluring, firm and round at the same time. She could be pregnant. I don't think she is, though. She is too new to us to keep it a secret—unless she doesn't know who the father is, either. But she let us drug her and fuck her.

I look at Vanessa, too. She is thin, graceful, as always. If anything, she has lost weight through the bust and lower abdomen. It hits me now that the past few weeks have been difficult for her. She probably didn't care about talking to me because she was suffering from grief before the anniversary of her parents' death. It wasn't anything to do with me.

But neither of them looks pregnant. Neither of them would have taken that Ecstasy if she were going to have a baby.

"Those shades look fly," Luke says to Erica.

"Thanks, Luke," Erica deadpans.

She is always so full of shit. No one is pregnant. She stares at the deck in silence. Luke fidgets next to her. Jason lamps and pulls on Dani's hair. She ignores him.

I realize I will have to paint some inane series for Aaron and Jeffrey's marina annex. I have not made any money in three weeks now. I bite back a stinging feeling in the corners of my eyes and look at Vanessa again, still driving slowly with the boat at full capacity. She can't be pregnant if she's skinnier.

Suddenly, irrationally, I hate them all.

We are coasting past Pass-A-Grille. Its briny scent overpowers

Dani's sullen cigarette.

"Oh! Look!" Kim says to Julie.

Everyone turns around. The coastline has slipped to the east. The marina is visible in the far distance. The balloons are, too.

"That's why you were there," Kim says. "Now why would they decorate that? You can see it all the way from here. Why not just put a sign, 'Come repossess my boat'?"

She pulls from a flask and passes it to Julie. Julie smiles and takes a swig. She tips her head forward and begins to wipe her mouth, when she realizes we are all looking at her.

I can see what she thinks. She thinks that one of us talked about last Wednesday, about our orgy, that we are looking at her and thinking about it.

She blushes a firebrand pink and freezes, her index finger dragging liquor off her lip. She drops her hand and closes her mouth and sits up very straight.

Kim notices and takes the flask back from her, glaring around the boat.

"You want a cigarette?" she asks.

"No, we're almost there. I don't smoke," she answers.

We are at the isthmus of Pass-a-Grille. Vanessa has stopped the engine. When she starts it up again, the boat jerks a bit, and Dani slaps Jason, who has accidentally pulled her hair with the lurching of the boat.

We are in open water now, far away enough from both Tierra Verde and Egmont Key to feel the magnitude of the Gulf. We stopped trying to talk after we saw the balloons. Everyone just looks at whatever is exactly in front of them.

The sky is clear as we arrive, a heartbreaking blue, unmarred with smoke in the distance. The Key shimmers, grainy and wobbling between the endless parachute of sky and the swirling green and blue of the Gulf.

Palms bend over the thin stalks of laurels. I cannot think how they got here. They bow into a path that leads to the crumbled Fort. Behind the Fort is a lighthouse, but the isolation is the allure.

No one is out here. We knew this would be true. We never worried about this. No one comes here anymore. This part of the world is forgotten. It is only ours now. I can still see Tierra Verde, the tiny, orange blocks of Spanish tile roofs across the Gulf.

Vanessa stops the boat. I help her drop the anchor. No one moves. Vanessa breaks into a grin, blinding in its unexpectedness.

"You have to get out of the boat now," she says.

Luke and Erica and Jason and Dani just stare at her dumbly. Julie is frozen still, braced against some new social barb. Only Kim, who is the drunkest, is gathering her things.

"You have to get in the water," Vanessa says. "I can't pull the boat right up to the sand. I won't be able to get it back into the water again."

She is smiling, explaining calmly, but I can tell she is greatly amused, and I realize she has never brought anyone out here with her.

Suddenly, it is so obvious to me that the Key is the real VIP room. Not the after-parties at Art, or the men's room at The Bait Bucket, the harem tents at House. This little island is the true qualifier. If you can make it here, you can make it anywhere. No one moves.

"How did Aaron and Jeffrey get on?" Erica asks.

"Ray has a raft that he used to float Alex's work in. Maybe they used that. Or maybe they hiked up their skirts and got their feet a little wet," she says.

She is teasing, but we aren't used to this from her.

"Why didn't you tell us we had to do this?" says Dani.

"I just didn't think to," she says. Her smile is gorgeous. "I'm sorry, but there's one way on this island now. I'll try to figure out a different way off."

"Babe, just take your shoes off," says Jason.

Julie stiffens at the affectionate dip in his voice. I feel ill at what we have done, at how my thoughts reek of selfishness when she is so obviously hurt by the fact that Dani exists. We led her into this.

It's so obvious neither of them is pregnant, too. I know their bodies, both of them.

Luke is picking at the hem of his shirt. Erica is staring blankly at the Key. He misheard her. She never said anything about anyone being pregnant or, if she did, she never said anything about Vanessa or Julie.

I suddenly feel an overwhelming sense of dread in the wake of Vanessa's good humor and Julie's dog-like fear.

We disembark from the boat. Dani sneers at Julie with such clear aggression that Julie startles. Vanessa puts a hand on her shoulder and smiles at her, takes her bag from her, so that she can get in the water.

I feel dizzy, dehydrated, seasick. I stare at the horizon, a fantastic in-between of bright blue upon deep blue. Vanessa is putting things in a canvas bag—sunscreen, a bottle of water, mundane things that seem obscene against the expanse of nature around us. Our friends are in the water.

I have to ask her, even though I know there is no answer, "Are you happy?"

She faces me and smiles.

"I like it here."

I come to her, wrap my arms around her. She burrows her head into my neck, her cheek brushing against mine, pressing it for a moment, then finding a roof under my jaw, so that our heads cradle together.

Her breasts press into me, soft, buoyant, and then her hips follow, in a sinuous line of torso that I hold more closely, until every indentation of her body fits against every convexity of mine, and she is mine, and I love her with a desperation I know is latched to my guilt, my feeling of failure, but, also, I love her.

"Vanessa, I want you to trust me. I want you to love me."

She stiffens only slightly. The arch of her back, curved with such simple delight against the broadness of my chest, loses its soft grace and becomes more fixed. The rest of her body remains mine.

"The other night was a big deal for me. I felt different than I expected afterwards. I felt closer to you, but not closer to Jason or Julie. Did you like it, too?"

She nods and giggles, such a rare sound.

"Yes. I liked it."

"I want you to tell me if anything unexpected happens because of that night." My voice is sticking to my throat, coming up my trachea slowly, straining like a clogged drain. "Any night, even. I want you to be mine, and you can tell me things. If you feel like I don't love you, I want you to know that you are wrong. If you get jealous ever, you can tell me about it."

I am glad for the slow slide of my voice. I need this odd stretching of time to help me through the next thing I say, to hide its guile, its careful syntax.

"If anything about us or us having been with other people or just . . . anything comes up, I want you to come to me and tell me, because I love you."

She looks up at me and disengages slowly, gently from my arms. She lowers her face and raises her eyes to mine, and I have a sinking sensation in my stomach that she is going to tell me that she is pregnant. A thousand thoughts flash at once. If I got someone pregnant, it is better that it's her than Julie. If she doesn't tell me, I still have to contend with Julie and Jason and countless others. Julie will suffer if Vanessa is pregnant. Julie will suffer if she is pregnant. I don't want anyone to be pregnant. I don't want to know.

She smiles at me. "OK, sure. Everything is fine, though. I had a good time, I swear."

I break into a sweat in my relief, and, even though I am not really off the hook yet, this answer is the first required step in the final answer I want—that my friends can just go back to being my friends.

She sees my body sag, though, and changes the subject, always so coy.

"So, it's pretty obvious Chrissy was going to try to rip off those ticket sales, isn't it?" she says.

"Yeah . . . they've had a hard time."

"It's pretty obvious that Ray didn't know she did it, either, isn't it?"

"Yeah, he's angry. He's going to need us today."

"Do you think Aaron and Jeffrey know?"

"I don't think Aaron and Jeffrey know anything," I say, as evenly as I can.

"I agree," she says.

I love her. She understands me better than anyone.

26.

His eyes swim. The water shines. The sun blinks. Everything is too obvious all at once. I rock at the helm of the dizzy boat. His eyes, teal, then turquoise, forecast high temperatures, low enhalinity. The water watches innocently, hoping for the best, and I hop over the gunwale in an azure splash and look back at him neutrally.

He is what other girls call sweet, always ready with a warm hug or a genuine smile, always ready to listen to people speak, to see and hear the good in them. He is full of iridescent oil.

I should get back in the boat.

No one is embarrassed, because no one knows enough to be embarrassed. Alex's work is atrocious, but the models are beaming with delight as each looks at her outfit. This is what Alex wanted. He wanted them to feel beautiful, but the pathetic quality of the work only highlights the fallacy of his concept.

He thought the universal beauty of humanity would create physical beauty, that the problem of duality would melt in the glow of stainless steel and happy faces, that some vital force would shimmer against the lifelessness of metal and somehow bestow radiance upon thick thighs and misshapen torsos, and, most audaciously of all, that if this were to happen, he would be responsible for it.

Aaron, naturally, loves this painful mediocrity and lets Alex wear his crown amongst the giggling harem of uninteresting girls. He wears yet another ridiculous kimono as a jacket, over a bikini bottom, and watches in satisfaction. He lolls his head back onto his neck and then rolls his chin onto his chest and looks at everyone, unthreatened, smug.

Kim calls the models for hair and makeup. She and Chrissy have set up two stations inside the first room of the Fort with mirrors and stools. The models clamor around each other, in front of the mirrors, but far away enough to pretend they aren't looking at themselves.

"Where are Dani and Chrissy?" I ask.

"Outside, fighting with their guys," she says.

I nod and take a sip of cheap, bubbly wine.

"Do you think you should go back and get people now? There are a lot more than we thought, right? How are you going to have enough time to do everyone's hair?"

"I always do people's hair last minute," I say. "I never know what I'm going to do until I see someone, remember?"

"OK, I just thought that we should—we never really talked about what we're doing. I don't know what you're doing."

Her words are rushed, nervous. She is rustling through makeup, her hands scrabbling like monkey paws.

"No one knows what they're doing," I say.

"Maybe—can Jason drive your boat?"

I close my eyes. I think suddenly of my parents, how my dependable father showed only a moment of personal interjection—a riot for him, but a token and moderate impulse in anyone else—and both my parents were crushed by a bullet train.

"No. Driving is . . . not for everyone."

Kim stares at me. She thinks I am going to say something else. I can't think of anything else. I finish the wine, tipping my head back. I hear my friends' laughter pealing in the tent outside the Fort.

Kim leans her chin toward me. Her eyebrows raise. She is trying to understand something about me. She doesn't need to understand anything, though. No one needs to understand anything. We only must live until we are no longer alive.

"OK," I say and I leave the cool walls of the Fort.

The scent of old stones disintegrates in the blazing sun, and I walk toward my friends. Only when I am at the tent entrance do I realize that I have just spoken for no reason, in response to nothing.

I feel larger, as if I am growing, like a sunflower. My lips curl back from my teeth like petals unfurling in the morning. My face turns upward, absorbing radiation and heat. Everything makes sense in a way that it hasn't before.

The top of my head will be near the apex of the tent soon. My hearing follows, upward. The noises that tunnel into my eardrums sound farther away. They are farther away.

I become warmer as I get closer to the sun. I am quivering with thousands of degrees of heat, but I do not burn. I simply become more powerful. I can hear wind breathing, clouds drifting, the kinetic turbulence of waves breaking, even just gently.

Other parts of the earth become visible. First, a lone hopscotch court of railroad tracks flashes and fades. A newer path diverts trains through a less populous area of burnt grasses and sparkling lakes, full of alligators.

I smell the far-off slick of blackness in the Gulf and see oil perpetually bubbling through its own skin. Tourists on the Atlantic coast, unaccustomed to the streets of a new town, lament the higher weekly rentals and mill aimlessly, slightly disoriented in the sun. They are still glad they aren't in Poughkeepsie or Ypsilanti or here, where there is nothing to do, because other people ruin everything.

My vision swings back to the desolation of the marina with its cluster of heartbreakingly ignorant, innocent people, waiting for me or anyone to arrive for them, and, then, I am in the park across the street from Art with my lone, bloody handprint on the blue tile of the fountain. The fountain's cherub spits water in the direction of the blackened gallery.

These visions appear in a stack of interchangeable cards. There is no such thing as time or gravity. Everything is always happening. Everything, hope, shit, everything that has ever happened floats.

I need to sit down. I sense that I am fine, but I am going somewhere. At the same time, I must remain. Something is happening that I have been expecting without realizing I have been expecting it. I do not want anyone to see it. I do not want these people, my friends, to see it.

There is a makeshift room in the corner of the tent, a swag of material that cordons off space where we can relax or have privacy once things get started. It is a sheet behind which my friends can do coke.

No one sees me. They are entranced by their own universes, drinking or arguing or talking over each other about nothing.

I feel as though I am gliding over the sand and I wonder how I will fit myself behind this curtain. I am so giant and radiant, as if I am the sun itself, with no need for feet or other corporeal ornaments to propel me. I am only bright, hot mass.

They are behind the sheet, though—who? I can hear their voices, one plaintively soothing, the other muffled and sobbing. Erica. Jeffrey. He is crying. His dog is dead, I remember. Today is the day we remind him that his dog is dead and that he almost killed all his friends and lost his business.

He is hiccupping into something that pads his sound. Erica is nearly frantic in her breathiness, but she carries the lilt of an attempt at calming him, the way one calms a child, in quick starts and carried whispers, all the while aware that nothing will stop the frenetic bellowing if that is what the child decides must happen.

He tries to say something. She stops him. He tries again. Once more, she shushes him. He sobs a jagged yowl. She frantically quiets him. There is a rustling as if she is either patting him or trying to swallow the sounds he makes.

The jubilant selfishness from the other side of the tent rings uninterrupted, punctuated by the occasional clang of metal, the joyful flirtatiousness and pride in Alex's voice, the thoughtlessness of Jason and Dani doing their best to annoy each other as Luke shows off for Julie. Ray plays along, while Chrissy stands tormented under a plaster smile that shows too many of her teeth, but she plays along, too.

Erica cannot gauge how self-absorbed they are, because she is the same. She just assumes everyone cares what she is saying and she shushes Jeffrey adamantly, rudely. Her voice blows something in a shouted whisper to him. I cannot hear her over the trumpeting in my ears, the gaudy, tympanic gleefulness of Alex and Luke, the lordly humming that slides off Aaron's skin and zigzags around them.

I hear Jeffrey, coarse and agonized, "Stop saying it was art. It wasn't fucking art. We killed our dog and we could have killed you."

"I don't believe that," says Erica quietly. "You're just hurting because you've almost realized your dream. Growing hurts."

I look down at my body. I am growing.

"No," Jeffrey responds. "We made a mistake. Killing your dog is not fucking art. It's fucking crazy," and he begins sobbing in deep, husky coughs that neither he nor Erica try to hide, so that when I walk away, not caring if they know I was there or not, they hear me, and shove the curtain to the side of its hastily clipped-up frame.

"Vanessa!" Jeffrey calls. "Come here!"

He says it as though he expects me to disregard him, but I turn and walk over to them. Erica stands there like a child atop a volcano, ready to be brave and sacrifice everything for nothing.

I stand next to her and look at Jeffrey calmly.

"You misheard us," he says plainly.

He stands planted in the sand, the white sheet around us. His breath is hot within the closed space. His eyes are rimmed pink. He is not trying to convince me. He is telling me what he will say if I say anything to anyone else.

I look at Erica. She looks down at her pigeon toes. I smile at her, but my smile is not mine—it is the smile of the sun, necessary, but capable of great damage.

"I didn't hear anything," I say.

Jeffrey puts his head in his hands and looks up at me with an affected, wistful smile.

"It's an emotional day for us," he says.

"I know," I say. I turn to Erica. "I have to go back. I was here too long, drinking."

I laugh and turn back to Jeffrey, "I'm not much in the mood for crowds, either, it turns out."

He smiles and puts his hand on my shoulder. "You're a good friend," he says.

"I haven't even done anything yet," I say.

"Their hair?" he says.

"I'm going to create an homage to the risks you've taken," I say.

I pronounce *homage* in French. Their faces coat with hard rubber fear again.

"Erica explained your philosophy of life as art, where conceptual unity matters more than influence," I say. "You're right. It doesn't matter if art imitates life or life imitates art. We came here to unify."

They nod, wide-eyed, impressed, and I want to laugh, but I can't, because I hate them. I realize that my emotions are not what matters, though. I have not had such strong ones in years.

I have an objective strength over this madness that I have not realized until now. I can make decisions based in ethics, without shame, because I have forgotten the nature of shame. Grief has stripped me of it.

I am able to create a world that runs, because I accept awful things. Aaron and Jeffrey have not proven an existential point by killing their dog. Alex's attempt at art does not overcome dualism because it makes average-looking girls happy.

Their efforts are insane—straining for transcendentalism when none exists, grasping for beauty where there is none. Their illusions are the essence of suffering.

We leave the curtain, and I look around the tent quickly. The models have departed to makeup. Ray and Chrissy argue quietly, rapidly, a few feet away. Jason leers at Julie, and Dani refuses to leave his side, yammering in his ear. Luke pretends to listen to Dani and watch Julie, too. He and Jason raise their eyebrows at each other, but he is watching Erica, insecurity shaking through his pores, as Erica and Jeffrey stand near Aaron in a huddle.

I know the rough hills and valleys of all their conversations at this moment. None of them are truthful.

"Ray," I say in a low voice.

He looks up at me, irritated that he is taken away from his point, his muddy flood of anger.

"We have to go back now, but I need your help with something. Can you go out to your boat and meet me there in a minute?"

He shakes his head at me, as if I am asking something

irrational.

"Please," I say. "I'll explain in a minute. I'm trying to make today easier for everyone. I'll explain outside."

He looks at Chrissy with such hate that I pity him. He did not ask for this, this thieving woman, these red-herring friends who overshadowed his needs with their selfish, misguided foolishness. Chrissy sinks hopelessly into herself as Ray glares at her and goes outside.

I grab Julie, almost roughly, by the arm, and guide her over to the partition where Erica and Jeffrey stood.

"I think you should leave," I say.

"What?"

The surprise in her eyes is palpable. Silver tears spring into her irises.

"I think you should leave."

My voice is an icicle, a cold, blue dagger, but I know I am right.

"You waltz into town and sleep with everybody's man and then think we should be friends with you. I think you should leave. Ray will take you back. You can have your money back."

"I . . . I didn't pay. I'm Kim's guest."

"She can leave with you if you feel more comfortable, but you have to leave now," I say.

She blinks at me. "Why?"

"I just told you why."

She swallows and her abdomen flexes for a moment, as if she will crumple, but she doesn't. She stands up and nods.

"OK," she says, bewildered, hurt beyond anything she expected. "Can I get Kim?"

I nod. She walks to the Fort. I follow her. My brain is beaming ultraviolet, flaring within my skull.

The urgency in Julie's movements does not escape Kim, who looks at me with such fury, I prepare to haul her outside and punch her in the face hard enough to knock her out if I must, but Julie puts a pleading hand on her arm and shakes her head.

Kim looks at her agape and looks at me. I nod my head, as if I expect them to hurry, because I do.

Kim walks away from Julie and toward me.

220

"You fucking bitch," Kim says to me. "What is wrong with you?"

"You don't have to leave," I say. "She does. You can stay in here."

"Oh, like anyone cares about Jason or Alex that much. Julie, just stay back here with me."

"Dani has to come back and get her hair and makeup done," Julie says. She looks scared, confused.

Kim sighs in disgust.

"Fuck it. Let's go," she says to Julie.

"You're an insecure bitch," she says to me.

I don't care what she thinks. I don't care at all. I just want Julie gone, out of the way, and away from Jason and Dani and Alex.

I walk out of the Fort and to the edge of the sand with them. We wade into the Gulf. When the water is waist high, I call to Ray, "They're going to go back with you. They need to leave."

Kim's shoulders raise up to her ears and she uses all her self-control to lower them again. Julie looks like a beaten soldier, walking home, broken and tired, after a long war. She is too soft to be here.

Ray looks bewildered. I laugh, loudly.

"They'll tell you what happened," I say.

"OK," he shouts back. "I'll see you in a few minutes."

I wave good-bye to him and turn back. I climb onto my boat and open up the hatch door on the bow. The boat slurps and bobs. The sun is beginning to lower in the sky toward mid-afternoon. No one even notices that we haven't brought anyone else over. Everyone is drunk. Everything is sizzling, shimmering, hot, and clear.

I survey the Key. A roost of stocky green herons blinks at me from atop the stilts of mangrove roots. I push my hair off my face and blink back. The heron closest to me squawks like a chicken. Its scream is natural, but they are nighttime fliers, sitting here in the heat, passive and passerine. They are pretending to be something they are not, because they think survival demands it.

Everything is different now. Nothing acts right anymore. I bend at the waist and stretch out my neck, leaning toward the nest, playing, reminding them of their stature. The squawking heron stops and flies away, its black-green belly slick and glinting. The other herons remain, unmoving, lightly puffed up.

I stalk past the herons and wind through the mangroves. I step onto the roots as they rise into the sand, holding overhead branches, so that my weight doesn't snap the spindles. I amble behind the Fort, looking ahead and below for falcons or snakes. The scent of salt lightly tops a green heart note in the air.

I pass the Fort and then I am behind the tent with my friends. I skip and hoist myself past both, still dangling in the mangroves, until I have a parallax view of their entrances and the space between them. A pair of models, each short with thin hair, walks back to the Fort after stubbing cigarettes on the ground. The other models are clustered in the door, hoping the smokers have news. They are waiting for someone to tell them what to do.

I am so dehydrated. My lungs are tissue paper. My cheeks are gummy. I pull myself higher into a mangrove. My biceps tremble. My triceps burn. I brace my foot against the side of the tree and boost up, tearing a muscle in my hip and scraping the opposite thigh.

Once on the branch, I am dizzy. The world turns pale yellow. I crawl farther out onto the branch. My knees leave shredded offerings on the bark. I am over the tent. I hear my friends' proud, braying laughter inside. I have missed the joke.

I pour gasoline on the edge of the tent. I crawl farther out on the branch and pour more in the center of the roof. A shallow, golden puddle winks in the filtered sun. I watch the tent slowly absorb it and clamber quickly to the far edge of the tent. It doesn't matter if anyone hears me now. What matters is that I hurry.

I stand on the branch. Vertigo chants through my skull, snagged with dehydration. I look up at the mangrove and run down the branch, toward the trunk, dumping the rest of the gas can. I crouch down at the branch's base, leaning into the trunk, and pull Alex's acetylene torch from my backpack. I walk back out, nearly losing my balance, and sit on the branch to push oxygen into the torch's chamber.

I don't even have to touch the flame to the tent. It goes up immediately.

Heat whips through the mangrove. I am back against its trunk. My scaffolding branch screams at me as it torches above the tent. I scramble to another branch and cower in the tree. My heart is thumping. My body finds the ductile poise of a marionette, waiting to respond to stimulus. I am hugging the tree. These fear responses are only signs of evolutionary fitness. My mind is not scared. I put the torch and the gas can away in my backpack.

The tent is no longer a tent. Instead, it is a blossom of flame. Where there were walls are now flapping bracteal leaves below the bloom, but then they conflagrate, too.

I hear Alex shout in surprise, "Go! That way!"

He is trying to save people, to lead them through the fire, like always, but he sounds so dim. They are inside a dome of flames, and then it's too late. The efflorescence tumbles inward. Everything collapses on them, these eight treacherous friends of mine.

Their shrieking is unimaginable, a refrain of awe and terror. I cannot tell whose voice I hear anymore, if the voices are male or female. They are the voices of suffering. Their bodies fall, at once. They have tripped over each other in fear, and even I cannot look anymore.

I drop from the other side of the tree, scraping my torso and falling into the mangroves, cracking the legs of the roots as I land. My breathing is rough from the gasoline and smoke and dehydration, but it is even and deep. Blood flashes from scrapes across my body, but none runs down my skin.

Ray will be back soon. I don't care about the models. They won't look for me, but Ray will. I have to get in the boat and open it up so hard I might actually blow something, but it doesn't matter as long as I can pass Ray, so that he doesn't see this and me at once.

The time he returns until the time anyone notices I am not

where they expect me is twenty minutes at most—if my boat is not here. Ray will call me. He will try to stop me from bringing more people here. He will call the Coast Guard to stop me.

If my boat is here, he will think I am in the rubble of bodies.

I look at the boat, the beautiful, hopeful gift from my predictable parents. It is only about a hundred feet away. I look out at the Gulf. I am already up to my waist in the water, standing amongst the splintered mangrove.

For the first time in two years, since the spill began, since my parents died, I am untroubled. I know suddenly with a profound, resonant knowing that the universe cleans itself. Well after I am gone, there will be purity here again.

If my boat stays here, I can make it to my house and gather whatever I need to survive. I am thinking Texas or Louisiana, haircuts and dye, light medical-spa procedures.

Then, I am thinking none of that.

I am looking at the Gulf, at its deep, welcoming calm, its glinting, gentle waves, and then I am wading farther into it, and then I am swimming, and then I am heading at a hard crawl to the northeast, where I will slip to the side of Ray, who will surely pass me at my human speed, but who will not be looking for me.

I am hurling one arm over the other, and, while the force of my stroke is strenuous, I do not feel overwhelmed.

About The Author

Rachel Moran is from New Jersey. *Paper Dolls* is her first novel.

Acknowledgements

Paper Dolls occurs in an imaginary hyper-version of a place I live sometimes. Many of the people there and elsewhere have inspired me:

Jake Behrmann, the cover artist, taught me to trust the process.

Jenny Marie told me to finish a draft before I turned thirty, so I did. She's also the only hairdresser I trust. Vanessa is a lifelong Floridian and a scissor whiz in tribute to Jenny.

Gina Vivinetto provided exceptional, incisive feedback. The novel is tighter and bolder because of her.

Miranda Schultz took great pains to ensure consistency in technical structure.

Frank Strunk III enchanted me with his 2006 Hard Wear collection. His artistic rendering of organic dichotomies exhibits merit that I don't even attempt to treat in descriptions of Alex's bumbling.

Alisha Vitale lost a chunk of hair to a candle in a club, inspiring Chrissy's accident at Art.

Aaron is named for **Aaron Edwards aka Guncle**, Brooklyn's most prolific underground doorman.

Dani is named for **Danielle Kelly**, my first friend.

The *New York Times* parody on the back cover paraphrases **John Fathom**.

Ben DeVoe is a bear. I better be sweet to him.

Discussion Questions

The man vs. nature conflict is rarely recognized by anyone in the novel. What do you think of the nonchalance toward environmental damage? Is desensitization excusable? Have you ever ignored an obvious problem? How did it affect you?

How does the economic impact of the oil spill affect the characters? Does it influence how they treat each other? Do you think it's OK to act like problems can resolve themselves? What is the difference between patient acceptance and refusing to acknowledge the truth?

Beyond the pragmatic location of the Gulf of Mexico, why is the setting so important? Consider how the heat affects Vanessa and Alex independently. Do you recognize stereotypes of people who live in Florida in other characters? How accurate are these stereotypes? Is 'doing nothing' a necessary part of transcending suffering or is it laziness? What responsibility do you have to engage in patterns of human accomplishment?

Animals offer the characters lessons they consistently ignore. What do you think of Vanessa's rationalization of Snuggles' death? Is it natural for the other characters to avoid genuine condolences to Aaron and Jeffrey? Why is it unnerving to see changes in birds and fish if humans still survive?

Do you think the novel is dystopian or transgressive? Why or why not?

Vanessa enters dissociative fugues and lacks deep emotion. Is she sociopathic or deeply grieving her parents' death?

Julie has distressing visions and abuses Klonopin. Is she delusional and drug-dependent or lonely from childhood neglect?

Compare the female characters' internal conflicts with Alex's anxiety attacks and low self-esteem.

What is the significance of Vanessa marking time by days and dates? How does her understanding of time compare to the apocalyptic predications Aaron, Jeffrey, and Alex each have? Do you think they really fear the world ending or are they avoiding other fears? Have you ever created drama to sublimate fear?

Julie is used or humiliated by men her whole life. How does this affect her sex drive and her ability to make friends? Have you ever felt powerless because of your need for physical or emotional affection? What did you do about it? What do you think is the best thing to do about it?

How do the characters use sex? What do the sex scenes in the novel have in common? Have you ever used sex for purposes other than emotional connection or mutual physical satisfaction? How did you feel afterwards?

What do you think of the characters' drug use? Why do you think they use drugs?

Vanessa knows she does not connect with other people as well as Alex. Does she resent this or admire him for it? How does it affect their relationship? Have you ever had a relationship where one person feels more deeply than the other? How did it affect you?

Alex struggles with his identity as an artist. Do you agree with his artistic ideals? What do you think about how the other characters treat him in regard to his art? Do you think he is a successful artist? Why or why not?

Erica cites several reasons why Aaron and Jeffrey set the gallery on fire and why those reasons make the party on the Key a bad idea. Are her reasons exclusive or could they all be accurate?

How do Erica's ideals impact her credibility with the other characters? Consider how she treats Alex when he submits *The McMansions at Deer Lake (Avon Park)* and, later, at House, when she says exactly what Vanessa was thinking about the utilitarian value of life.

The other characters view Vanessa and Alex as having a significant private relationship. Does Vanessa agree with this? How does Alex's approach to their relationship change? What do you think Vanessa's motivation is for participating in the orgy?

What does Vanessa's response to her pregnancy show about her? Why do you think she chooses to keep her hospital ordeal private? Is her failure to tell Alex just another betrayal within a group of treacherous friends or is she justified in keeping it to herself? Are other betrayals in the novel justified?

How would you characterize the relationship between Aaron and Jeffrey? Consider how they interact after the explosion at Sand Key, how each treats Alex throughout the novel, and how each acts at the party on the Key. Do you know anyone who triggers certain behavior in you or a friend? How do you feel about that person?

Discuss the different lies the characters tell each other. Are some of these lies more acceptable than others? Do you think intention or effect matters more?

What is Vanessa's guiding ethical principle? Consider her responses when she discovers each of her friends' treachery and her calculated division and isolation of her friends at the novel's end. What does she not know that makes her choice to spare Ray a discrepancy?

Does the ending of the novel support that Vanessa's original ethics are right or wrong? How?